THE MANSIONS OF MURDER

THE MANSIONS OF MURDER

Paul Doherty

CRÈME de la CRIME

This first world edition published 2017
in Great Britain and the USA by
Crème de la Crime, an imprint of
SEVERN HOUSE PUBLISHERS LTD of
19 Cedar Road, Sutton, Surrey, England, SM2 5DA.
Trade paperback edition first published
in Great Britain and the USA 2018 by
SEVERN HOUSE PUBLISHERS LTD

British Library Cataloguing in Publication Data
A CIP catalogue record for this title is available from the British Library.

ISBN-13: 978-1-78029-100-0 (cased)
ISBN-13: 978-1-78029-582-4 (trade paper)
ISBN-13: 978-1-78010-914-5 (e-book)

All Severn House titles are printed on acid-free paper.

Severn House Publishers support the Forest Stewardship Council™ [FSC™],
the leading international forest certification organisation.
All our titles that are printed on FSC certified paper carry the FSC logo.

MIX
Paper from
responsible sources
FSC® C013056

Typeset by Palimpsest Book Production Ltd.,
Falkirk, Stirlingshire, Scotland.
Printed and bound in Great Britain by
TJ International, Padstow, Cornwall.

HISTORICAL NOTE

By the late autumn of 1381 the Great Revolt in England had been successfully crushed. Young King Richard II was eager to make his authority felt, even though he continued to act under the brooding shadow of his uncle, John of Gaunt. London had been purged of all rebels and the city soon recovered from its occupation by the peasant armies. The courts reopened, a Parliament was summoned to sit at Westminster and the great lords began to gather, ready to flex their muscles as the murderous rivalries which divided them surfaced yet again. The nobles knew that whoever controlled London would also control Westminster, the Crown and the great offices of state. The lords played out their bitter enmities by using and exploiting the violent gangs of the city, the 'rifflers', who swarmed through the slums either side of the Thames. The lords regarded these as a huntsman would his pack of dogs so, when they whistled, the packs would gather to bay for blood . . .

To Alan Mair
"Keep running the good race to take the prize"
(I Cor. 9:24)

PART ONE

***Scrippet* (Old English)**: he who sets the watch

'Blood stains the face of the moon, dark shadows mist the sun' – or so the Benedictine chronicler in the majestic Abbey of Westminster defined the times, the year of Our Lord 1381. A season for portents, auguries, dreams and prophesies. Strange lights seared the night sky above the King's own city of London. People stared and wondered. The Great Revolt had been cruelly crushed. The bloody wine-press of the noble lords had ground it to nothing. The Masters of the Soil such as the likes of Norfolk, Beaumont, Fitzalan of Arundel and, above all, John of Gaunt, uncle of the young King Richard II and self-proclaimed regent of the realm, made their power known. The war in the shires was drawing to a bloody end. The peasant rebels, with all their high-sounding titles and claims to power; the Great Community of the Realm, the Upright Men, and their street warriors the Earthworms, were nothing more than a fading memory. Those rebels who had survived the great hunt and savage persecution by the lords could only quietly pray for hundreds of their comrades whose corpses still rotted on gallows and gibbets as far north as Alnwick and as far south as Dover. The Great Cause was finished. The dream was dead. No new Zion would come down from heaven and sink its foundations into the muddy banks of the Thames.

However, as the Westminster chronicler was quick to point out, the Great Revolt might be finished, but human wickedness, especially in London – the new Babylon – flourished richly and swiftly as cockle amongst the wheat. Peace reigned, but it was a peace which allowed every form of sin to crawl out of its hiding place. London had been brought back under the authority of the Crown. Parliament sat at Westminster. The Commons exercised their authority from St Stephen's Chapel or the great chapterhouse of the abbey. However, Crown, Lords and Commons, not to forget the masters of the city who sheltered in the Guildhall, were fearful of a new danger. A great scourge was now raising its head as peace and harmony allegedly returned. The great gangs of London, the rifflers and the roaring boys, were also making their presence felt. These legions of the damned, as the chronicler described them, were not supposed to exist. People could reject them and their wicked doings as the work of those who gossip and chatter, claim that the danger they posed was all shadow and no substance. Nevertheless, the gangs were there, like the great rats which plagued the sewers. They did not like to be caught out in the open, but their brutal acts were clear enough for all to see. The chronicler emphasised this important fact. Hadn't his own abbot expressed this riddle, a paradox for all the good brothers to ponder on? How the great London gangs did exist, but they only moved or acted by courtesy and favour of the lords: Gaunt, Arundel and the rest, who could whistle up their packs of wild dogs whenever they wished.

Of all the gangs and covens of rifflers, none was more feared than the Sycamores under their leader, Simon Makepeace, also known as 'The Flesher'; a brutal soul, tavern master, mine host, and owner of the Devil's Oak, close to the Thames in Queenhithe ward.

The tavern squatted like a great, fat, bloated toad with dirty, leprous warts, at the heart of a maze of alleys and runnels which reeked to high heaven of dirt and filth. The tenements lining these needle-thin paths were propped up by makeshift struts and rotten beams, their windows sealed with iron-bound shutters. Nevertheless, people lived here, the midnight folk, crammed as fast and as thick as lice on a slab of putrid beef. The denizens of these hellish dwellings clustered around make-shift braziers full of smoking, dusty charcoal. The stench of singeing clothes and unwashed flesh curled everywhere. The braziers provided a little light, some warmth, as well as being a source of putrid food. The tenements were places of perpetual twilight, where figures crawled – dark, crouching shapes against the poor light – so it looked as if Judgement Day had dawned and every obscure grave was giving up its dead.

Once night fell, men, women and children slunk out to hunt for whatever they could, along with the great, grey rats, though even these rodents sensed that the staircases and stairwells in these mouldering mansions were most dangerous, teetering on the verge of collapse. Instead both dwellers and vermin used the Jacob's ladders, rickety staircases built on the outside of the tenements.

Hell's buttery, as this part of Queenhithe adjoining the Thames was so aptly known, was a shadowy, dismal place full of steaming filth. Everything loathsome and decaying could be found here. Dens of depravity where murder had taken up residence under smoke-stained ceilings. Thieves and prostitutes, pimps and cunning men crawled amongst the cockroaches, which scampered in vast hordes across the rotting floors, where dirt swilled ankle-deep. Along the narrow runnels stood decaying alehouses, their taprooms nothing more than amphitheatres where a wooden circular fence about five feet high ringed a sand-filled arena. Here the huge grey rats from the nearby wharves were pitted against ferocious terriers and, when the rats had been specially starved, against each other.

All of London's grotesques gathered to watch: the likes of Daniel the Damned with his huge dead eyes in a coarse, bloated face, who offered to bite off the head of a rat for a penny and that of a mouse for a farthing. Daniel had clashed with some of the Fleshers' followers and had promptly disappeared, never to be seen again. Killings were commonplace. Murder in all its gruesome forms a daily occurrence. Just before the Great Revolt, one of the rotting tenements in Hell's buttery had abruptly collapsed. Officials of the ward decided to clear the site and they filled sack after sack with human bones found beneath shattered floorboards, above crumbling ceilings and between plastered walls.

One place amidst all this squalor was owned and controlled by the Flesher. Gossiping locals called it the 'Mansion of Murder', a three-storey building set in its own square of overgrown garden, fenced off by palings at least two yards high; each post was surmounted by razor-sharp spikes to deter anyone foolish enough to try and force entry. The only gate into the garden was iron-bound and studded: bolts at top and bottom held it fast whilst the main lock, although dirty and chipped, had been fashioned by the most skilled locksmith.

The Mansion of Murder had once belonged to the Guild at St Dismas, a group of men and women who tried to work amongst the dispossessed in Hell's buttery. The Guild had been forced to withdraw after three of its members had been found floating naked in the Thames, hands tied behind their backs, their throats slashed from ear to ear. Once the Guild had left, the mansion had immediately been seized by the Flesher, owner of the nearby Devil's Oak tavern. He had cleaned and swept it, raised the high paling fence, and had the great gate rehung and secured. No longer a House of Mercy, the mansion was a blasphemous mockery of what it had once been. According to those paid to glean news and information along the quaysides, this house of murder had been stripped of furniture, hangings and any ornamentation. Just three galleries of dusty wooden floors, plastered ceilings and flaking walls. At either end of this sinister dwelling stood a winding staircase. A kitchen, buttery and chancery chamber ranged along the ground floor, with more chambers on the galleries above.

The mansion also had cellars, which stretched the entire length of the building: dark, grim rooms once used for storage. The street sparrows who collect rumour, God knows how, claimed these cellars housed two war mastiffs, hell-hounds, long, sleek and short-furred, with bulbous heads and huge jaws. The Flesher kept these within and so transformed the House of Mercy into a place of terror. Those who crossed the Flesher, or failed this ugly-souled captain of the night, were taken to the Mansion of Murder, thrust through its one and only door, every other entrance being bricked up, whilst the windows on all three floors were mere lancets. The Mansion of Murder became a prison, though the captive did not survive long. Once the door was locked and bolted, the hounds soon learnt that new prey was available. Starved and ferocious, they'd slope up the cellar steps, eager for the hunt. People sometimes heard their growling, their horrid howling at some unearthly hour. Others claimed to have heard the screams and death cries of those the Flesher had imprisoned there.

However, what could be done during a season when there was blood on the face of the moon and a dark mist across the sun? A time when the King's writ did not run along the warren of filthy runnels next to the riverside in the ward of Queenhithe. What objection could be raised? The Flesher, if anyone had the temerity to question him, could cite the law. He would argue that the former House of Mercy was now his property. Consequently, he had the right to protect it and to use guard dogs to ensure it remained safe and secure, especially in this time of troubles when the law was, perhaps, not as strong as it should be. Moreover, he – or rather his lawyer Master Copping – would argue that it was hardly his fault that intruders, housebreakers, murderers and trespassers who broke into his valuable property paid the price.

On the eve of the Feast of All the Angels, the year of Our Lord 1381, Eudo Ingersol, mailed clerk in the secret employ of the city council, leaned against the door of the Mansion of Murder now firmly locked behind him. He tried to calm the terrors seething within him; his throat was dry as sand, his heart pounding so hard he found it difficult to breathe. The Flesher had tried him and found him guilty. Ingersol had been brought here to die.

The clerk peered through the darkness, eyes and ears straining. Then he heard it: the low rumble of a bark, the snarling and growling of the great war dogs in the cellar below, now alert to a new victim, of the fresh meat that he would supply for the hunt. Eudo wiped sweat-soaked palms on his leather jerkin. He did not have his dagger with him, he had left that at St Benet's, whilst Raquin, the Flesher's other henchman, had made sure he carried no weapons. A heart-chilling, blood-freezing howl echoed through the house. Ingersol crouched down. He fought to control his breath as he crossed himself. The ominous patter of clawed feet and that harsh breathing of the mastiffs echoing as they sloped up the cellar steps to hunt him.

Early in the morning of the feast of St Luke, the year of Our Lord 1381, Martha Ashby prepared herself for the day. Martha was housekeeper and confidante of Reynaud Filleby, parson and parish priest of St Benet's, an ancient church, its great sprawling graveyard almost stretching down to the Queenhithe wharves along the Thames. Martha had waited patiently for the first glow of sunrise when the bells of St Benet must begin their pealing, their clanging summons to attend the Jesus Mass and so greet the dawn. Parson Reynaud was strict in this, even if he ignored or flouted the more serious mandates of both Christ and Holy Mother Church. Martha would have to follow her usual routine. She climbed the steps up to the first gallery of the priest's house. She walked quietly down the passageway to the left, knocked on the door of Curate Cotes' chamber and, receiving no answer, opened it: the room was empty. The window shutters were pulled back, the small four-poster bed undisturbed, the curate's gown slung over the coverlet, his chamois slippers still pushed under the bedside table.

Satisfied that all was as it should be, Martha hurried to Parson Reynaud's chamber to the right of the staircase. She knocked and, without waiting, opened the door. Again the chamber lay silent, the shutters undisturbed, as well as the sheets and coverlet on the great four-poster bed. No candles glowed on their spigots and the capped taper on the bedside stall had not been lit. Mistress Martha tried to control her curdling anxiety and apprehension as she hastened down the stairs. All seemed to be going well, but Martha had certainly learnt how life was fickle and cruel.

She went into Parson Reynaud's chancery chamber and picked up the key to the devil's door, the postern on the west side of the church. She slipped this into the pocket of her gown, which she carefully patted, and hurried out of the house. Martha locked the door behind her and hastened down the coffin path which wound through the ancient graveyard. On either side lay the thousands of dead buried there since the church had been built at least two centuries ago, or so Parson Reynaud had informed her, a veritable forest of tomb crosses, memorial stones, funeral plinths, and all the other insignia of the houses of the dead which ringed St Benet's. All of these were to be removed as Parson Reynaud carried through his own proposed harrowing of this ancient cemetery.

The graveyard was a truly haunted place, with the darkness

now thinning and a stiff morning breeze bending the long, coarse grass, bramble and gorse which grew so vigorously across the cemetery, as if to hide and smother all signs of death and decay. A ghostly place, so Parson Reynaud had declared, where the shades of the dead could often be seen trailing around the tombs and grave plots. Mistress Martha, however, was of a more practical disposition. She believed such wraiths were just the wisps and shapes created by the thick river mists which crept in from the Thames to smother this sombre place in its chilling embrace. Such a mist was now seeping in as dawn broke and the birds in the ancient yew trees began their own morning matins.

Mistress Martha paused halfway down the path: she glanced quickly around and shivered. This was God's Acre, the last resting place of Christ's faithful departed: it should be a sacred and consecrated sanctuary, yet Martha knew different. The housekeeper stared out over the sea of shifting gorse. In the poor light, the cemetery looked more like the place it truly was: a whitewashed sepulchre, all seemingly proper without but, in truth, full of all kinds of dark filth and rottenness within. Martha opened her eyes, drew a sharp breath to calm herself and hurried on. She reached the devil's door as planned and tried the key, but could not make it grip as it was locked on the other side. She leaned against the hard wood, then straightened up as she heard approaching footsteps. Glancing to her right she saw the bobbing lantern light and shadowy shapes hurrying through the murk.

'Good morrow!' she called.

'Good morrow, Mistress Martha. God's blessings on you.'

Sexton Spurnel, a small, thickset, fussy man hurried up, all breathless, in one hand a lanternhorn, in the other a key ring.

'I've been to the postern door at the front.' He leaned closer, his bearded lined face anxious under a mop of dirty-grey hair which, Martha believed, hadn't been washed since the bathing days at the end of Lent. The sexton stared pleadingly at the housekeeper, the cast in his right eye even more pronounced.

'All the doors,' he hissed, 'are locked. I've tried the main entrance, the postern door to the side, the corpse door and now this.' He almost pushed Martha aside as he tried a key.

'It won't go in,' Martha declared.

'Like the other three.' The sexton rattled the key in the devil's door. He took it out and pushed it back in.

'I've tried it,' Martha offered.

'This is no different,' the sexton wailed.

'From what?'

Both housekeeper and sexton turned to greet Curate Cotes, who came hurrying through the half-light with Nathaniel Cripplegate, leader of the parish council, close behind him. Martha considered both men to be a startling contrast to each other. Despite the poor light, how Curate Cotes had spent the previous evening was more than obvious: his scrawny black hair, thick with grease, was a tangle; his pasty face even paler; his bloodshot eyes and stubbled chin eloquent testimony to heavy drinking and hours of carousing. Ale and food stained the curate's shabby black cassock, whilst his breath stank like a brewer's yard. Cotes seemed all a-flutter, muttering questions about the whereabouts of Parson Reynaud.

'He is not in his bed,' Martha declared.

'And he doesn't seem to be in the church either.' The sexton added: 'If he was, he would certainly hear the clattering of these keys. I mean, I have now tried all four doors.'

'Something must be very wrong.' Nathaniel Cripplegate slipped through the pool of light thrown by the lanternhorn. 'Oh yes,' he repeated, 'something must be very, very wrong.'

Martha scrutinised the council leader carefully and quietly wondered if he would appreciate it if she bestowed a blessing on him. Cripplegate was a widower, and Martha often wondered who looked after him, as he was always so neat and precise in both his dress and appearance. Despite the early hour, Cripplegate's grey hair, moustache and goatee beard were neatly clipped, his sallow face oiled; his deep blue cotehardie, with matching hose and ankle-high leather boots, was of the finest quality and spotlessly clean.

'Can't you do something?' Curate Cotes pleaded with Cripplegate. 'After all, you are a locksmith – a very skilled one, too, much respected by the guild.'

'I am not a miracle worker,' Cripplegate murmured.

'So what do you suggest?' the sexton demanded.

'We should force a door,' Martha spoke up quickly. 'And it should be this one. The others, like the main entrance to the church, are of solid oak. Parson Reynaud always said they turned the church into a fortress. Oak is hard to shatter and very slow burning, but this one,' Martha tapped the door, 'is made of wooden slats. All we have to do is break two of these free and we will be able to reach the lock and the bolts inside.'

The rest quickly agreed. Sexton Spurnel hurried across to the small death house deep in the cemetery and returned with a hammer, axe and crowbar. Martha heaved a sigh of relief as the rest hastened to help the sexton. Using axe, hammer and crowbar, they hacked at the stout wooden slats near the lock. Eventually these were wrenched free so the sexton, at Cripplegate's bidding, could slip his hand through the gap and turn the key in its lock. He stretched his arm to loosen the bolts at both top and bottom. The sexton then kicked the battered door open and, lifting the lanternhorn, led the rest into the cold, inky darkness of the nave. No candle burned or cresset torch flared. Curate Cotes was so nervous his teeth chattered as he whispered the same prayer time and time again. The sexton moved to the candle-chest just inside the entrance, beneath the now blocked-up leper squint. He crouched down, unlocked the box and took out four tallow candles, which he lit from the lanternhorn, giving one to each of his companions. Curate Cotes took his and cautiously walked towards the coffin, which had been churched the previous evening. He lifted the candle to get a clearer view and screamed.

'It's gone!' He screeched. 'Look, it's gone!'

The others gathered around and stared in horror at the coffin. The purple-gold pall cloth had been pulled to the floor. The casket lid had been unscrewed and thrown some distance away but, most surprisingly, the linen-wrapped cadaver had disappeared. Nothing inside but the casket's white-cushioned interior, peppered with the scraps of herbs sprinkled on the now vanished corpse. Cripplegate glimpsed the scrap of dirty parchment pinned to the discarded lid. He prised this loose and held it up.

'For its return,' he read, 'at a time and place of my choosing, with no trickery and deceits, fifty gold crowns.'

'In God's own name!' Cripplegate breathed. 'A king's fortune. But why all this? Who is responsible? What—'

He was cut short by Martha's piercing scream. She had wandered across to the corpse door before going into one of the chantry chapels along the north transept. Like the other chantries, this was a small, carpeted chamber with all the furniture such a chapel needed, a place of prayer dedicated to a local saint. Martha now stood, one hand over her mouth and nose as she pointed to Parson Reynaud, sitting in the celebrant's chair just within the doorway. The old priest lay slumped in the seat, his pasty-white face twisted in the shock of death caused by the death wound, a cruel slit deep in the left side of his chest. The stench from the corpse was offensive. The sheer horror of the old priest's life being cut short so brutally in such a consecrated place created a deep sense of creeping evil. Curate Cotes crouched down to half sit on the prie-dieu just outside the chantry chapel, where a penitent would kneel to be shriven by the priest sitting on the other side of the trellised screen.

'I'd best open the postern door,' Sexton Spurnel whispered, desperate to escape the horrid scene. He hurried down the nave, into the deep shadows which cloaked the main entrance, his hurried footsteps rapping through the silence.

Martha was about to crouch down to study Parson Reynaud, this old man whom she had tried to serve, when Sexton Spurnel's scream heralded further horrors. They hastened towards the bobbing light of the lanternhorn. The sexton had placed this down on the ancient cracked paving stones; he now knelt before the corpse of a man slouched in the sexton's chair just within the doorway. The victim sat rather crookedly, his unshaven face caught in the sharp rictus of death, one hand lolling over the armrest, as if reaching for his warbelt on the floor, the other almost touching the deep wound on the left side of his chest.

'Daventry,' Martha murmured. 'Daventry, Arundel's man. He visited Parson Reynaud yesterday.' Her fingers flew to her lips. 'Murder, sacrilege and blasphemy, oh sweetness!'

'What!'

'Master Cripplegate, Curate Cotes. The arca in the sacristy!'

All three hurried back down the nave and into the long, cavernous sacristy. The door to this hung open and, even before they placed their candles on the table, they could see that the trap door hidden in the far corner had been thrown back.

'I am now in charge,' the curate screeched.

'No you are not!' Cripplegate pushed by him and went down the cellar stairs. 'In heaven's name!' Cripplegate's voice echoed up. 'The arca has been opened, not a farthing remains. We have seen enough. We can do no more. Sexton Spurnel, fetch the sheriff's men . . .'

'Go forth Christian soul, may the angels of God greet you so you do not fall into the hands of the enemy, the Evil One, the Son of Perdition.'

Athelstan, Dominican friar and parish priest of St Erconwald's in Southwark, blessed for the last time the freshly turned burial mound which now housed the mortal remains of 'Fat Margo', as she was popularly known in the parish, though in the Book of the Dead, the Record of Remembrance, she was recorded as 'Margaret Grenel, widow, seamstress and embalmer of corpses.'

'Now you have gone to your eternal reward,' Athelstan murmured, staring down at the heavy wooden cross on which Crispin the carpenter would carve the dead woman's name and the date of her death, 'The Feast of St Michael, 29 September, the Year of Our Lord 1381.' Athelstan handed the asperger's rod and bucket back to Crim the altar boy and stared round at the parish council grouped behind its leaders, Watkin the dung-collector and Pike the ditcher. He nodded at Ranulf the rat-catcher and others of the parish now eager to return to the church before flocking to the Piebald tavern and the tender ministrations of its owner Mine host Jocelyn, the one-armed former river pirate. Fat Margo in her will, a scrap of parchment written some three years earlier, sealed, tied with ribbon and deposited in the parish chest, had left her small house and all its moveables 'for the parish community to be merry at table and faithful in their devotion to St Erconwald.' She had specifically added, to Athelstan's great amusement, 'that the parishioners toast her memory, to wish her God speed in her journey to paradise on the very day of her burial.' She also added that they 'do not think or say any ill of her on account of what might be revealed.'

'God knows what Margo meant by that,' Athelstan murmured.

'Pardon Father?'

Athelstan broke from his reverie and stared at the lined, close face of Mauger the parish clerk, who stood, church ledgers in one hand, his bell of office in the other. Athelstan glanced quickly at all the parishioners gathered around the freshly turned grave mound. He glimpsed Ranulf the rat-catcher who, the previous evening, when Margo's corpse was churched, had told the parishioners gathered for a church ale in the nave of St Erconwald's a ghost story about a rat-catcher. Apparently Ranulf's associate was visited by the devil and given the gift of being able to know what every rat was saying. He also knew what the rodents were doing, nibbling at larders, sniffing at babies or gnawing on corpses in the graveyard. Athelstan's parishioners had expressed their horror and delight, and the conversation soon turned to how Fat Margo hated rats and kept her house spotlessly clean, so much so that she was reluctant to allow anyone, including Athelstan, into her neatly scrubbed kitchen. In all, Ranulf had thoroughly enjoyed himself, though he now looked much the worse for wear. The rat-catcher's two champion ferrets, Audax and Ferox, were scrabbling, eager to be released, desperate to be despatched down some crack or crevice in their constant, bloody war against the horde of rats which plagued Southwark and beyond.

'Father, is it finished?' Athelstan caught Watkin's pleading tone.

The dung-collector and his henchmen had schooled their rugged, wind-whipped faces into masks of seeming piety, but they were impatient to be gone. Matters spiritual did not have much of a hold on Watkin and Pike, these two stalwarts of the parish council. They were not avid Gospel-greeters, and would soon show their disapproval if parish services became prolonged for more than necessary.

'You are impatient to say farewell to Margo as you are to greet her,' Athelstan teased. Both parishioners stared open-mouthed at the riddle Athelstan had posed.

'We are thirsty,' Moleskin the boatman called out. 'Father, it will soon be time for the Angelus bell.'

'So it will be,' Athelstan agreed. '*Procedamus in Christo* – let us proceed in Christ. Back to the church it is.'

The funeral procession lined up. Crim led the way, his capped candle, on its stick under a metal shield, fluttering bravely in the autumn breeze. Behind Crim, Mauger ponderously rang his bell, alerting the faithful to the funeral cortège. Athelstan glanced around as he gripped his psalter more tightly. Autumn was certainly making itself felt. The glossy green of summer was fading. The wild flowers were past their full glory and the ground was littered with growing mounds of discarded brown leaves. The breeze was not so warm. The sweet fragrances of the fresh grass which had sprouted so lovely and lush were tinged with corruption. Michaelmas had come and gone. Soon they would celebrate the October feasts and the rhythms and cycles of the seasons would continue. Parish life settling down for the long approach to Advent and the preparations for Christmas.

'And so life in all its riches will run its course,' Athelstan murmured as he glimpsed Cecily the courtesan and Clarissa her sister slipping away from the line of parishioners with Simon the skinner and William the weaver.

The funeral procession passed the old death house, now the home of the madcap beggar man Godbless and his omnivorous, filthy goat Thaddeus. Godbless constantly talked to the goat, as he was doing now, oblivious to the mourners passing his makeshift cottage and well-tended vegetable patch. The cortège left through the lychgate on to the great concourse stretching before the church. Athelstan caught sight of his close friend and constant dining companion the great, one-eyed tomcat Bonaventure on the prowl to the right of the church, where an old water duct was used by different vermin scurrying in and out of the building. Bladdersmith the beadle had opened the main door and stood on the steps with Judith the mummer next to him. She gazed expectantly at Athelstan, who smiled falsely to hide his exasperation. Judith was zealous in the extreme and pestered Athelstan constantly about staging a mummer's play based on the legend of Bigorne and Fillegut, the mythical beasts who devoured lecherous husbands. The story of the play centred on a meeting between these and their counterparts, Chice-fache and Pinchbelly, who gobbled down sharp-tongued wives. Judith had shared her ideas with the parish, who were equally enthusiastic about staging the play. They were already settling scores by choosing who would be best for what part, Watkin and Pike being foremost in the brewing mischief. Athelstan had decided to keep both these worthies under scrutiny. They were up to some devilment, though Athelstan couldn't detect what, except that Watkin had bought a magnificent new dung cart, specially constructed by Crispin the carpenter. Apparently Watkin had, God knows how, sealed an indenture with the good burgesses of Queenhithe to assist in the clearing and cleaning of their sewers, midden heaps and lay stalls.

'Father?'

Athelstan blinked and glanced round. He was so lost in his own thoughts he had abruptly paused just within the doorway of St Erconwald's whilst the rest of the procession had streamed ahead, threading its way through the door of the rood screen. Athelstan walked quickly down the nave. Benedicta the widow woman hurried beside him, her lovely olive-skin face full of concern, her eyes bright with agitation. Athelstan stopped at the foot of the sanctuary steps.

'Benedicta, what is the matter?'

'Father,' she grasped his wrist. 'You must come with me.' She leaned closer. 'You must see this.'

'You've been in Margo's house? You were—'

'Father, never mind that. You must come, please!'

A short while later, Benedicta led her parish priest down Spindle Avenue and into Margo's comfortable red-brick cottage which stood in its own garden plot. Benedicta hastily unlocked the door and, plucking at Athelstan's sleeve, took him across the solar, through the kitchen and buttery, and into a small scullery which housed the back door and stairs leading down into the cellar. Athelstan noticed how the trap door had been reinforced with strips of iron whilst locks and bolts ranged along all three sides.

He followed Benedicta down into the square, box-like

chamber, which glowed with lights from the wall cressets and candle spigots on the table, where two men sat with goblets and platters before them. Athelstan walked towards this and froze. He had seen embalmed corpses before and realised the grey-haired, stout man and his younger colleague – possibly his son, were cadavers: cleared, cleansed and skilfully embalmed. The bodies had been prepared, then dressed again and placed on these two chairs. Athelstan sniffed; putrefaction had not set in, although the faces and hands looked as if they had been fashioned out of wax, whilst the eyes of both corpses had receded deep into their sockets. Again Athelstan checked but there was no stench of corruption. Indeed, a grille high in the wall allowed in fresh air, whilst herb pots placed around the chamber and in wall crevices exuded a sharp sweetness.

Athelstan stared in amazement at these two figures. The sheer ordinariness of the situation chilled him. The men were dead, probably for some time, yet they sat as if expecting their souls to return at any moment. He also noticed how the platters before them contained stale crumbs, whilst wine dregs could be detected in the two goblets. The corpses sat slightly towards each other, as if deep in conversation, one hand close to the knife beside the platter, the other leaning against the table edge: the elder man wore a distinctive mail-studded wrist guard, though the younger corpse only bore the mark left by one on his right wrist.

'This is what Margo was referring to in her will,' Athelstan whispered. 'Something about not thinking ill of her when we made the discovery.' He gestured at the gruesome scene. 'This is it.'

Benedicta just stood petrified, fingers to her lips. 'I came in here.' She whispered. 'Everything was so tidy. I was listing what she had left. I went into the buttery and saw the trap door. It's just so ordinary,' she breathed out, 'that's what I thought. Two dead men sitting at a table, yet they seem alive. I did hear rumours . . .'

'About what?'

'Brother Athelstan . . .'

The friar and Benedicta turned as Mauger came clattering down the steps. 'Brother . . .'

The bell clerk stopped in amazement, then fell to his knees as he realised the full truth about the two grotesques sitting at the table.

'Saints and sinners,' Mauger gasped. 'Lord have mercy! Christ have mercy! Lord have mercy on us all.' Mauger sat back on his heels, staring at the macabre sight. 'I wonder, yes they must be.' The bell clerk got to his feet and nervously approached the table, staring at the faces of the embalmed corpses.

'What?' Athelstan asked.

'About eighteen years ago, I think it was that, Father. Yes, eighteen years ago, John of Gaunt organised a great chevauchée into Normandy. The commissioners of array were sent out searching for all able-bodied men, especially archers.' Mauger pointed to the far corner where two yew bows rested next to bulging quivers of yard-long shafts. 'All able-bodied men were summoned to the standards in Moorfields,' Mauger continued. 'If I recall parish gossip, Margo's husband Henry, and Walter their son went with them, marching down to Dover before being shipped across to Calais. According to Margo, both husband and son were killed in France leaving her a widow . . . but they didn't go. She must have murdered them . . .' Mauger's voice faltered.

'She was most skilled,' Benedicta declared. 'For years Margo prepared corpses for burial for our parish and neighbouring ones. She was loved, respected. I never dreamt she harboured such a secret.'

Athelstan went and sat on an overturned barrel, staring at the gruesome scene that was at once so ordinary and yet so chilling. He tried to recall what he knew about the merry soul who had lived in this cottage along with these ghosts. Margaret Grenel, to give her full and proper name, attended Mass on Sundays and feast days. She involved herself in parish festivities, though he could never recall her coming to be shrived. Athelstan shivered as he murmured a prayer for her soul.

'Poor woman,' he whispered. 'Her husband and son being commissioned for war – as in so many families; yes, even mine,' he added bitterly. Athelstan wondered what had truly happened here. The King's wars would often provide a path to freedom for many men. They were delighted to receive the royal writ and flock to the standards for a life allegedly made more exciting with the prospect of plunder and ransoms as well as escape from the crushing boredom of ordinary life. After all, Athelstan ruefully reflected, hadn't he, what seemed like an eternity ago, inveigled his own brother to join him in the King's array across the Narrow Seas? He and Francis/Stephen had been fascinated at the prospect of glory, the riches to be won, of being knighted on the battlefield, a fitting thanks for some act of bravery. Instead they had descended into Hell's own nightmare. Athelstan's beloved brother had been killed, his corpse brought back for burial at a Carthusian house close by the pilgrim's route to Canterbury. Athelstan's life had been shattered, not only at the loss of his brother, but his parents, broken hearted, falling ill and dying out of sheer grief.

'She must have objected, tried to stop them.' Athelstan hastily blessed the gruesome scene. 'They must have been obdurate,' he continued, 'both father and son, so she decided to kill them, probably with poison. Once they were dead she would remove their heart, stomach and entrails. Drain the fluids, packing the corpses with aromatics, herbs and spices, similar treatment being given to the skin, especially the face.'

'Can this be done?' Benedicta exclaimed.

'Yes, believe me, I have seen it done. Go into the city, Benedicta. Visit some of the churches. You'll hear about knights killed fighting alongside the Teutonic Knights in Lithuania, and even further east. Their corpses were embalmed, carefully preserved and shipped back for burial in some of our London churches. I understand it is not as difficult as people think. In Italy they have even found corpses perfectly preserved, through no artifice but simply the composition of the ground they were buried in. I suggest Margo was very skilled and had considerable experience in the management and preparation of cadavers.'

'Oh Lord, what shall we do?' Mauger moaned.

'Yes, what shall we do?' Athelstan echoed. He went and sat down on the third high-backed chair close to the table. Using his finger, he traced the stains left by the wine cup. 'These are fairly recent,' he murmured. 'Margo must have come here to dine, to talk as if her husband and son were still alive. God have mercy on them all.' He sketched a cross in the air. 'The human heart is a veritable maze within a maze of emotions, dreams, nightmares – and whatever else flits through this vale of tears.' Athelstan peered closer at the two grey-faced corpses, noticing the half-open eyes, the texture of hair, moustache and beard. He repressed an abrupt shiver of fear and a gnawing unease, a deepening uncertainty about what he was actually seeing. Despite the obvious horror, there was something else hidden away in this dreadful cellar.

'I suggested that she murdered them. On immediate reflection, I am not too sure.'

'What do you mean, Father?'

'Well, Benedicta, I was too hasty. First, Margo may have been many things, but she wasn't an assassin. I don't think she had a murderous heart. In fact, I don't believe she had a wicked bone in her body. So why would she kill her husband and son? That would be the work of some monster from Hell. Secondly, why embalm and keep them here? Was there something else she was trying to hide? Were these two men killed and she was unable to explain their deaths – hence this? Thirdly, Margo made no attempt to hide this from us once she had died. In fact, she actually warned us in her will that we would come across something unexpected, and not to think ill of her, which means she regarded herself as innocent.' He shook his head. 'But that doesn't explain the death of these two men or why their corpses are here.'

'What shall we do?' Mauger moaned.

'You have already asked that,' Benedicta snapped.

Athelstan glanced quickly at the widow woman, his sole comrade and keen-witted confidante. Benedicta seemed deeply preoccupied, as if she too was uncertain about what had happened.

'I do wonder if there is more to this than meets the eye,' she murmured.

'I agree,' Athelstan replied, getting briskly to his feet. 'Oh Mauger, why are you here, how did you know?'

'I overheard Benedicta insisting that you leave the church. I sensed you were coming here. Since Margo's funeral was over . . .' The bell clerk's voice trailed away as if he was totally distracted.

Athelstan stared at Mauger: a fairly youngish man with black hair parted down the middle which fell to his shoulders. He was dressed in jerkin and hose, a pair of gloves pushed into his belt. He wore mud-caked boots, his lined face all puckered in concern.

'Do you know something, Father?'

'What, Benedicta?'

'Margo crossed the river to receive treatment at St Bartholomew's hospital. She left the keys to her cottage with the parish, yes?'

'Agreed,' Mauger spoke up. 'She left her will and keys in the parish chest.'

'When I came here,' Benedicta continued, 'I had a feeling that someone had visited this house.'

'A thief?' Mauger asked quickly.

'I don't know.' The widow woman shook her head. 'I had the feeling that the house had been searched. Just a suspicion.' She half smiled. 'We women are much neater and more precise in what we do.'

'Explain,' Athelstan insisted.

'Well, go back upstairs in the buttery, kitchen and solar. You'll find small objects have been moved. You can see where they once stood for some time, but then they have been shifted. Go on, Father, have a look.'

Smiling to himself, Athelstan went back up the steps into the buttery and kitchen. Looking around, he agreed with Benedicta. Margo had been very precise and neat. He suspected that when she embalmed a corpse she did so in the solar, then cleared up afterwards, although most of the work was usually completed in the parish death house. It was as if Margo, because of the grisly work she did, made sure everything else in her life was neat, orderly, even fragrant. Small flower vases stood on sills and ledges, whilst pots of herbs had been placed in wall crevices. The fireplace was neatly swept and the irons carefully hung. Athelstan walked around and realised Benedicta was correct. It would be logical to have the occasional pot or vase moved a little to the right or left, but he noticed all of them were out of line, as if somebody had been looking for something. He recalled the trap door and went over and studied it carefully. He noticed the padlocks and bolts, as well as the large chest which had once covered the sealed entrance. Murmuring to himself, Athelstan returned to the cellar. Mauger still crouched there, looking anxious and furtive. Benedicta was staring at the two corpses, as if fascinated by them.

'Benedicta, did you pull away the chest, and where did you find the keys to the locks on the trap door? Surely they were not with the key to the house? Margo only deposited her will and one key in the parish chest.'

'I follow my parish priest,' Benedicta grinned, 'and try to be thorough in everything. I looked at the chest and thought, what was that doing in a buttery? I opened the lid and it contains, as you can see, nothing but blankets.'

'Of course,' Mauger whispered, 'such a chest is usually kept in the solar.'

'I thought the same. I pulled it away and saw the trap door. I then thought that Margo would not keep its keys too far away. If you feel beneath the chest, there is a nail. I found the keys to the locks tied to that. In fact, as I pulled the chest away, I heard a chink, though there is nothing in the chest to make such a noise.' She opened her purse on her belt and took out two small keys on a ring. 'You'd best keep these, Father. Now, Mauger,' she turned back to the bell clerk, 'why are you here? You never did answer Father?'

'Tiptoft,' he replied, still distracted. 'Sir John Cranston's courier.' The bell clerk shook himself from his reverie and sprang to his feet. 'Oh Lord, I forgot in all the hustle-bustle. Brother Athelstan, Tiptoft is waiting for you at the church. Sir Jack needs you urgently at St Benet's Woodwharf in Queenhithe.'

'A den of iniquity,' Benedicta breathed.

'So there must be mischief brewing there,' Athelstan declared. 'Look – Benedicta, Mauger, not a word to anyone about this. Lock and seal both this cellar and the house. I am going to meet Sir John, but I will ask Tiptoft to take an urgent message to Brother Philippe, who has now returned to the mastership of St Bartholomew's. I need him to study these corpses.' The friar blessed the chamber. 'Now I must go.'

Athelstan headed off to collect Tiptoft; he was ensconced with the parish council in the Piebald tavern. Cranston's messenger, dressed in the usual light green livery of a royal verderer, was all a-quiver with the 'horrid news'; he was regaling Athelstan's parishioners, who were always agog for any scandal, with it. How the church of St Benet's Woodwharf was now a house of corpses: men cruelly stabbed to death whilst something equally evil had been discovered in the crypt . . .

'But worst of all,' Tiptoft proclaimed, as Athelstan paused to listen just within the doorway, 'the arca has been broken into and the Flesher's money stolen!' Athelstan could almost feel the pall of deep fear descending on this usually merry taproom. Athelstan beckoned Jocelyn over.

'The Flesher?' he queried.

'Brother, the Flesher was baptised, though he is such a demon I doubt if he ever was! He was raised from the font as Simon Makepeace. He is called the Flesher because of his previous life.' Jocelyn stared quickly around. 'I think he's slaughtered everything that crawls under God's sun, both man and beast. He captains the most violent gang of rifflers in the city. He is the bane of Queenhithe—'

Jocelyn's description was cut short by Tiptoft's cry of recognition as he glimpsed Athelstan. The courier drained his tankard and pushed his way through the throng, his ghostly-white face beneath his fiery red, nard-streaked hair wreathed in a grimace.

'Brother Athelstan, Sir Jack awaits you with a veritable litany of murders.'

The courier almost pushed Athelstan out of the tavern, with Moleskin the boatman close behind, offering to take them for free across the Thames, an offer neither Athelstan or Tiptoft could refuse. Moleskin was eager to know more about these gruesome murders and all the mayhem and mystery at St Benet's.

The boatman summoned up others from his Guild of Watermen and Oarsmen and swiftly recruited a crew to row his great, six-oared barge from the Southwark side to St Paul's wharf. Athelstan and Tiptoft clambered in, made themselves as comfortable as possible, and Moleskin cast off. A choppy, cold journey. The bargemen seemed more interested in questioning Tiptoft about the gory details he'd glimpsed in St Benet's than concentrating on the sullen, swollen waters of the Thames. Athelstan found it difficult to remain calm: the barge pitched and fell as it battled the power of the river. He tried to distract himself by glancing to either side at the myriad of small vessels which darted here and there like water beetles. Occasionally a magnificent cog would break through the thinning mist, some great merchant ship of the Hanse, with sails bulging and flags fluttering. War barges, crammed with hobelars and mailed archers, made their way to the different quaysides, the captains on the prow blowing horns as a warning to the smaller craft – the herring boats and purveyance skiffs – to pull away. Athelstan wiped the spray from his face and stared up at the sky. It was a fairly cloudy day; autumn was sweeping in with all its fading glory.

'Jesus mercy,' Moleskin muttered.

Athelstan, sitting in the canopied stern, looked round the leather-stretched hood. They were now approaching the Woodwharf, pulling past a barge making its way from the quayside, a massive, high-prowed craft painted blood-red from stern to poop, six oarsmen on either side, all hooded in deep cowls and dressed completely in inky garb. On the high stern of the barge stood its master, the Fisher of Men, clothed in the robes of a Benedictine monk. He wore a mask over his face, and mailed gauntlets on his hands. No one knew who he really was. Some maintained he was a hospitaller who had been to Outremer and come back with the dreadful disease of leprosy. Others whispered that this was true, but that he had been cured by a miracle. This eerie, midnight figure, aware of Athelstan's stare, turned and raised his hand in greeting before turning back to his henchman, Icthus, who stood just behind the Fisher. An equally eerie sight, Icthus, despite the river cold, was dressed only in a linen tunic. He took his name from the Greek word for fish, because that is what he looked like, with his webbed hands and feet, his completely hairless face, sloping brow and cod-shaped mouth. He was a born swimmer, as fast as the great silver-skinned salmon or twisting porpoise. As now, he always stood ready, at his master's bidding, to slide overboard to bring in some corpse bobbing in the waters, the victim of an accident, suicide or murder. They would take what they culled from the river, the slime-covered corpses, back to their Chapel of the Drowned Men on its deserted quayside just past La Reole. Once the cadavers were cleaned and purified, they would be publicly exhibited, their descriptions proclaimed so grieving relatives, if there were any, could come and claim the corpse and pay the appropriate fee.

The rowers of this funeral barge were all grotesques and misfits, who hid their twisted bodies and malformed faces behind masks and visors. Moleskin believed they were the best rowers on the river, and Athelstan watched as they bent over the oars, chanting a death song as their craft cut through the water. The friar wondered if they were involved in the mysterious business at St Benet's, the spire of which Athelstan could now glimpse as Moleskin's barge aimed like a lance towards the quayside. Once they had come alongside, the friar, Tiptoft, Moleskin and his merry crew promptly disembarked. Athelstan would have immediately despatched the courier with urgent messages for Brother Philippe at St Bartholomew's, but Tiptoft gripped the friar's arm and squeezed.

'Brother, we are about to enter the kingdom of the damned, the realm of chaos, and so thread the devil's valley. I must accompany you.' Tiptoft tapped the hilt of his short sword in its deerskin sheath. 'Brother Athelstan, Sir John would have my head if anything happened to you.' The courier was deter-mined, so Athelstan shrugged and let him have his way. They entered the devil's warren, the alleyways of Hell, narrow strips of dirt-caked ground which twisted like snakes between the overhanging rotting houses and decaying walls. They entered a stygian darkness where the sunlight was never glimpsed and the air reeked of every putrid stench. The lanes were deserted and lonely, though occasionally some figure flittered through the murk, a dark, darting shadow in the gloom. A place of dread where the very silence was fraught with danger.

Occasionally a dog would howl, whilst behind mouldering fences Athelstan heard the snuffle and grunt of half-wild pigs. Rats swarmed across the streets as if they owned this man-made

Hades. A door was swiftly flung open and then crashed shut. A wooden shutter rattled on the building opposite and a strident voice shouted, 'King's men; Cranston's courier with Athelstan who cherishes the poor.'

At last they cleared the maze and entered the great, cobbled concourse in front of St Benet's – an ancient church in many styles with towers, transepts and side chapels added on to the great soaring nave built centuries earlier. A grim and forbidding house of prayer, broad, sweeping steps led up to the main entrance, with a narrow postern door to its left. On either side of this ancient church stretched the parish cemetery, a sea of tumbled crosses, headstones and tomb markers. The cemetery, however, looked as if it was being cleared. The postern door abruptly opened and Sir John Cranston, Lord High Coroner of London, strode out in all his velveteen glory. 'Sir Jack,' as he liked to announce himself, was dressed in a dark blue cotehardie over a high-collared linen shirt; the silver buttons down the middle gleamed in the sunlight. He wore hose of the same colour and texture, pushed into stout leather riding boots, with spurs which jingled like a host of elfin bells. The coroner had his broad warbelt displaying sword and dagger strapped around his generously endowed waist. On his head a beaver hat, his white-whiskered face oiled and trimmed, beaming with the joy of a man who loved the comforts of both table and the bedchamber. The coroner stood stretching himself, cloak thrown back, hands on his hips. Athelstan called out from the entrance of the alleyway and raised a hand in greeting. Cranston, grinning from ear to ear, trotted nimbly down the steps, strode across, nodded at Tiptoft and embraced Athelstan in tight hug. He kissed the friar on each cheek then stepped back.

'Welcome little monk.'

'Friar, Sir John.'

'As I said, welcome.' Cranston beamed.

'And the Lady Maude? All is well? The two poppets, your household?' Athelstan gently poked Cranston in the stomach. 'Nor must I forget the Irish wolfhounds, Gog and Magog?'

'All are well. Lady Maude is truly a cypress under which I shelter, whilst the twins grow strong and straight like the cedars of Lebanon. They still believe,' he added wearily, 'that Gog and Magog are there to be ridden. It's so good to have them back.' Cranston narrowed his eyes. 'It was so blessed,' he repeated, 'to meet them in Canterbury.'

Athelstan smiled and glanced away. He, Sir John and most of the parish of St Erconwald's had made a most singular pilgrimage to St Thomas a Becket's shrine in Canterbury. Here, Cranston had met his family again after their long stay in the countryside during the turbulent bloody days of the Great Revolt. Cranston and the entire parish had returned refreshed and renewed, and it was just as well, as more murderous mysteries emerged from the seething life of the city. Cranston brought one hand down on the friar's shoulder.

'My friend,' he murmured, peering down, 'how are you?'

'In a while, Sir John, but what is happening here?'

'A bubbling broth of murder, theft, blasphemy and sacrilege.'

'Sir John?'

'Let us walk very warily into this.' Cranston jabbed a thumb, pointing back at St Benet's. 'There is an inscription carved above the doorway there. I believe its translation runs, "This is a terrible place, the House of God and the Gate of Heaven." Believe me, Brother, the first half of that proclamation is true. The second half beggars belief. So come, my little ferret of a friar, watch and listen.'

Athelstan pulled a face, crossed himself and asked Cranston to despatch Tiptoft to Brother Philippe at St Bartholomew's. Once the courier learnt the message by rote and left, Athelstan followed the coroner up the steps and through the door, into the vestibule of St Benet's. A place of shifting light and moving shadows, Athelstan immediately sensed the sinister gloom which pervaded this place, cold and dank, whilst the poor light made it even more threatening. Flaxwith, Cranston's principal bailiff, stood on guard just inside the door with his cohort of stalwarts. Samson, Flaxwith's mastiff, which Athelstan regarded as the ugliest dog north of the Thames, yipped in delight at Cranston's appearance, and would have leapt on the coroner but for the leather leash around his thick, muscular neck which kept him close to Flaxwith's boots. The chief bailiff indicated with his head toward a cluster of shadowy figures gathered around the baptismal font.

'Leading parishioners,' he whispered.

'Take them into one of the chantry chapels,' Cranston growled. 'They are not to leave until I have questioned them.'

Athelstan waited for these to go, then walked over to study the painting on the wall where the parishioners had been gathered. Athelstan loved the different frescoes that decorated the London churches. Indeed, thanks to his own parish artist, the Hangman of Rochester, Athelstan was becoming quite a peritus, an expert on the different styles. He could see that the painting close to the baptismal font was very old and clumsily illuminated, the scene almost scrawled, its colour fast fading. Nevertheless, this ancient fresco vividly depicted a world turned upside down. A jester sat enthroned, crowned with a cap sporting pointed ears and bells; his monkey-face was a mask of mockery as he presided over a topsy-turvy world where all reality was cleverly twisted. A cohort of mice hanged a cat. Hares with human faces rode to the hound. Chickens terrorised a fox whilst a weasel kissed a falcon. Athelstan wondered if this was the world he was now entering? A church where bloody murder had been committed, a holy place which housed horrid blasphemy, because so-called Christian souls had committed the most appalling acts.

Cranston tapped him on the shoulder and led Athelstan across the vestibule to a figure slumped on the sexton's chair to one side of the main door. At first Athelstan thought the man was asleep. Cranston pushed the lanternhorn closer so Athelstan could inspect the corpse in all its gruesome horror. The friar hurriedly sketched a cross in the air as he crouched to study the cadaver.

'Giles Daventry,' Cranston murmured. 'One of my Lord of Arundel's henchmen. More of that later. Just look and learn, Brother.'

Athelstan, murmuring a prayer, did so. Daventry was a fairly young man, his black, greasy hair untended, his harsh face and chin unshaven. He sat, or rather slouched in the chair, one hand over its armrest, the other pointing towards the deep death wound in the left side of his chest. Daventry was dressed in a leather jerkin, woollen hose and scuffed leather boots; his warbelt lay on the floor beside him. Daventry's face was frozen in the rictus of violent death, startled by its suddenness as he sat in that chair, legs apart. The dead man's flesh was cold, hardening, whilst the blood which had spurted from the wound as well as through his nose and mouth had congealed as it dried.

'Here is a fighting man, yes, Sir John?'

'I agree.'

'He has been dead some time, so he probably came into the church yesterday evening. We don't know why, nor the reason for him sitting in the sexton's chair, but he does so after taking off his warbelt, which he placed on the floor beside him. Now, from the very little I know, the henchmen of great lords are soldiers, men steeped in violence; conse-quently – like the mastiffs they are – alert to any danger. But this is not the case here. Daventry is relaxed. His killer approaches and he still remains relaxed. Daventry senses no danger. The killer leans down, his knife concealed, then he strikes. But who, why and whatever are the mystery.'

Athelstan scrutinised the cracked paving stones around the sexton's chair, but he could detect nothing amiss, no scuff marks or sign of the chair being pushed backwards and forwards. Athelstan shook his head and blessed the corpse.

'There's more?' he murmured.

'Of course.'

Athelstan sighed, got to his feet and followed the coroner down the long, gloomy nave. It reminded Athelstan of a tithe barn used by his father: a dark, high shed lit by cresset torches fixed to a row of pillars either side, as well as by the lancet windows high in the wall. Transepts had been built on to the north and south side of the church. Each of these contained small chantry chapels behind dark, oaken trellised fencing. At the far end of the church rose a sombre rood screen, which divided the sanctuary from the nave. To the left of this stood the lady altar and to the right the Chapel of St Benet, the patron saint of the parish. Cranston first took Athelstan over to the coffin, which stood on trestles before the rood screen entrance. Athelstan gazed in astonishment at the empty casket, its lid unscrewed and thrown to one side along with the purple-gold burial pall, the white-cushioned interior gleaming in the light. Athelstan leaned closer and smelt the herbs that had been crammed around the cadaver.

'Look on that and weep,' Cranston intoned. 'Notice the coffin, Brother, made of the finest elm wood. The bronze bolts, handles and screws are the work of a craftsman. Believe me, Brother, this empty coffin could spark bloodshed and the most murderous affray across London.' Cranston dug into his pouch and took out a soiled scrap of parchment. Athelstan read the message. How the corpse would be returned at a certain time and in a certain place of the writer's choosing in return for a ransom of fifty gold crowns.

'The devil's ransom,' Athelstan murmured.

'And the devil to pay,' Cranston agreed. 'That casket once housed the mortal remains of Isabella Makepeace. What a name! She was the mother of London's most vicious and notorious riffler, known to all and sundry as the Flesher. A man who fears neither God nor man. A great thief, Simon's problem, and it always has been, is that he cannot distinguish between his property and everybody else's. He takes what he wants and he will not be checked, be it the property of the Crown or Holy Mother Church. A soul conceived in sin, he was born to sin most vigorously. The Flesher will regard this empty coffin as an act of war.'

'Yes, yes,' Athelstan intervened, 'I have heard about the Flesher.'

'And you will be told more later – but come, the deceased Parson Reynaud awaits us.'

Cranston took Athelstan across to the chantry chapel close to the lady altar. Its curtain had been pulled back. Parson Reynaud sat crookedly in the celebrant's chair on the inside of the trellised screen, a prie-dieu on the other side; anyone wishing to be shrived would kneel there and await absolution. Athelstan studied this arrangement, a common one in many churches, including his own. He pinched his nostrils at the fetid smell. He then knelt down and swiftly blessed the corpse, murmuring the requiem as he studied the old priest's wiry grey hair, the lined face with the toper's nose and thick, blood-encrusted lips. Like Daventry, Parson Reynaud squatted legs apart, one hand lolling down, the other close to the heart-wound deep in the left side of his chest. The dead priest was dressed in a thick green woollen cloak thrown around his shoulders, a jerkin and hose of the same colour with the softest slippers on his feet. The fingers of both hands were decorated with jewelled rings and an intricately carved bracelet circled his left wrist. Athelstan also noticed the gold filigree chain around the parson's neck; from it hung a silver heart with the inscription, 'Love conquers everything' etched on to it.

'A man of the world,' Athelstan murmured. He peered closer at a second chain with a coffer key hanging on it.

'Remember that, Brother.'

Athelstan glanced up at the coroner.

'Why?'

'In a while, what do you think?'

'Well, he wasn't killed to be robbed,' Athelstan gestured at the jewellery. 'So we must look for some other motive. This priest intended to shrive penitents or meet someone. He must have come in just before dark yesterday evening. The killer was either waiting or followed him in. He approached and, as swift as a pouncing cat, drove a dagger into the old priest's chest. God rest him. Someone should administer the last rites.'

'Let the curate do that,' Cranston retorted. 'We are busy enough and I have more to show you.' Athelstan leaned on the screen to get up, once again noticing the sober yet very costly raiment on the old priest, as well as the expensive jewellery. Athelstan immediately recalled that gruesome scene in the cellar of Margo's cottage.

'That's it,' Athelstan snapped his fingers. 'That's it, that's it!'

'What, little friar?'

'Their clothes, the Grenels' clothes. They were clean, they were new.'

'Grenel?' The coroner shook his head. 'That name echoes down the years. What, oh my goodness, yes . . .'

'Sir John, not now.' Athelstan shook his head. 'Let us concentrate. It would seem an assassin swept through here late last evening.'

'And one who loves gold.' Cranston plucked at Athelstan's sleeve and led him up across the sanctuary into the sacristy; a long chamber with a table, chairs, stools, aumbries and a stack of shelves screwed to the wall. Athelstan immediately glimpsed the trap door thrown back and the heavy, iron-bound coffer with its weighted base standing to the right of this. The concave lid of the arca had been tipped back and, as he knelt beside it, Athelstan noticed the two intricate but quite distinctive locks.

'This must have held a treasure,' Athelstan murmured. 'That's why it was fashioned like this, with special locks fitted. One of the keys to open it still hangs around that dead priest's neck, yes? And the other?'

'Around the fat, thick-skinned throat of the Flesher, Simon Makepeace. I believe he is now in council with Fitzalan at my Lord of Arundel's Thameside mansion. He will arrive here in a truly murderous rage. I will explain that later, but finally . . .'

Corbett led Athelstan back down the nave through the shattered devil's door and out into the cemetery. They followed the path round to the back of the church and the cracked, worn steps leading down into the crypt, its heavy double doors flung back. Two of Flaxwith's bailiffs stood guard over four pathetic bundles of bones, each partially covered with a shabby canvas corpse cloth. Cranston and Athelstan went gingerly down the chipped, moss-strewn steps. At Cranston's insistence, the corpse sheets were removed to reveal four skeletons; shards of dry skin still clung to the bones, tufts of hair to the skull. Cranston knelt down and turned all four over so Athelstan could see the horrid blow to the back of each head.

'From the little I know,' Cranston squinted up at Athelstan, 'these humble bones belong, in God's eyes, to four young women. Each of them was killed by a hatchet blow to the back of the head.' He pulled a face. 'Now that's the mark of the Flesher. He loves to kill with a cleaver to the face, which splits the head from brow to chin or,' he waved a hand, 'a clean cut to the back of the head, hence his name.'

'And you think this is the Flesher's handiwork?'

'Probably.'

'And these remains are whores, prostitutes, street workers?'

'Yes, Brother, happy girls from the stews and brothels along the Thames.'

'And how were they discovered?'

Cranston pointed towards the dark, yawning crypt. From where he stood, the friar could glimpse the high fence or palisade, and one mound after another of skulls and bones lying beyond it.

'Flaxwith came down here more out of curiosity than anything else. Of course Samson followed. Now that dog may have the ugliest face, but he also has the most tender nose. Flaxwith's dog can sniff out dead human flesh better than anything which crawls or flies beneath God's blue sky. Samson trotted round the outside of that palisade till he reached the gate, where he paused, barking and pawing at the wood. Flaxwith let him in and Samson began to nose amongst the remains just inside. Flaxwith brought a lantern and glimpsed these four skeletons piled close together.' Cranston sighed, blowing his cheeks out. 'I suspect there are more remains like this in both the crypt and that God-forsaken cemetery. From the little I know, apart from his mother, the Flesher truly hated women, and loved nothing better than to become violent with them.'

Athelstan murmured a prayer and sketched a blessing above the skeletons. 'And there is no other indication of who they were or where they came from? Nothing else was found?'

'Brother, you see what Flaxwith did and, before you ask, if our priest or his sexton knew about this?' Cranston shrugged. 'Flaxwith received a very vague answer; apparently this crypt is never locked or bolted. There is only one entrance to it through the cemetery. Let's face it, Brother, there are no pockets in a shroud; nothing of value on a corpse, certainly not in St Benet's. So why should anyone enter a crypt? Most people would avoid such places as they would a leper house.'

'Unless they want to hide the effects of their heinous sin of murder.'

Athelstan gazed down at the skeletons. 'None of these have been in the soil for long. There's no mark or tinge of the grave, the mud and clay which become part of the bone. To a certain extent they are still white and gleaming. Sir John, I suspect these four have not been buried for long. They may have been dumped in some pit and, once the flesh was corrupted, dragged out and thrown in here . . .'

PART TWO

Hemp office (**Old English**): the condemned cell

Brother Philippe, keeper and master of the King's own hospital of St Bartholomew's, stood on the execution platform beneath the soaring gibbets known as 'The Elms' overlooking the great, open meadow of what was once known as 'Smooth Field', the great meeting place of the city. Above him, the nooses of the gallows hung like deadly black necklaces against the sky. Brother Philippe had seen so many die here; as today, he had been called as a witness, as well as to offer the Sacrament, before the condemned man was turned off.

Brother Philippe hated execution day. He stared out over the crowd, most of whom had come to watch another human being die. All the weird and the wonderful from London's underworld, be it Whitefriars, Hell's buttery, the Devil's Kitchen, or any of the other dens of despair which housed the lawless tribes of London's Hades. Brother Philippe's eyesight was not as good as he might wish, but he glimpsed the shifting sea of colour and pinched his nostrils at the myriad of smells wafting around him: smoke, fire, burning meat, cheap perfume, heavy sweat and the foul smells of the midden heaps. The Benedictine gripped his psalter more tightly as the sheriff's men abruptly shouted, 'Turn. Turn the ladder.' The executioner, the Hangman of Rochester, a member of Athelstan's parish at St Erconwald's, gripped the gibbet ladder but then paused. The hangman stared up at Roslin, the notorious robber indicted for numerous felonies and crimes perpetrated the length and breadth of the city. Brother Philippe followed the hangman's gaze.

Poor Roslin, a housebreaker who, by his own admission, had chosen to burgle – or at least try to – a merchant friendly to the Flesher. Roslin had been captured as he came out of the window of Goldsmith Blundel's house, and his booty seized which, for a fee, was returned to its owner. The Flesher's men had handed Roslin over to the sheriffs in order to claim the reward, as well as teach Roslin and everyone else that no robberies took place without the express permission of Master Makepeace. Brother Philippe chewed on his lip. He really must have words with Blundel about this matter; after all, Brother Philippe had recently done business with that powerful London merchant.

A thunderous roar from the crowd startled the physician from his reverie. The condemned man had now reached the top of the ladder, where he had been bound hand and foot, the noose fitted expertly around his neck. However, Roslin seemed determined to postpone his death for as long as possible, by delivering a homily on his nefarious career as one of the city's most notorious housebreakers. Once again, Brother Philippe stared out over the crowd. He was certain he glimpsed the fiery red hair of Tiptoft, Cranston's courier. The crowd shifted and surged slightly forward. Crucifixes were held up high in the air by the different guilds of those who flocked to The Elms on execution day to offer consolation to the condemned, their family and friends. Roslin had cheekily confessed he had neither friends nor family, but the Guild of the Hanged and the Society of the Good Thief still gathered at the foot of the scaffold to sing songs of mourning and the psalms for the dead. Ale carriers, water-bearers and beer boys pushed their handcarts and shouted for business. Itinerant cooks carted their moveable stoves, grills and braziers, which gave off a pungent smoke, turning the air sickly with the rancid stench of the ancient meats being cooked. Hot-pot girls pushed their way through, with platters of steaming food from the many cook shops which fringed the open expanse of Smithfield. Pleasant faced and smiling, they tried to outbid the itinerant cooks, both with the freshness of their own appearance and the food they were serving. Pimps, sharp-eyed for any profit, led their string of whores for any buyer desperate enough to purchase the raddled bodies of these scarlet-clad prostitutes. Naps, foists, pick-purses and cunning men swarmed through the crowd, eager for any mischief and easy profit. Knights on their way to the tournament ground on the far side of Smithfield passed by in a blaze of heraldic colour and clash of armour, their great destriers snorting noisily as they pawed the ground.

'That's it, that's it. Turn him off!' the sheriff's man bawled. The Hangman of Rochester, eyes fixed on the prisoner, listened to the quickening beat of the tambour players on the steps of the execution platform. A hunting horn brayed and the hangman swiftly turned the ladder. Roslin fell like a stone until the noose abruptly tightened and a loud crack heralded the felon's neck had been broken. Immediately the mob which had come to witness the hanging broke up: some streaming back towards the stalls, piggeries or cattle pens; others eager to shelter and drink in the many ale booths, taverns and hostelries around the great field. A few of those who regarded the effects of a hanged man, be it his clothes or his flesh, as containing powerful properties, tried to climb on to the scaffold. They had drawn knives, blades and razors, and held these at the ready to slice a finger, cut some hair, shred a piece of clothing or peel a portion of the dead man's skin. The sheriff's men fought these off but they still persisted. The sorcerers, warlocks and wizards in their shabby black robes, dusty wigs framing faces ghastly-white with black kohl rings around their eyes, were determined to secure their macabre spoils. They fought and jostled the sheriff's men.

Brother Philippe decided he'd done enough. After all, he was not supposed to be chaplain at this execution. The nominated priest was Parson Reynaud of St Benet's Woodwharf, but he had died in the most mysterious circumstances, so Brother Philippe had been summoned to assist. The affray on the execution platform was growing worse, so Brother Philippe hurriedly blessed the hanging corpse now twisting and creaking at the end of the rope. He felt his elbow grasped, turned and smiled at the Hangman of Rochester.

'Come on, Brother,' the hangman urged. 'The sheriff's men are determined not to lose this fight. They are under strict instructions to gibbet Roslin's corpse on the approaches to London Bridge. The dead man incurred the wrath of the great ones of this city. I understand Parson Reynaud was to deliver Roslin the harshest of homilies.'

Brother Philippe nodded understandingly. The hangman gently insisted on escorting him off the scaffold; as he did so, the executioner explained how the physician must not be worried about Roslin, who was now past all caring, whilst the felon's death had been mercifully swift. The hangman added how he always arranged the rope and ladder so the condemned had their necks snapped in a few breaths rather than be slowly strangled. Brother Philippe, of course, had heard all of this before. The executioner's expertise at quickly despatching London's criminals to God's high court was now legendary. Indeed, the same could be said for the hangman's skill as a painter; his frescoes and wall paintings decorated St Erconwald's, as well as other churches in Southwark and beyond.

Out of the corner of his eye, Brother Philippe closely studied this eerie-looking individual, who had once been a parish anchorite. The hangman was garbed completely in black, which only emphasised his snow-white face, deep-set eyes and the long, corn-coloured hair falling down to his shoulders. Lost in thought about the sheer strangeness of his fellow men, Brother Philippe followed the hangman from the gallows site. They clasped hands and the physician watched the executioner stride back to claim Roslin's corpse. The Benedictine then turned towards the cavernous entrance of St Bartholomew's, only to find his way blocked by four men. Three of these were rifflers dressed in leather jerkins, woollen hose and stout marching boots. They looked unkempt, with long, tangled hair, bushy beards and moustaches. They sported an escutcheon on their right shoulder, which displayed a tree in full bloom; the branches were a deep brown, the leaves a bright, glossy green. They stood aggressively, thumbs thrust into the shabby warbelts fastened around their waists. Brother Philippe, refusing to be cowed, peered more closely at the insignia.

'Is that an elm tree?' he questioned. 'They once used the elms here in Smithfield to hang felons.'

'It's an oak tree.' The fourth person, dressed in the costly robes of a lawyer, stepped in between the physician and the rifflers.

'And you must be these gentlemen's legal representative?' Brother Philippe murmured.

'In a sense, yes. These are the Sycamores – retainers, household servants and henchmen of my master Simon Makepeace, owner of the Devil's Oak, a magnificent hostelry in Queenhithe ward with a splendid view over the river.'

'You can also get a splendid view of Smithfield from the top of the execution ladder.'

'Ah yes, Master Roslin.'

'And you are?'

'Josiah Copping. Lawyer, attorney and legal adviser to Master Makepeace.'

Brother Philippe stared at this little mouse of a man with his scrawny hair, worried black eyes, snub nose and thin, disapproving mouth. The lawyer beat his fingers impatiently against his stomach, whilst his companions showed their impatience by tugging at warbelts and shuffling their boots, looking about, as if fascinated by the colourful stream of people hurrying across Smithfield.

'I can see you are a busy man, Master Copping. I certainly am. What do you want from me, a physician? I must say you all look fairly healthy, although you three sirs,' Brother Philippe pointed at the rifflers, 'drink too much. You are red in the face and your noses are swollen—'

'Jewels,' Copping broke in. He now lost some of his simpering pleasantry.

'Jewels?' Brother Philippe questioned.

'You took an amethyst which gleamed a deep imperial purple to Goldsmith Blundel. You exchanged it for a sum of pounds sterling—?'

'Who told you that?'

'Master Blundel.'

'He really should be more discreet, I mean as a banker.'

'Master Blundel was grateful to my master, who helped capture Roslin and found the amethyst on his person,' Copping shrugged, 'along with other precious items. Apparently Master Blundel had been closing for the day. He was distracted for a short while and Roslin, like the shadow he was, seized what was on display at the back of the shop. He tried to escape but the hue and cry were raised. Apparently my master's men had a hand in his arrest. Roslin was caught, handed over to the sheriff's comitatus, and the stolen goods, including that amethyst, were returned to their rightful owner. My master admired it and asked Goldsmith Blundel where he had obtained the amethyst. The good merchant named you.'

'Most indiscreet. I shall certainly have words with Master Blundel.'

'So you did sell it to him?'

'I best go now – and tell your dogs,' Brother Philippe pointed at the rifflers, 'that I am a Benedictine monk, a royal physician on personal terms with my Lord of Gaunt, as well as His Grace the King. Just as importantly, I am also a personal friend of Brother Athelstan and Sir John Cranston, Lord High Coroner of London.'

Copping raised a hand and snapped his fingers. The rifflers stepped aside and Brother Philippe swept on.

'Oh, Brother?'

The physician turned.

'Grenel, did Margo Grenel give the amethyst to you?'

'Why not ask her yourself?' Brother Philippe snapped and walked on.

'Tell me,' Athelstan caught Cranston by the wrist as they walked back up the sanctuary steps towards the sacristy where Flaxwith had summoned all those Cranston wished to question. 'Tell me,' Athelstan repeated, 'why I saw the Fisher of Men on his great barque making his way across the river?'

'A new craft,' Cranston half chuckled. 'The Fisher has christened it *The Leviathan*. Yes, he came to see me to report on what he hadn't found more than what he had. But more of that later.'

Cranston led Athelstan into the sacristy, where Parson Reynaud's household had gathered. Martha Ashby, the house-keeper, had brought across a jug of light ale and a platter of croutons toasted lightly and smeared with herb cream cheese. The introductions were made and Cranston sat down at the head of the table, Athelstan to his right, whilst Flaxwith closed and guarded the door. Both coroner and friar gratefully accepted the refreshments. Cranston immediately began to eat. He ignored the ale, but now and then took a generous mouthful from the miraculous wineskin hidden so expertly beneath his cloak. Athelstan half smiled as he sipped and nibbled at what had been set before him. Cranston was playing his usual game: creating a silence which would both deepen and sharpen to test the keenest wits, whilst allowing both himself and Athelstan to study those gathered to answer their questions. Athelstan nodded at Martha as she took her seat at the far end of the table. A pretty, homely woman of no more than thirty-five summers, the housekeeper was garbed in a dark brown dress clasped high at the neck. Its sleeves were unbuttoned and unrolled slightly back to reveal elegant wrists and long, fluted fingers, the nails slightly painted. Martha's thick, rich auburn hair was neatly clipped under a short, white linen veil. She wore little jewellery, apart from a ring on her right hand. An astute, highly intelligent woman, Athelstan reflected, very much like Benedicta: good looking and good natured, kindly and welcoming, but with a steely will and a keen wit.

Curate Cotes, slurping at his tankard, was neither of these. The priest looked as if he had gone to bed drunk and unwashed, only to be dragged unceremoniously from it. Sexton Spurnel, a small, thickset man, sat nervously, one hand grasping his tankard, the other combing his thick moustache and beard. A worrier, Athelstan reasoned, very unlike Cripplegate, the leader of the parish council, who exuded a quiet confidence. A prominent member of the locksmith's guild, Cripplegate sat all neat and poised, his sallow, grey-moustached face carefully composed. He ate slowly, lost in his own thoughts, though now and then he would join the desultory conversation going on around the table.

Cranston coughed as Athelstan opened his chancery satchel and laid out his writing implements.

'We should begin,' the coroner declared.

'Sir John, first,' Athelstan pointed at the curate. 'Master Cotes, you will see to the anointing and blessing of the two corpses?'

The priest, his mouth bulging with food, nodded.

'Can I remind you,' Athelstan continued, 'that no Mass, or indeed any of the sacraments can be celebrated in St Benet's until the Bishop of London has purified and re-consecrated your church?'

'It's not my church,' the curate slurred. 'It's a den of thieves.'

'Enough of that,' Cripplegate declared. 'Brother Athelstan, I've already sent a messenger to Archdeacon Tuddenham. We will cooperate fully with the bishop and all the requirements of canon law.'

'Good, good,' Cranston declared, 'and you, sir,' he pointed at the curate, 'will show me and mine every respect. This is in fact a court, and I am the King's coroner.'

'And I am a cleric, you have no right—'

'I have every right!' Cranston bellowed, bringing his ham-like fists down on to the table. 'I couldn't care if you are related to the Holy Father in Rome. Murder has been committed in your church and you will be questioned.' Cranston glowered down at the curate, who sat slumped, suitably cowed, or appearing so, at the coroner's outburst.

'You haven't changed,' Cotes whispered, 'has he, my friends?'

The silence that ensued was abrupt and deep. Athelstan straightened up and cursed his own tiredness. He wasn't truly concentrating on what was happening. He sensed there was more to these people meeting around this table, not just the murderous mystery of St Benet's, but something else. Cotes's remark was meant to provoke memories of the past. Athelstan stared around. Was there a bond between these parishioners, or some of them, and the King's coroner? Had their lives brushed before and, if so, how and when?

'Let's begin,' Cripplegate demanded.

'Good, good,' Athelstan soothed, 'let us start with the empty coffin. It once housed Mistress Isabella Makepeace, yes?'

'Mother of Simon Makepeace,' Cripplegate declared. 'A venerable lady, past her eighty-fifth summer. She resided in her own chambers at the Devil's Oak.'

'The tavern owned by her son, Simon?'

'Yes, Sir John.'

'Known to others as the Flesher?'

'I cannot speak for others.'

'So, Mistress Makepeace dies,' Athelstan pressed on, 'and she's brought here?'

'Yes,' Martha replied. 'The corpse was brought in on

Monday. I dressed it for burial in the parish death house, a bleak enough place. Parson Reynaud churched it yesterday evening.'

'And you screwed on the lid, sealing the casket?' Athelstan asked.

'Yes,' she answered, 'and Master Makepeace came to pay his last respects to his mother. He placed red roses in her coffin. He ordered me to seal it. I did so in his presence. He stood and watched me close the coffin for burial.'

'And then?'

'I took it over,' the sexton declared. 'Mistress Martha, myself, Curate Cotes and Master Cripplegate also attended the churching. We placed the coffin on a wheeled sled and pushed it across to the church to where Parson Reynaud was waiting just before the rood screen.' The sexton drew a deep breath. 'The ceremony took place. The corpse was churched and left to the angels before the high altar. We never guessed what was going to happen.'

Athelstan nodded understandingly, even as he recalled one of Cranston's sayings: 'People's lives are like onions. You peel the top layer and realise the thickness and multitude of the skins beneath.' Athelstan was intent on peeling this particular onion to its very core. He stared at Martha, her pretty, slightly rosy face, the full parted lips and the merry, dancing eyes. Yes, Athelstan thought, it was time to peel this onion a little further.

'Mistress Martha?'

'Brother?' Her smile widened.

'You live in the priest's house?'

'Yes.' Her smile faded. 'My own room, a bedchamber. Seventeen years ago, Parson Reynaud hired me. We sealed an indenture kept in the parish archives. I looked after him and his house. I also, when I could, helped out in the parish; that's what I did.' She added meaningfully, 'Nothing else.'

'Though the good parson did his best to widen your duties,' the curate jibed. 'You were most sought after.'

'By you and him,' she replied coolly. 'But I put him in his place – and remember, Sir Priest, I have had to do the same with you, Curate Cotes. But, there again, you were so

deep in your cups, you probably cannot remember such
occasions . . .'

Cotes coloured and stared down at the tabletop. Athelstan
glanced quickly at the others, but they all hid behind a mask
of studious indifference.

'Mistress,' Cranston smiled at this very pretty but strong-
willed woman, 'we thank you for your honesty and directness.
What are your antecedents? How did you—'

'I can answer that,' Cripplegate declared.

'As can I.'

Athelstan whirled round and stared at the figure who had
quietly opened the sacristy door. Flaxwith had been standing
to one side and now blocked the visitor on the threshold.
Athelstan rose and glimpsed the shadowy shapes behind their
visitor.

'I am sure you can.' Cranston heaved himself up and,
accompanied by Athelstan, gestured at Flaxwith to stand aside
as he confronted these new arrivals.

'You should announce yourselves,' Cranston smiled. 'After
all, you are the bell clerk, aren't you?' He jabbed a finger at
the intruder. 'I know who you are. I certainly recognise the
mouse-like features of Josiah Copping, bell clerk of this parish,
clerk and legal advisor to Master Simon Makepeace, owner
of the Devil's Oak. A true wolf in sheep's clothing, aren't you,
Josiah, and where were you yesterday evening?' Copping,
standing on tiptoe, peered over Cranston's shoulder at the
others gathered around the sacristy table.

'I asked you a question.' Cranston advanced threateningly.

'I was in my house in Tumbleweed Lane,' Copping answered
hastily. 'I . . . we have heard the dreadful news. My master
is busy at Lord Arundel's mansion which lies—'

'I know London,' Cranston barked.

'I represent Mater Simon's interests. I need to be present
at this meeting. After all, my lord, the Earl of Arundel,
has the right—'

'Of advowson.' Athelstan spoke up. 'The right to appoint
the priest and curate to this church?'

Copping looked Athelstan up and down. 'Ah, you must
be the Dominican?'

'Yes, I must be.'

'You can join the meeting.' Cranston grabbed Copping by the front of his expensive robe and almost pulled him into the sacristy. 'You, gentlemen,' Cranston bellowed at the rifflers, their hands falling to their warbelts, 'can take your hands away from your swords. You can stay outside in the nave and say some prayers – it will do you all the world of good. And don't steal anything, or I will report you to the Flesher, as well as hang you on the gates to London Bridge.' Cranston slammed the door in their faces and pushed Copping towards the table. The lawyer hurriedly squeezed on to the bench beside the sexton.

'You were saying,' Cranston declared, 'or both of you were, about Mistress Martha's appointment here?'

'Oh, for the love of God,' the housekeeper exclaimed, 'I am a widow! My husband died when I was very young. He was a member of Nathaniel Cripplegate's Guild. He was a locksmith as well as a very distant relative to Parson Reynaud.' She added warningly, 'I kept house for the priest and that was all.'

'And last night,' Athelstan demanded, 'what exactly happened?'

'Mistress Makepeace's corpse was churched,' Curate Cotes declared, trying to assert himself. 'Compline was sung by myself and Parson Reynaud.'

'You gabbled through it,' Martha retorted, 'as you always do.'

'I believe the friar was talking to me.'

'I am eager to talk to anyone who will tell us the truth,' Athelstan smiled. 'But Martha, you tell us.'

'Compline was sung, Parson Reynaud returned to the house where Daventry was waiting. They were closeted in Parson's chancery chamber. Parson Reynaud then returned to the church and the chantry chapel of St John to hear the confessions of any parishioners who wanted to be shrived.'

'And you?'

'Brother, I retired to my bed.'

'And Curate Cotes?' Athelstan turned to the priest, who sat slumped against the table.

'I decided to visit certain parishioners.' The curate ignored the muffled laughter from the sexton as well as Cripplegate's sly smile. 'Afterwards I retired to the Devil's Oak to have something to eat and drink. I became tired, so I slept there,' he shrugged, 'until this morning.'

Athelstan was about to glance away when he caught the curate's change of expression, flitting and swift as a heartbeat, a knowing, clever look at Sir John. But then, as if the mask had slipped, the curate assumed the look of a born toper, still mawmsey with drink. Cranston now sat head down, slouched as if on the verge of one his brief naps, when he abruptly glanced up. 'The coffin, the old woman's coffin – it definitely held a corpse?'

'Of course,' Spurnel scoffed. 'I personally witnessed the casket lid being secured. I and the others lifted the coffin and pushed it on a sled from the death house to the church.' Others murmured their agreement to this.

Cranston got to his feet. He took a slurp from his miraculous wineskin and began to pace up and down the sacristy, forcing his audience to turn and watch him.

'So, you were all in your beds last night?' A chorus of agreement answered his question. 'Very good,' Cranston paused, 'and that includes you, Master Copping?'

'Yes, as I have said, I was indoors and remained there.'

'Mistress Martha, you had retired to your bed. You knew Parson Reynaud and Daventry had gone down to the church?'

'Only that the parson had. I really had no idea where Daventry was and, to be perfectly honest, I didn't really care.'

'Quite so, quite so,' Cranston agreed. 'But this morning, Mistress, you rose and found Parson Reynaud not in the house?'

'Not an exceptional situation,' she retorted. 'Sometimes Parson Reynaud went visiting. Sometimes,' she waved a hand airily, 'he drank and slept in the church.'

'What was exceptional,' the sexton interposed, 'was what happened this morning – usually a door was left open and people inside will respond to knocking and shouting. Today was different. I, Master Cripplegate and Martha found all four doors locked and bolted.'

'Explain,' Athelstan demanded.

'I tried the postern door at the front, not to mention the main door, then the corpse door. I met Martha at the devil's door. I could see that all four had their keys in the locks when I tried to insert mine. All four were also bolted, which is exactly the situation I found when we broke in this morning.'

'Broke in?'

'Three of the doors are solid oak. The devil's door is more recent and made of panelling – that's the door Martha had tried. She has a key to it.'

'Parson Reynaud,' Martha declared, 'insisted I have a copy of a key to one of the church doors. I use it occasionally. This morning was different. I could not insert the key whilst the door seemed tightly bolted from within.'

'We eventually decided to break the panelling,' the sexton continued, 'smash our way through so we could turn the lock as well as draw the bolts at top and bottom.' Spurnel coughed to clear his throat. 'Once we were in the church, we were confronted with one abomination after the other. The Parson and Daventry murdered. The coffin violated. The corpse gone and the arca robbed.' Spurnel gestured at the empty chest, still standing forlornly close to small barrels of altar wine.

'But you checked all the doors, once you were in?'

'Each and every one, including the devil's door, which we forced. Brother, I swear, every single door was bolted both top and bottom, the key turned fully in the lock.'

'So you would have us believe,' Athelstan declared.

'Brother,' Master Copping retorted, 'we are not here to make you believe anything. We are,' he held a hand up, 'as mystified as you are.'

'So,' Cranston intervened, retaking his seat, 'each door has two keys, no more?'

'Yes,' the sexton replied. 'Parson Reynaud held one set, I the other. Parson Reynaud always locked the church at night; you will find the keys on him.'

Cranston nodded at Flaxwith, who hurried out. He returned with a ring of keys, which he handed to the coroner, who dangled it in front of the sexton.

'Are they all in order?'

Spurnel took the ring, studied it closely, then passed it to Cripplegate for examination.

'Everything is in order,' the leader of the parish council murmured.

'Hand them to me,' the curate murmured. 'Can I keep them?'

'No, you can't,' Cranston snapped, and grabbed them back. He turned to Flaxwith. 'Where were they?'

'Deep in the pocket of Parson Reynaud's robe, Sir John.'

'Continue!' the coroner ordered.

'Whoever,' the sexton declared crossly, 'locked all four doors in the evening, I, as sexton, would open the church the next morning. Today, however, proved to be a real mystery.'

'Then let's define this mystery,' Athelstan retorted. 'We have an ancient church, its windows are high and narrow, and it has no other entrance or secret passageway, yes?'

'Brother,' the sexton shook his head, 'I would go on oath, no such secret tunnel or passageway runs in or out of our church.' The others agreed, shaking their heads in denial at such a possibility.

'And so this mystery becomes even more tangled. We have Parson Reynaud, an old priest, but wiry and strong.'

'Brother Athelstan, I agree,' Curate Cotes declared, smirking behind his hand. 'He was certainly active enough, as a number of the young ladies will attest.'

'He was an old soldier,' Cripplegate added. 'He served in the King's array.'

'And he wasn't alone in this church?' Athelstan declared. 'Daventry was an associate; either he came in with him or was close by. Both the parson and Daventry were stabbed cruelly to the heart. It must have been a swift cut, a sudden slash, the work of a professional assassin. What makes it more curious is there isn't any sign of any resistance or trace of a struggle? You would all agree with that? Good.' Athelstan nodded at their assent. 'Their killer, and I assume it is the same person, then opens the arca, the great money chest, and removes . . .' Athelstan paused and gestured at the chest. 'How much was in that arca?'

Silence greeted his question. Cripplegate and his companions stared stonily down the table.

'We asked a question,' Cranston declared quietly.

'My master,' Copping coughed, 'Master Simon kept his – or some of his – treasure here. He thought it would be safe in the arca of a sacred place, especially where the chest had two distinctive locks, he holding one key, Parson Reynaud the other. You must have seen it. The key is still on a chain around his neck—'

'How much?' Cranston barked. 'In God's name, how much to the nearest penny?'

'In gold and silver coin,' Copping whispered, 'about five thousand pounds sterling, perhaps even more.'

'A king's ransom!' Cranston exclaimed, whistling beneath his breath.

'And Master Simon now knows this has been stolen?' Athelstan asked.

'As he does about the death of the parson and Daventry,' Copping declared. 'You can imagine how angry he is. At the moment, he does business with Lord Arundel, but he and his henchmen will be here soon enough.'

'So,' Cranston pressed on taking a generous gulp from the miraculous wineskin, 'it would look as if the same person killed two able-bodied men without any trace of resistance or mark of violence. One of these certainly, Daventry being a man of war, skilled in arms. Both men would be alert; there is no trace of either being the victim of some sleeping potion or too much wine?'

'That's true,' Spurnel spoke up. 'As I left the church last evening, I passed both going in there. They seemed to be in good spirits.'

'They went in together?'

'Yes, Brother, nothing significant. Daventry was as we found him. I thought he would check on the arca then leave, whilst Parson Reynaud sat in the mercy chair to hear and shrive some penitent.'

'And did anyone come?'

'I saw no one,' Martha replied, 'but there again, I didn't see the parson or Daventry walk in together. I retired early to bed, as I believe everyone else did.' She glanced mischievously at the curate. 'Wherever that bed might be.'

'Very well.' Athelstan folded back the sleeves of his gown, a gesture to cover his complete confusion about what he was being told. He could detect nothing wrong, no loose thread to pull.

'All of you went your separate ways,' Athelstan murmured, 'and darkness descended. I cannot prove this, but I suspect Parson Reynaud and Daventry were murdered swiftly, one after the other. Once both had been killed, the assassin turned on the arca, robbed it, opened the coffin and plucked out that poor woman's corpse. But how he moved both plunder and cadaver is a mystery.' Athelstan pushed away his writing tray on the table before him. 'That must have been difficult. Two ungainly weights. A corpse and heavy sacks of coin. You would agree?'

'Of course,' Copping declared, 'it must have happened like that.'

'Heavy sacks of coin,' Athelstan repeated. 'Queenhithe at the dead of night is not the place to be carrying clinking bags which would have echoed like bells to the wolfsheads who swarm here. And, of course,' Athelstan continued, 'there is always the danger of being seen or being stopped. Oh yes, a true mystery.' He got up and, with Cranston's help, lifted the arca on to the table. Athelstan sketched a quick blessing in the air. 'My apologies please, but I shall return.'

Athelstan left the sacristy and hastened to where Parson Reynaud's corpse lay slumped in the mercy seat. He hurriedly found the silver chain around the dead man's cold, fat-creased neck and undid the clasp to pull off the key. Once back in the sacristy, Athelstan tried the key on one lock but it did not fit, though it slid easily enough into the second. Athelstan turned it and watched the lock spring up, the heavy, sharpened steel bolt, which would fasten deep into the tight groove carved into the edge of the coffer lid. Athelstan examined both locks carefully. 'The work of a true craftsman,' he murmured. 'Fashioned out of the finest steel with a strong spring, the bolt wedges into the groove to keep the heavy lid securely fastened to the body of the coffer. The wood is of the sturdiest oak and the entire arca is bound by bands of steel.' He smiled and pointed at Cripplegate. 'Your work, sir?'

'No, but I wish it was.' The locksmith rose, leaned over and stroked the polished lid. 'Believe me, Brother, this arca was specially fashioned. The locks are definitely the work of a master craftsman and, of course, there are those in London.' Cripplegate smiled thinly. 'To be honest, I envy such skill.'

'Do you recognise the work?'

'No, Brother, I don't, but skilled craftsmen can be found in other cities both here and across the Narrow Seas. Indeed,' Cripplegate tapped the arca with his fingers, 'I would wager, though I cannot prove it, this arca might be the work of some Hanseatic craftsman.'

'How long has the arca been here?' Cranston asked, pointing at Martha.

'Sir John, I don't know. Certainly as long as I have been.'

'I would agree,' Spurnel added. 'The arca has been here for years. I would regard it as part of the church.'

Athelstan chewed the corner of his lip as he stared at the treasure chest. He had heard of similar practices, where the powerful merchants preferred to deposit their monies away from prying eyes, yet still keep it immediately available. Goldsmiths could be over-inquisitive about the source of monies, as well as dishonest, whilst foreign bankers such as the Bardi faced the ever-present danger of their goods being seized by the Crown.

'Mystery within mystery within mystery,' he whispered.

'Pardon Brother?'

'Well, it's obvious, Master Copping. Murder, theft, the opening of the arca without using the keys specially fashioned for its lock. One key was found on the person of the dead Reynaud, but the other is in the firm grasp of Master Makepeace, yes?'

'It certainly is.'

'Yet that arca was robbed, that coffin pillaged, but the felon responsible left this church with all its doors bolted and locked from the inside, as if he could walk through solid stone carrying his gruesome trophy and ill-gotten gains. Sir John, we need to search even further as well as ask more questions.'

The coroner rose and pointed at the sexton. 'Why are there skeletons in the crypt; fresh bones with blows, clefts to the back of their skulls?'

Cranston's words immediately created a watchful silence.

'My Lord High Coroner is correct.' Athelstan brushed his robe. 'I accept there are cemeteries all over London, charnel houses and crypts full of bones. Nevertheless, the remains we found here are grouped together. I believe they were first buried in the cemetery for a short while, then tossed into the crypt without a by-your-leave?'

'Sir John, Brother Athelstan,' Spurnel gabbled springing to his feet, 'as my colleagues here will attest, the cemetery of St Benet's is a sprawling wastelend . . .'

'Look,' Cripplegate spread his hands, 'our cemetery is unbounded and stretches around the church like a great meadow.'

'It's a wild place,' the sexton blurted out, 'more of a wasteland than anything else.' Athelstan could see the sexton was deeply agitated. Cranston had certainly touched a rawness in the man's soul. 'Anyone can bring a corpse here,' the sexton continued. 'The crypt lies open; you could hide a dead body there, though of course the stink might alert you. However, Sir John, Brother Athelstan, I cannot mount a constant guard over our cemetery. Can you?' He pointed dramatically at the friar. 'Do you know, Brother, who lies buried in your cemetery?'

Cranston glanced at Athelstan, who winked back. The sexton was correct; even St Erconwald's was not free from what happened in the graveyards of many London churches – rambling, desolate places used by every kind of mischief-maker. Wizards, warlocks and witches would gather to dance beneath the midnight moon. They would light their fires and even plunder graves for human remains to use in their filthy rituals. Thieves would conceal stolen goods, and assassins the occasional corpse – the victim of a hapless accident, suicide, or murder. There were also those who simply wanted to get rid of their dead without paying their dues to God, man or the city. Yet this was different. Athelstan was building a picture of a truly wicked Parson Reynaud, a man who used religion as a cover for his own iniquity; a villain hand in glove with a leading wolfshead and riffler.

Athelstan glanced quickly around, but what role did these

people play? Were they Parson Reynaud's accomplices or his victims? Had one of them, or all, turned on their wicked parish priest and carried out justice, or at least what they regarded as justice?

Benedicta stood in the musty cellar beneath Margo's cottage and stared around the now empty chamber. Both corpses had been secretly removed, under Mauger's strict supervision, to the parish death house. Few as possible would know of the macabre scene they had stumbled upon here.

'Only God knows the secret ways of the human heart.' Benedicta repeated one of Athelstan's favourite aphorisms. She sat down on one of the chairs Margo had so carefully placed around the battered table. Benedicta smoothed this with her hand. According to Margo's will, this table and all the remaining moveables would be left to the parish. Benedicta wondered what truly happened here, still surprised at how this quiet, reserved, lonely parishioner had harboured such a secret. Margo had kept to herself, taking on the duty of corpse dresser, preparing cadavers to be churched and blessed in St Erconwald's and other parishes. In return Margo had received the coffin fees. She also worked as a seamstress but, apart from that, little else. People had mentioned how her husband and son had been excellent archers, master bowmen, but very little was known about them. The widow woman stared around. Margo seemed to have given most of her possessions away before moving across to St Bartholomew's Hospital about eight weeks ago.

'Yes, that's it,' Benedicta murmured to herself. She recalled Margo just before she left for the city; she was undoubtedly very ill: thin, even emaciated. Margo had confided to Benedicta how the humours in her belly had turned malignant and she could not stop the flow of blood or escape the constant pain. Brother Athelstan had furnished her with letters to Philippe, keeper of the hospital. On one occasion the friar had crossed to visit his ailing parishioner, but returned saying that Margo had been put into a deep sleep with the assistance of a powerful opiate. A week later, Benedicta had gone across to visit the sick woman. She found Margo sitting up in bed but very weak and delirious, babbling about the tales of Arthur and the magic of the Round Table and the treasures to be found there. Brother Philippe had confided to Benedicta that Margo would die within a week and, when she did, Watkin and Pike crossed the Thames to collect her corpse. Margo was brought back to St Erconwald's to be churched and blessed. The requiem had been celebrated, followed by swift burial in God's Acre. The poor woman's will, lodged in the parish chest, had left little of monetary value but, as Athelstan had said, 'We are all born without pockets and we go to God without pockets.' He added that for people like Margo, that was not difficult. She had lived without any real wealth. Nevertheless, Benedicta recalled Athelstan's surprise when he discovered how Margo had been able to afford costly care, physic and sustenance at St Bartholomew's.

Benedicta heard a sound from upstairs. 'Mauger!' she murmured, getting to her feet. She climbed the cellar steps, then stopped, heart in mouth, and stared at the three masked strangers standing between her and the cottage door. They wore hoods that masked their entire heads and faces, with slits for eyes, nose and mouth. They were garbed in dirty leather jerkins, patched hose and worn boots, but their warbelts were well furnished with sword, throwing knife and dirk. One of them carried an arbalest, primed and ready, whilst his two comrades wielded nail-studded maces.

'What do you want?' Benedicta gasped.

'Apparently the same as you. You are here to search, aren't you?' The man's voice was low and guttural. The crossbow came up, its jagged, pointed barb close to Benedicta's face.

'I am a friend of the deceased,' Benedicta replied sharply. 'I am looking after the few paltry items she has bequeathed to our parish, not to mention the sale of this cottage which, standing as close as it does to the Southwark bath-houses and stews, will not amount to much.' Benedicta's clipped, sharp tone made the riffler lower his crossbow.

'Who are you?' he demanded.

'More to the point,' Benedicta retorted, 'who are you? What right do you have to be here visored and hooded? What are you looking for?' Benedicta wiped clammy hands on her gown and deliberately stepped forward to confront these mysterious, sinister visitors. 'Who are you?' she repeated. 'This is my friend's cottage, now recently dead.'

'The jewels. The jewels, the precious stones,' the man rasped.

'What on earth . . .?'

'Toothsome, she is.' One of the rifflers stepped forward and put a hand out to claw Benedicta's breast. 'She'd fetch a good price amongst the ships.' The man's hand fell away as a crossbow bolt whirred through the air and smacked into the wall behind Benedicta. The wolfsheads turned. Mauger, Watkin and Pike pushed themselves into the room; each was armed with a crossbow. Watkin and Pike held theirs up as Mauger primed his with a fresh bolt.

'You should leave,' Mauger threatened.

'You shall leave,' Watkin echoed. 'And you shall stay away from our cemetery and our priest's house.' He loosed the lever on his crossbow and another barbed bolt whirled dangerously close to the intruders' heads.

'We'll leave,' the leading riffler rasped. 'But no more bolts or threats.'

'Agreed.' Mauger and his companions stood aside as the intruders swept by them in a swirl of sweaty cloaks and rasping, harsh breath.

'In God's name!' Benedicta leaned against a wall and dabbed a perfumed rag at her face and neck. 'By the Mass,' she breathed, 'what was all that about?'

'You'd best come.' Mauger grasped her gently by the arm. 'Mistress, I am sorry for your distress, but there is more. You must come.'

Mauger and his companions would say nothing more, so Benedicta followed them out into the street along the narrow, twisting coffin paths towards St Erconwald's. Benedicta, still not recovered from the shock of being threatened and abused, felt as if she was in a dream. Her mood deepened as she caught glimpses of the dark people who lurked deep in the shadows of the God-forsaken rotting houses she passed. A young girl, wearing a jester's mask, pulled a baby in its cot on a makeshift sledge. She did this with one hand whilst holding the leash of a three-legged dog that hopped along beside her. Beggars, faces round and white as the moon, screeched for alms, skeletal arms pushed out like the claws of a bird. Whores and their pimps touted for business. A gust of wind carried all the filthy stenches, even as the foul air was riven with screams, yells and curses and the strident crying of children.

Benedicta and her companions kept close, crossbows primed. They only relaxed once they broke free of the warren and entered the broader lanes leading down to the high-towered parish church. They reached the cemetery wall and went through the carved lychgate into the graveyard. Godbless was there, with Thaddeus standing patiently beside him. The beggar man had left his makeshift cottage and decided to cook a meal amongst the wild, high grass, warming a pannikin of goat's cheese.

'They have been here,' Godbless wailed. 'Demons from Hell. Three of them. Lucifer's captains. All masked and hooded, each living in one of Hell's blazing flames. They have dug the earth and harrowed the dead. They've crept across God's Acre,' he moaned, 'they were most violent. They were followed by the bagpipers of Hell, the fiddlers of the Underworld and Satan's own contortionists.'

'Mad as a March hare,' Mauger murmured. 'Come on, ignore him.'

Benedicta pressed the beggar man's hand and left him wailing. They hurried along the winding coffin path which cut across God's Acre to where Margo had been buried: her grave had been truly desecrated, the fresh soil clawed out as if dug by some beast, which had also plucked the coffin from its resting place. The lid had been wrenched off. Margo's thin corpse sprawled indecently, its linen shroud ripped to shreds.

'The same wolfsheads who attacked me,' Benedicta whispered, trying to curb the clammy fear which, despite the late autumn sunshine, chilled her body in a damp sweat. 'Who?' She turned to Mauger. 'Who would desecrate a poor woman's grave, abuse her corpse and ransack her pathetic belongings?'

'And if that's not bad enough.' The bell clerk plucked at Benedicta's sleeve, then told Pike and Watkin to gather Margo's corpse for reburial before leading the widow woman up out of the cemetery to the priest's house. Benedicta glimpsed Crispin the carpenter, busy repairing the door which Benedicta had closed and locked earlier that day. The door had been wrenched off its thick leather hinges. Inside, everything had been overturned and emptied: coffers, caskets and panniers ripped open, the bedloft violently ransacked, Athelstan's thin straw mattress slit and emptied. Benedicta's anger welled up so swiftly and strongly it forced tears to her eyes, as she gazed around this usually serene place that housed a man she deeply loved.

'I'll see those villains hang,' Benedicta exclaimed. 'But that will have to wait. Mauger, summon the entire parish council. Everything must be put right before our little friar returns . . .'

Athelstan was busy along the nave of St Benet's Woodwharf. The Dominican had seized a moment to inform the coroner about what he had discovered in Margo's cottage. Strangely enough, Sir John just looked surprised and whispered as if to himself, 'So that's what happened to both of them.' He refused to elaborate, saying the very walls had ears, whilst the Grenels were part of a greater tale he had to share with Athelstan. For the moment, the coroner insisted, they should concentrate on the mysteries before them. Athelstan agreed, and insisted on examining both corpses again, the friar making precise notes on the posture, dress and death wound of each of the victims. They then moved to the empty coffin, noticing that this had not been too damaged during the sacrilegious theft. Athelstan was more puzzled by how the corpse had been removed and taken out of the church. They eventually finished their examination, and had returned to the sacristy to scrutinise the arca when they heard doors opening followed by shouts and cries and the echo of booted feet along the nave. Cranston and Athelstan hastened out to meet a group of men who had gathered around the empty coffin.

'Who, Cranston?' One of the group stepped out of the shadows, raising a mailed fist at the coroner. 'Who did this? They will regret it as they die, and that will take them days. I—'

'Master Makepeace!' Cranston took a generous slurp from the miraculous wineskin and dramatically thrust the stopper back. He then moved his cloak so that Makepeace could see his warbelt. 'No threats!' Cranston warned. 'No threats from you at all. You may be the Flesher. You can call yourself London's own champion, but to me you are just a sly wolfshead who, so far, has managed to escape the hanging he so richly deserves.'

Cranston snapped his fingers. 'You and one of your companions may approach me and my noble secretarius Brother Athelstan, Dominican friar and parish priest of—'

'Of St Erconwald's in Southwark.' The Flesher finished the sentence as he lumbered forward to confront the coroner. He stood there, swaying on the balls of his booted feet, thumbs pushed into the broad black swordbelt clasped around his bulging waist. Athelstan stared in fascination at London's most notorious gang leader. The Flesher, he thought, looked the part: he was garbed in tawdry finery, a magnificent gold and blue houppelande with a high-collared edge fringed with ivory silver thread. The Flesher's boots were of the finest Moroccan, as was the warbelt with its sheathed sword and the dagger pouches. He sported gilt-edged spurs which jingled noisily, yet there was nothing pretty or soft about the Flesher. If a man's soul showed in his face, Athelstan quietly conceded, then this gang leader was twice as fit for Hell as any sinner could be. Simon Makepeace was an ugly man, with his egg-shaped head, broken nose and protuberant ears, which looked as if they had been chewed by a pig. He had heavily veined, hanging jowls, and his short bull neck was scarred with knife cuts, as was his unshaven face beneath a thinning mop of greasy black hair. He stood, his deep-set crafty eyes studying Cranston closely. Now and then his gaze would shift to Athelstan and his face bulged in what looked like a mocking smirk.

'Just one,' Cranston declared. 'I will meet you and one of your companions. Any more and I will have you all arrested.'

The Flesher leaned closer. 'On what charge?'

'On wasting the Lord High Coroner's time. One!' The Flesher took off a mailed gauntlet and snapped his fingers at the dark shadows who had followed him across from the coffin. A man stepped into the light and Athelstan heard Cranston's sharp intake of breath. The Flesher's companion looked truly sinister: he was garbed completely in black leather, jerkin, hose and boots, which only emphasised the man's corpse-like appearance; his face was as white as snow, with sunken cheeks; his thick eyebrows and lank, long hair were as inky as soot. He had large eyes which glittered balefully at them. A fighting man, Athelstan concluded, and one ready to take on the world. He came and stood close to the Flesher, turning slightly so he glanced at Cranston out of the corner of one eye.

'Raquin!' Cranston exclaimed. 'Gideon Raquin. Origin unknown, parentage unknown, country unknown, and yet a villain I know only too well.' Cranston gestured at both the Flesher and his henchman. 'Two cheeks of the same filthy arse. How long have you been in London, Raquin?'

'Since midsummer.' Raquin's voice was harsh, sharp and guttural. The only reaction to Cranston's studied insult by both men was a shuffling of booted feet, fingers brushing the hilt of sword and dagger. They let their hands fall away as Athelstan stepped forward and sketched a blessing in the air.

'Master Makepeace,' he declared, 'for what it is worth, I am truly sorry that your mother has died. I am distraught that she has not been allowed to rest in peace. You must have learnt about the horrors which have occurred here?'

'Yes, yes I have.' The Flesher's shoulders sagged as the tension lessened. Raquin stepped back out of the light. Cranston pointed at the retainers still standing close to the coffin.

'Tell your bullyboys to stay where they are. You, sir,' he nodded at the Flesher, 'along with your shadow, may join me and my secretarius in the sacristy.'

'And how is my Lord of Arundel?' Cranston asked as he closed the door and sat down at the top of the sacristy table.

'Very well,' Raquin retorted. 'And looking forward to the next Parliament being assembled at Westminster. He has certain questions to ask my Lord of Gaunt as well as other ministers of the Crown . . .'

He broke off as the sacristy door was thrown open and

Copping came in, hurrying to sit like a lapdog beside his master, whilst Martha brought in a tray of tankards.

'Fresh ale,' she murmured. 'I thought you could slake your throats.'

'There was a time,' the Flesher retorted, 'when you'd slake your own throat, Mistress Martha.' The Flesher was all vanity, eager to show off. Athelstan glanced at the housekeeper. Beneath the bustle, the work-day wimple and head veil, Martha was a very good-looking woman. In her youth she must have plucked the strings of many a man's heart. She did not even bother to acknowledge the Flesher's salacious comment, but placed the tray on the table, filled the tankards, served them and swept out of the sacristy. She was no sooner gone than there was a rap at the door, and Cripplegate along with Curate Cotes and Sexton Spurnel crept into the sacristy.

'None of you is needed,' Cranston growled. 'And I don't remember inviting you, Master Copping, but –' he flicked a hand at a tray – 'it accounts for why Mistress Martha brought in the extra tankards.'

Athelstan nodded, and whispered to the coroner how it would be best for all concerned if they stayed, and that included Mistress Martha. Cranston agreed and despatched Spurnel to bring the housekeeper back.

Martha returned, murmuring how she was busy, pointing to the barrels of altar wine still stacked against the wall of the sacristy.

'We won't need them for a while,' she declared. 'Parson Reynaud always liked to keep them close, so it's best if they are moved to the priest's house. Strange . . .' she added, taking her seat.

'What is, Mistress?'

'Well, Brother, the thieves who broke into the arca never tried to steal anything else, be it the wine, the chalices, the cruets. Even the altar cloths would have fetched a good price.' She sighed prettily, fanning her flushed face with her hand. 'What can be done?'

'Discover who these thieves were,' Cranston retorted, before taking a generous gulp from his wineskin. He pushed the stopper back, rubbed his hands, and began a pithy description of what they had discovered at St Benet's: Parson Reynaud stabbed in the heart at the mercy pew; Daventry, Arundel's man, murdered in a similar fashion on a chair close to the main door; the corpse of Isabella cruelly filched from its coffin; the arca chest opened and all the money stolen. There was also the question of the skeletons, at least four in number, with axe blows to the backs of their skulls.

Cranston paused, hands clasped as he stared at the Flesher, but the riffler's ugly face betrayed nothing, though his vein-streaked neck seemed to bulge in fury. He reminded Athelstan of a venomous toad getting ready to spit. Raquin lifted a hand to hide the smirk on his cadaverous face, whilst Sexton Spurnel, responsible for both the charnel house and God's Acre, reddened, shuffling his boots noisily as he stared down at the table.

'It's a mystery,' he mumbled.

'What is, Master Spurnel?' Cranston smacked the flat of his hand against the table top.

'Well, it's a mystery.' The sexton lifted his head. 'I mean, Parson Reynaud wanted the cemetery cleared.'

'Why?'

'I don't know, Sir John, but you've seen God's Acre around St Benet's?'

'Yes, it must be one of the largest cemeteries in London, but you don't know why Parson Reynaud wanted to clear it?'

'No, as I've said, I tried to have words with the parson,' the sexton continued. 'Our cemetery is large and open. It's easy for people to hide a corpse there, either in the undergrowth or simply by digging a shallow grave . . .' The sexton's words petered out.

'And can you throw any light on this?' Cranston pointed at the Flesher and Raquin. The riffler leader just shrugged. 'I asked you a question,' Cranston demanded.

'We left such matters to the parson,' the Flesher growled. 'Both the cemetery and the crypt lie open. Corpses could be left there. It's nothing to do with me.'

Cranston sat back on his chair, staring at the Flesher. Athelstan was more fascinated by Raquin, who slouched, one bony hand over his mouth. He continued to stare unblinkingly at the coroner, with a deeply hostile, hate-filled glare. Athelstan had never met such a sinister soul and felt a great malice emanate from the Flesher's henchman. He reminded the friar of a sorcerer in his black garb, with his hollow cheeks and sunken, deep eyes, glittering with a malicious glee, his grizzled hair hanging down like a tangle either side of his snow-white face. Raquin moved his skeletal fingers, a slow, rippling movement, as if that long hand contained a hidden dagger. Athelstan's unease deepened. He felt a real flare of fear. He and Cranston were in the presence of a most malevolent and malicious enemy. Athelstan could also sense that Cranston was disturbed by Raquin, too; indeed there seemed to be some bond between the two men – a curdling, unresolved enmity from the past.

'So,' Cranston tapped his fingers against the table, 'none of us knows anything about Parson Reynaud clearing the cemetery, or why he kept it so open, and the same is true of the crypt?'

'It would seem so,' Raquin sneered.

'And Daventry, why was he here?' Cranston demanded. Silence greeted his question. 'Why?' Cranston repeated menacingly.

'We don't know,' the Flesher retorted. 'My Lord of Arundel has the advowson to this church. Daventry was a member of his household. My Lord of Arundel probably sent him here on some errand or other, so you'd best ask him.' He smirked. 'I am sure he will give you a worthy answer.'

'And who might kill my Lord of Arundel's messenger?' Athelstan demanded. 'And why?' Again, silence.

'Or steal the corpse of Isabella Makepeace?'

Apart from the Flesher's whispered curses, the assembled company didn't even stir, except for Martha who slowly rose, pushing the chair back, smoothing out the creases on her gown.

'Brother Athelstan,' she declared quietly, 'before God, and I am sure I speak for my companions here at St Benet's, we know nothing about these horrid events.' A murmur of agreement echoed her words, though the Flesher, Raquin and Copping remained sullenly silent.

'So all is well here, yes?' Athelstan declared sarcastically.

'Outside at night the dead sleep beneath a silver, silent moon, whilst here in this so-called sacred place, nothing can explain the mysterious blasphemies confronting us?' He glared at the riffler leader, who sat so repellent and repulsive.

'And no one can resolve,' Cranston thundered, 'how the arca in this church was opened? Two keys are needed for that.' Cranston held up the one taken from Parson Reynaud's corpse. 'We have this; the other, sir,' Cranston pointed at the Flesher, 'is still in your possession, yes?' The Flesher undid the clasp of his tunic, loosened the chain around his neck and slid both chain and key down the table.

'Little use it has now,' he growled.

'Who fashioned the arca locks?' Athelstan asked.

'A craftsman amongst the Hanseatics, he is now dead. Both keys were unique, as were the locks they fitted.'

'And that key never left you?'

'Up until now, friar, never.' The Flesher rubbed the side of his face. 'I treasured it and always kept it close.'

'Not even Ingersol could get hold of that,' Raquin spoke up, grinning at Cranston. 'Whatever his name, he liked to call himself the dagger man, the Sicarius. Some dagger man!'

Athelstan was surprised at Cranston's reaction. The coroner lurched from his seat, breathing heavily, one hand on the table, the other scrabbling for his knife sheath on the warbelt hung over the back of the coroner's chair.

'Sir John?' Athelstan, worried that his friend was suffering a seizure, sprang to his feet, even as the Flesher and Raquin got to theirs, cloaks going back to reveal their warbelts. Mistress Martha screamed. Cripplegate went to comfort her. Sexton Spurnel cursed beneath his breath, Curate Cotes sat still, narrow-eyed, watching everything, whilst Copping hurried to stand behind his master and Raquin. Cranston took a deep breath, calming himself before grasping his warbelt and strapping it on. Raquin still grinned, though the Flesher was more wary, as if he sensed his henchman had provoked the coroner too far. Athelstan was truly mystified at what lay behind all this.

'You,' Cranston pointed at Raquin, 'you tallow-faced, blistered tongue rogue . . .'

'I hear you, Sir John,' Raquin lisped.

'You and your master can leave,' Cranston continued. 'I am finished for the while, but I may follow you. Makepeace, I have the authority. Perhaps I will visit the Devil's Oak before long and search that house of sin from cellar to attic. I know why you let both the graveyard and crypt lie open here at St Benet's. You kept both as your sewer to throw in and hide the victims of your wickedness. Now, I swear, one day I will see you hang. I am the King's own coroner in London and never forget that.'

The Flesher made to object; Raquin's smirk had now disappeared.

'Shut up!' Cranston shouted. 'Shut up and sit down.' Both men did so. 'For the rest,' Cranston gestured around, 'take care of the corpses.' Cranston turned, nodded at Athelstan to follow, and swept out of the sacristy into the ghostly nave with its looted coffin and stiffening corpses.

Once outside, Cranston stood on the top step, breathing in deeply and shaking his head. 'Believe me, Athelstan, when I was a boy I had a nurse, Tabitha the Terrible, or so I called her. Tabitha liked nothing better than to frighten me to the very marrow of my soul with one macabre tale after another, especially at bedtime. Never mind prayers or psalms! Tabitha was the nearest woman I have met who was a witch in the true sense of the word. Anyway, she told me a story about twin cats, all spotty with black-blue skin and weird, glaring eyes. According to Tabitha, these cats prowled the world by night, sucking the breath of infants until they were husks of bone and skin, and how both cats had a special thirst for my breath. Well, when I think of Raquin, let alone meet him, that deep, childhood fear returns. God knows why; it's just a feeling in the heart of my soul that either he will be the death of me, or I of him.'

'Pray God it's the latter,' Athelstan whispered, staring anxiously at this closest of friends, now steeped in a dark mood he had rarely witnessed before.

'Leave me for a while,' Cranston smiled thinly. 'Let me calm my thoughts.'

Athelstan sketched a blessing and walked down the nave.

He turned right out of the church into God's Acre, stretching like a great common around St Benet's. Even in the full light of day, this field of the dead did not seem like a sacred place, but a dark, dank forbidding meadow with its forlorn, crumbling monuments. The ground was broken and littered by tough brambles, sturdy weed patches and bristling patches of bush and briar. Most of the crosses and headstones were much decayed; here and there a more recent burial was marked with a cleanly cut memorial stone but, in the main, the rest stretched in long lines of soil-packed mounds. At the far end of the cemetery, a trellised fence separated that part of the burial ground from the stately, three-storeyed, black-tiled priest house, built of grey ragstone. Picking his way carefully, Athelstan went deeper into the cemetery, towards what he thought must be the mortuary, a long, red-bricked chamber with a slated roof and three lancet windows either side of the garishly painted double door. Athelstan noticed the paths wending down from the priest's residence and the death house, the coffin paths which would be difficult to thread in the dead of night; any intruder would soon find themselves in difficulties. The place had a sinister, sad atmosphere, and when night fell it must become a place of nightmares.

Athelstan walked on past the now shattered devil's door. The friar noticed how a long row of empty burial pits lined that side of the church. Nothing more than deep holes in the ground, some half-filled, the others with heaps of crumbling soil beside them. Wheelbarrows, sleds and carts stood forlornly about. Eventually Athelstan reached the steps leading down to the charnel house. The doors to the ancient crypt hung open, the skeletons Flaxwith had brought out still lying in their pathetic horror. Athelstan studied these, then glanced around. Sexton Spurnel was correct. God's Acre at St Benet's was a wasteland, its crypt and open charnel house piled high with white, crumbling skeletons, skulls, shards of bone and other relics of the mouldering dead.

'You could murder my entire parish,' Athelstan whispered to himself, 'and bury them here without trace. God knows what this hideous place secretly hides, what blasphemies it shrouds?' Athelstan returned to the front of the church, where

Cranston stood threading his ave beads through stubby fingers. He glanced at Athelstan and winked.

'Well met, monk.'

'Friar, Sir John.'

'Let us adjourn to my personal chantry chapel.'

'You mean the solar at the Lamb of God in Cheapside?'

'Of course.' Cranston tripped merrily down the steps. 'Come, my little friar, let me educate you about the Flesher and his villainous coven.'

PART THREE

PART THREE

Dilp (**Old English**): a trollop

They hurried through the tangle of streets leading up into the heart of the city. Cranston walked purposefully, Athelstan trailing behind, distracted by what they passed. Now and again the friar caught sight of faces, pale and haggard, peering out from doorways or windows, only swiftly to disappear in a clatter of wood or chains. Cranston deliberately took Athelstan into what he called 'a maze of utter misery', which cut through the city, separating the rank corruption of the riverside from the warm, enveloping wealth of Cheapside, Poultry and the Inns of Court. They crossed sluggish ditches choked by coarse grass and rank weeds. They passed under the shadow of rotting houses, along alleyways which reeked of the most rancorous filth, where grey-furred rats fought each other for the rancid spoils of the midden heaps and lay stalls. They entered the 'black dens', the 'labyrinth of lamentations'; here nightmares gathered and fearsome apparitions could erupt in the dark. 'Mazes of murder', as Cranston called them. 'This,' he hissed at Athelstan, 'is what the Flesher controls. Look around, friar. The surging London mob crouches hidden here with its raging bloodlust, which can swell and spill out whenever Master Makepeace wishes. If he wanted, he could unlock this labyrinth and summon out all its monsters.'

They hurried along through the runnels and alleyways on to the streets, which broadened out as they reached the wealthy heart of the city. Here stalls and booths displayed the resplendent wealth of the Middle Sea and beyond: clothes, jewellery, household goods; all manufactured by skilled craftsmen, be it leather from North Africa, cloth woven in Liège, Arras and Hainault, or a finely turned cup from Cologne. London's great commercial thoroughfare was a most frenetic place: the perfumed air was riven by shouts and cries, whilst the eye was constantly distracted by the different sights and sounds.

Near the Tun, close to the great Conduit, Guildhall bailiffs had caught two housebreakers red-handed. The malefactors had been stripped naked and their clothes burned. Blackened ash, light cinder flame and fetid smoke were whirled up by the breeze. The two felons, forced to their knees, faced summary execution. Cranston and Athelstan could not pass. They had to stop and watch as a bailiff whirled his broad-blade cleaver and expertly severed both heads. The onlookers scattered, fearful of being splattered by the blood which squirted out of the severed necks, the heads bouncing away even as the torsos toppled over. The heads were collected and set on poles, the flies immediately swarming around them, the dead eyes glaring up as if watching them approach. Only then did Cranston grasp Athelstan by the arm and almost pulled him away.

'Sorry about that, Brother,' he murmured, 'but it's an ordinance of the city. All officials, especially the Lord High Coroner, must witness justice being carried out, bloody as it may be if you are in the vicinity. Right, my little monk.'

'Friar, Sir John.'

'All the same, there you go.'

And before Athelstan could protest, Cranston almost lifted his companion on to a stone plinth, then climbed up beside him. 'Now, my little ferret of a friar, what do you see?'

Athelstan stared out over the sea of drifting colour. 'Sir John, it's like watching different strands in a woven tapestry.'

'Precisely, my little friar. Now,' Cranston stared around, 'look, do you see that funeral procession, the coffin bobbing on the shoulders of those cowled mourners? Now it could be a genuine funeral, or the coffin might contain a victim of the Flesher's murderous rage being taken to some cemetery or charnel like that at St Benet's. I would wager a gold coin that our notorious Flesher patronises more than one church. Or,' Cranston was now warming to his subject, 'perhaps the coffin contains stolen goods being carried to this ship or that warehouse. Turn a little to the right. Do you see the travelling relic seller standing on an overturned cask, preaching about the wonders he's seen; dragons in the mountains of Syria or giants who prowl the forests of the ice kingdoms? Now, Brother, look at the number of urchins who gather to hear the relic seller's words of wisdom. In truth they are foists, sharp-fingered pickpockets hungry for the unwary, ready to lift a purse. The relic seller is their master; he draws the crowd in and his scholars ply their skills. Close by, do you see the argument which has broken out between the minstrel in his multi-coloured jerkin and that itinerant cook with his smoking grill in the wheelbarrow? They are in fact brothers-in-arms who argue merrily to the enjoyment of passers-by who stop to listen in. However, they should keep their hands on their wallets. It's the same trick, Brother: create a disturbance, draw in a crowd and give your accomplices free rein. Nearby are old friends, the Cheapside whores resplendent in their orange and red wigs; not far away lurk their pimps, sharp-eyed with even sharper knives. All of these, Brother, pay allegiance and dues to Master Makepeace the Flesher. Woe betide anyone who does not pay the devil's tax or refuses that prince amongst rifflers his due. So,' the coroner helped Athelstan down, 'we continue to my chantry chapel.'

Cranston's 'chantry chapel' was the serene private solar in the Lamb of God, Cheapside's most magnificent tavern. Mine hostess ushered Sir John and Athelstan to the coroner's favourite window seat, overlooking a splendid garden with its flowerbeds, herb pots, shady arbours and reed-fringed stew ponds, where golden carp, one of the great delicacies of the tavern, swirled in the light green water.

The solar was a delightful chamber. The windows in the outside wall were filled with painted glass, richly hued tapestries decorated the pink-washed walls; all of these proclaimed stories from scripture which extolled the virtues of wine, although, as Athelstan conceded to himself, Sir John needed little encouragement to drink the blood-red Bordeaux. Cranston undid his warbelt and cloak, eased off his high-heeled spurred boots and sank back gratefully into the settle of the window seat. He snatched his beaver hat off, threw it on his cloak, then wiped his solemn white-bewhiskered face and hands with the perfumed towel that Mine hostess had supplied.

'Sir John, you are well?'

'Little friar, I need to tell you a tale – but first,' Cranston sat up, 'let us feed the hungry demon within.'

Mine hostess returned, hustling back with a jug of Bordeaux, goblets, and a bowl of minced venison cooked in a savoury sauce, along with fingers of the softest white bread and a dish of cooked vegetables. Cranston ate and drank as if starved. Athelstan blessed his food and picked at the dishes, he was not so much hungry as curious about what Cranston was about to tell him.

'In the beginning,' the coroner began, wiping both his fingers and mouth on the napkin, he took a generous gulp from the goblet and glared across the deserted solar, 'yes, in the beginning,' he murmured, 'I was a young knight, a King's man. On the feast of the Annunciation, the Year of our Lord 1363, I and a war barge of Tower archers received my final orders to meet a Hanseatic ship, *The Glory of Bremen*, at Queenhithe quayside. The German merchants were acting as intermediaries. The old King and his elder son, the great warrior who styled himself the Black Prince, father of our present King Richard, God bless him, had waged war sharp and cruel in pursuit of the French crown. Both the King and his heir were killers to the bone. They loved war. They would stir up strife in heaven. Anyway, you know the story. We English inflicted defeat after defeat upon the French and forced them to sign peace treaties in which France promised to pay the English Crown vast war damages.' Cranston took a sip of the wine. 'Edward and his son drained the Valois like a thirsty man shakes the very dregs from his goblet. Certain monies were outstanding, so the French agreed to hand over the Rose Casket containing the Twelve Apostles. No, no,' Cranston lifted a hand at Athelstan's interruption, 'let me explain. The Rose Casket had once been the property of the doomed Templars. It had been discovered in the Temple Mount of Jerusalem by Hugh Payens, who founded the order. The Rose Casket was an exquisitely crafted coffer with a beautiful concave lid, fashioned out of sandalwood and smelling as sweet as any heavenly fragrance. The casket was covered with intricately carved trailing roses, with petals of the purest gold and stems of the finest silver. Inside, resting on a purple samite cushion, were twelve precious stones: a diamond, an amethyst, a ruby, and so on. Stones so extraordinarily magnificent, each was worth a king's ransom. These were the Twelve Apostles, held in the Rose Casket by the French Crown in a special tabernacle at the royal chapel of St Denis. The English demanded these as payment. The French were forced to agree. The Hanse merchants would act as go-betweens, so *The Glory of Bremen* brought the Twelve Apostles to Queenhithe. I was to collect the treasure and transport it to the Tower.' Cranston picked up the goblet and cradled it in his hands. 'A fog-bound night, Brother, cold as cold can be. A river mist swirled like a host of ghosts. No one knew of our assignment.' He sighed. 'Or so they told us. We left *The Glory of Bremen*; our barge was a high-prowed war-craft called *The Song of the Sword*. We made good progress, moving out into mid-river, lanterns glowing; every so often a horn would bray to warn other boats to pull aside.' Cranston paused, the goblet halfway to his lips. Athelstan was surprised to see tears in the coroner's light blue eyes. 'Good men, Brother. Perhaps one or two of them may have been bastards, as I will explain, but our company were archers – skilled, able men, loyal to the Crown and each other. Veterans such as Henry Grenel and his son Walter. Oh yes,' Cranston smiled bleakly, 'those two were there. They vanished that night, not seen again till what you saw earlier today. There were others. A few of these you also met this morning; they too served on that war barge.'

Cranston drank noisily, staring into the middle distance as he became immersed in the past. 'Satan's tits, Brother, they were all there, each and every one a Tower archer: Sexton Spurnel, Nathaniel Cripplegate and Curate Cotes. Archers, Athelstan. Men of the royal war band. Well, until that evening anyway. Afterwards the cohort was dissolved . . .'

'Sir John,' Athelstan intervened, 'what happened? You mention the men we met this morning. All three were once under your command?'

'Tower archers, Brother. Royal bowmen. Sworn members of a select garrison. An honourable post, a token of great trust, or so I thought at the time. Anyway,' Cranston cleared his throat, 'we were mid-river. The Rose Casket with the Twelve Apostles lay in a sealed royal chancery bag. We thought all was safe. Men strained over the oars. I was standing in the stern, the captain of archers on the prow, two bowmen with him, one holding the beacon lantern, the other blowing on the hunting horn. All was quiet, when suddenly two other barges appeared on port and starboard. They surged in, swift as arrows finding their mark. They rammed us on both sides, even as their crews, hooded and masked, all garbed like the night, swarmed aboard *The Song of the Sword*. I drew my weapons and hurried to confront a stream of assailants, when I suffered the most cruel blow to the back of my head. I found myself falling and that was it. When I awoke, two days later, I lay in a bed in a whitewashed chamber at St Bartholomew's Hospital, with the most lovely woman bending over me.' Cranston smiled faintly. 'That was how I first met the Lady Maude. She was a member of the Guild of St Veronica and, along with other young ladies of good families, did charitable work amongst the poor and sick committed to the hospital. Now the effect of the Lady Maude's tender care is quite obvious to see. At the time, however, I was more concerned by what had happened than any wound and who was tending it.'

'And?'

'Little friar, a true disaster! *The Song of the Sword* had capsized. The Rose Casket and the Twelve Apostles had disappeared. Most of those in the royal barge were dead or missing, and that included the Grenels, both father and son. Some of the crew survived, including myself, Cotes, Spurnel, Cripplegate, and a few others. The old King and his eldest son were furious. Of course, somebody had betrayed us. As regards our attackers, it was a question of much suspected, little proved. However, the finger of suspicion was pointed strongly at Simon Makepeace the Flesher, along with his evil henchman, Raquin. Apparently both barges vanished as swiftly as they'd appeared out of the river mist. No one along the Thames claimed to have seen or heard anything about them.'

'Too frightened?'

'Possibly. The Flesher had just emerged as the foremost leader of London's rifflers. More precisely, if you study a map of the Thames and where we were attacked, it was not far from the water-gate of the Flesher's tavern, the Devil's Oak, which had opened the previous year.' Cranston shook his head. 'As for evidence, you are right, people are terrified of the Flesher and no one dare talk, even now. Athelstan, if someone was convicted of being part of that attempted robbery, then they are guilty of high treason and would suffer the most excruciating death.' Cranston sipped at his wine. 'Looking back, it was like a nightmare. One minute, I am standing in the stern of a barge and all is well, the next I am facing the fury of Hell.'

'And you still suspect the Flesher?'

Cranston leaned closer. 'Little friar, I don't suspect.' He patted his chest. 'I know the Flesher and Raquin were involved. Both men should hang.'

'But who informed the Flesher, provided him with all the details about the royal barge, its armaments, cargo, time and place? And, whoever did, should be very careful.'

'What do you mean?'

'Well, Sir John, if a member of your crew betrayed you, they were running a terrible risk. After all, they were on that barge on a freezing, misty night, where sword and dagger play would be brutal and swift. If there was a Judas amongst you, he too would face the same danger as you did. So none of your crew fell suddenly sick beforehand?'

'None.'

'But as you have said, somebody must have betrayed you?'

'Little friar, for eighteen years I have asked myself and others the same question, without a scrap of success.' He paused. 'I hear what you say about the danger our Judas faced; however, I still suspect one of those, or all of those we met this morning: Cotes, Spurnel and Cripplegate.'

'Strange that they are now members and officers of the same parish church.'

'Not really. They were all born and raised in Queenhithe. They joined the King's array together and served shoulder to shoulder beyond the Narrow Seas. Anyway,' Cranston sighed, 'we have no real idea who betrayed us.'

'But you suspect the Flesher, you virtually claim that he

was responsible. I've asked this before – surely you have some evidence?'

'Nothing, just a feeling about something I may have glimpsed but, apart from that, not a scrap of real proof. Just riverside tittle-tattle, chatter amongst the dark-dwellers and night-walkers about how the Flesher lusted after the Rose Casket and its contents. You see, Athelstan, at the time there was a great deal of gossip about the French having to pay war damages and the old King's demands for the Twelve Apostles. The Flesher does have friends and allies at Court . . .'

'Were any of the attackers wounded, captured or killed?'

'According to witnesses, and they could add very little to what I already knew, our attackers were highly organised and, if they had any casualties, they took their dead and wounded with them. And that's the Flesher, a villain with fingers and toes in every pie but impossible to pin down. Oh, we could bring a host of indictments against him, but his lawyer Copping would demand proof, whilst any witness who opened his mouth on Monday would have his throat slit by Tuesday. The Flesher sits in the darkest of corners and spins his sinister web. He did the same on the night of the great river battle. He and Raquin were responsible: they haven't forgotten, and they realise I certainly haven't.'

'Could someone else be responsible for the attack?'

'Possibly. Some curious tales did begin to surface. At one time even the French were suspected of trying to get their treasure back by stealth. I dismiss that as arrant nonsense; the source of such a story could well be the Flesher trying to protect himself. You see, Brother, the Rose Casket and the Twelve Apostles disappeared completely. Nothing has been seen or heard of them since that night, which probably means no one had them, either here or abroad.'

'And the Grenels?'

'They too fell under suspicion. Their corpses were never found – well, not until this morning. So yes, they were suspect, and yet matters grow even more mysterious. Something I have already referred to.' Cranston leaned closer, his voice barely above a whisper. 'The English Crown let it be known what had happened. It alerted all its officers and agents, not to mention our merchant community throughout the kingdom and beyond. The Crown charged every loyal subject with the solemn duty of reporting anything they learnt about the Rose Casket and the Twelve Apostles. If both were offered on the open market, or glimpsed in a private house, the Crown was to be informed. The proclamation was hedged with the most hideous punishment for anyone who failed in this matter, whilst offering the most generous rewards to those who could supply valuable information.' Cranston drummed his fingers on the top of the table. 'Nothing, Athelstan. The Twelve Apostles and their casket disappeared completely. And there's the mystery: why steal such a treasure but never offer it for sale? If the Flesher or anyone else had stolen it, eventually, one way or the other, we would have learnt that the Rose Casket and the Twelve Apostles were on the open market.'

'The treasure could have sunk with the barge?'

'Possible, but the river was truly scoured. You see, the barge didn't sink completely. It was badly damaged and listed heavily. Expert swimmers, men like Icthus, were sent in to search it from prow to stern. All they discovered were that the ropes which bound the royal chancery pouch had been cleanly sliced by a knife.'

Cranston fell silent, staring moodily at his empty platter. Athelstan was about to press him further on the Flesher, when the door to the solar swung open and the two beggars who haunted Cranston whenever he appeared in Cheapside slipped into the chamber; Leif, the one-legged mendicant, as he styled himself, and Rawbum, his constant companion, a former cook dismissed from his employment for being drunk and sitting down on a pan of boiling oil. These two miscreants edged their way forward. Leif half crouching, staring at Cranston's face. Rawbum, rubbing his backside with one hand, the other stretched out like a claw, eager for a coin.

'There is a monster appeared in Moorfields, north of the city,' Leif hissed. 'We need to inform you, Sir John . . .' Leif hopped back, Rawbum following, as Cranston rose threateningly to his feet.

'Although a dwarf,' Leif gabbled, 'the monster's head and

face are large enough for a giant. He has black eyes, flared nostrils, heavy stubble and fangs for teeth—'

'Yes, yes,' Athelstan interrupted, ushering them towards the door, 'but you can see Sir John is preoccupied.'

'The monster has fingernails, crooked and yellow.' Rawbum blithely took up the tale. 'He has the appearance of a prowling dog and he can devour a man in a single gulp.'

'Go,' Athelstan whispered hoarsely. He dug into the tattered wallet on the cord around his waist, drew out two of his precious pennies, and thrust these into the hands of the unfortunate beggars. They both stopped their lurid tale, turned, and promptly disappeared back into the taproom beyond.

'Thank you.' Cranston sat down as Athelstan came back to the table. 'I could not tolerate those two. My good humour is all but drained, Athelstan, whenever I recall the good men killed that night, not to mention the humiliation and disgrace at losing such a precious cargo.'

'But you were not blamed?'

'No I wasn't, Brother. As I have said, I received a crack on the head and disappeared beneath the fast-flowing river. I then surfaced and a fishing boat almost knocked me under again. I was dragged aboard and taken to Queenhithe. The old King, the Prince of Wales, declared they were convinced that I did all that I could . . .' Cranston paused, as if listening to a bell-like voice bellowing from the taproom that 'conserves of violets, roses and borage, along with a few drops of camphor, are good for those of a moist humour.'

'Lady Maude,' Cranston murmured, 'used such remedies on my bruised head, as well as feeding me delicious dishes such as tender chicken poached in wine, carp grilled over charcoal, along with soup of almonds.' The coroner smacked his lips, a dreamy look in his eyes. On any other occasion Athelstan would have laughed at Cranston's constant absorption with good food, yet the coroner remained oddly deflated, as if the defeat he had suffered some eighteen years earlier had returned in all its hideous strength. Abruptly, the coroner's mood changed; a puckering of the lips, a half-smile as if to himself, his right hand going out to caress the pommel of his sheathed sword, as if he was going to use that to swear some solemn oath.

'Sir John?'

'Before God, Athelstan, I tell you I do not know for sure who actually attacked us, or the Judas who betrayed us, nor can I prove that the Flesher and all his wickedness was responsible. However, and I am only telling you this as a penitent to his father confessor, wanting to be shriven,' the coroner drew a deep breath, 'the attack was swift and brutal. I saw a man race along the edge of the enemy barge and jump on to ours. He had a helmet on with a visor that closed over the mouth, but it hung open. I am sure the face I glimpsed was Raquin's, but I dare not mention that in public. The lawyers would regard it as an attempt to pass the blame on to an enemy without a shred of evidence to prove my allegation.' Cranston wove his fingers together, 'Raquin was hungry for my death that night. I still regard him as the greatest threat. God have mercy on me, but I believe I must kill him or he will undoubtedly kill me.'

Athelstan shivered as he clutched his goblet, eager to sip the thick, red wine.

'And now, as for the rest . . .' Cranston pushed away the platter in front of him. 'First, my little friar,' Cranston deliberately tried to lighten the mood. He quietly cursed himself for allowing his own morbid fears to surface: he could tell Athelstan was becoming deeply anxious. 'Parson Reynaud! Trust me, Athelstan, I do not have the best opinion of your fellow clerics. However, Parson Reynaud was a priest who knew all about sin for all the wrong reasons and in all the wrong ways. A man sworn to celibacy, Parson Reynaud was well known to the Daughters of Joy.' Cranston grinned. 'Ladies of the night to you, my little friar. Courtesans, young women who regard themselves as a cut above the common street whore. They have a mansion in Reynaud's parish which they call the House of Delights, in Grape Street. Our good parson was a frequent visitor, a man who strove to live life to the full. Parson Reynaud, like his ally the Flesher, was a former soldier; he served as a chaplain in the royal array in the old King's forays through France. Accordingly, Reynaud would have seen sights which would whiten anyone's hair. Perhaps that's where he left the path of righteousness. I doubt very

much if Reynaud took the Scriptures seriously, except for one
verse, "Do not worry about tomorrow." Parson Reynaud
certainly didn't.'

'But he performed his priestly commitments, shriving his
parishioners and celebrating Mass?'

'Oh, of course, he had to. Parson Reynaud was well known
to the Bishop of London and his formidable archdeacon, Master
Tuddenham. They would have pounced like a hungry cat on
a mouse if Reynaud did not fulfil his priestly duties to justify
his income, and his house, as well as all the other comforts
such priests insist on.' Cranston nudged Athelstan. 'Present
company excepted, of course?'

'Of course.'

'Now the advowson, the right of appointing both parson
and curate to St Benet's Woodwharf, is held by the Fitzalans,
the Earls of Arundel. The present lord is well known, even
notorious for his meddling in matters politic. The Earl of
Arundel would love nothing better than to topple our self-
proclaimed regent, uncle to the King. Now Fitzalan has granted
all rights of advowson to his henchman and former comrade
in the King's array, Master Simon Makepeace, also known as
the Flesher.

'Let me tell you a little more about that sinner.' Cranston
took a deep gulp of wine. 'Simon Makepeace is probably one
of the greatest villains under God's sun. We are not too sure
of his origins. Born in Queenhithe, he served with Fitzalan's
retinue in France, where he excelled himself as a killer and a
thief. Indeed,' Cranston wagged a finger, 'I have heard it on
good authority that the Flesher committed such heinous crimes
that the mayor and citizens of Rouen placed a generous bounty
on his head, dead or alive. Apparently, Makepeace became an
écorcheur, a flayer who liked nothing better than to peel the
skin of his victims till they confessed where they had hidden
any treasure.'

'Heaven forfend.' Athelstan breathed. 'A flayer? I've heard
about them, devils incarnate. The most violent of men;
criminals freed from jail on condition that they fought in the
King's array.'

'Such as Master Makepeace, Brother. Anyway, about nineteen

to twenty years ago, our killer returned to London and settled in Queenhithe. He soon won a reputation for ruthless ferocity. He became a leader amongst the rifflers, a lord of the mob who would not be challenged or checked. One man tried to oppose him, a merchant, Gilbert Croyland. Do you know what the Flesher did? He provoked Croyland and his son into a fight; he killed them both, then took their severed heads to every tavern in Queenhithe and beyond. The Flesher claimed self-defence. He could produce a score of witnesses who would swear to that, whilst no one would dare gainsay him. The Flesher insisted that Croyland's wife and daughter carry the severed heads before him on a tray.'

'But the sheriff, the Guildhall?'

'Too frightened, Brother – not only of Makepeace, but the ominous dark shadow behind him.'

'Arundel?'

'In a word, yes. The Earl of Arundel openly proclaims that Makepeace is an honest citizen and a valued member of the Fitzalan household. You see, the Flesher is the mailed gauntlet, Arundel is the fist within. He needs Makepeace to control the London gangs, the mob, that many-headed monster which lurks in the dark, nightmare corners of this city. Over the years, the Flesher's powers have increased. True, in the months leading up to the Great Revolt, the Flesher became more discreet. He did not wish to cross swords with the Upright Men and their ferocious street warriors, the Earthworms. Makepeace kept to the shadows, paying lip service to the Crown and city council, whilst offering secret support to the Upright Men or, at least, the illusion of support. Once the revolt was crushed, the Flesher continued to extend his power.'

Cranston rose and stretched. He walked to the door, opened it and then came back. 'I thought as much,' he murmured, retaking his seat. 'The Weasel has arrived, one of the Flesher's street spies. He controls a veritable horde of them. The Weasel is one of the best, and he is called that because of his skill at twisting his way through this city. Nevertheless, he is an ugly bugger and, despite his best efforts, stands out in a crowd.' Cranston scratched his head. 'I am sure there are others of his tribe lurking in the taproom, but Mine hostess, a most redoubtable woman, will keep them away from the keyhole. So,' Cranston rubbed his hands together, 'to return to my indictment. Arundel controls Makepeace, who controls the rifflers, exercising his authority and power from his hellish tavern, the Devil's Oak, close to the river. He has fingers and thumbs in every pie, be it crooked dice-throwing or our red-wigged ladies of the night. He can call up the legion of the damned and field a mob within the hour. He also controls St Benet's and Parson Reynaud. God knows what mischief those two got up to before the good parson went to join the choir invisible. You see, Athelstan,' Cranston wetted his lips, 'London's full of villains. The whores do a roaring trade, Parson Reynaud was certainly not celibate, but the Flesher is different. According to gossip, Master Makepeace likes to become violent with his women. Those skeletons Flaxwith unearthed in the crypt, whatever Sexton Spurnel's claims, were the victims of the Flesher's murderous lust. A cleaver blow to the face or the back of the head would account for the violence we saw. Of course, I haven't a shred of evidence to substantiate my allegation. Nothing to prove my suspicions, except on one night there was a pretty whore and the next, after she had visited the Devil's Oak, there wasn't. She'd vanished and remained vanished like the dew on a hot summer's day. Oh yes, our Flesher is a truly sinister soul who rules by fear and that, one day, might be his undoing.'

'Sir John, what do you mean?'

'Oh, I will come to it in a while. Just mutterings, grumbles, a growing tide of discontent with the Flesher, even though he still controls through terror. Let me explain.' Cranston leaned back on the settle. 'Close to the Devil's Oak stands a most forbidding, sinister, even macabre dwelling. The night-walkers and shadow-shifters call it the Mansion of Murder. It stands in its own grounds, about three storeys high. To all intents and purposes it is well kept, but still a very empty building. However, according to what I have learnt, the Flesher uses this mansion to terrorise all of Hell's buttery, that stretch of cramped, rotting, fetid tenements along Queenhithe's wharf. People who cross the Flesher, who fail to do what he orders, are locked up in that dreadful mansion and exposed to great war dogs. They are savaged, mauled and cruelly killed; their corpses, nothing more than mangled remains, are thrown into the Thames.'

'In God's sweet name,' Athelstan breathed, 'wickedness incarnate. Sir John, surely you can intervene?'

'Can we, Brother?' Cranston declared moodily. The coroner used his fingers to emphasise his points. 'First, we have no complaint, no evidence of a crime, nothing to link the Flesher to the death and disappearance of anyone. Secondly, the Flesher is the leader of the most powerful gang of rifflers in London. He is a true robber who wields complete authority over his tribe of thieves. As I have said, they used the Great Revolt for their own purposes. Now it is over. The King's peace has been restored, the common enemy has disappeared. The great lords gather in Parliament and the gangs have re-emerged, flexing their muscles, and the Flesher is foremost amongst these. He takes his orders from Fitzalan of Arundel, who absolutely hates Gaunt and would love to see our regent's head lopped off on Tower Hill. Now Gaunt has had a stroke of great fortune.'

'Sir John?'

'Gaunt has a great ally, no lesser person than our young King. Richard has a particular detestation for Richard Fitzalan, Earl of Arundel. Our King, God bless him, believes that foxy-faced Earl is a born traitor, an intriguer who does not wish him well.'

'Why?'

'Brother, you must never tell this to anyone but, remember after the revolt, our young King decided to stage a series of ceremonies where he would sit in cloth of gold wearing the Confessor's crown and carrying the orb and sceptre? Around him would gather the leading officers of state and the Knights of the Body?' Cranston smiled. 'I am both a royal officer and a Knight of the Body. I am allowed to wear weapons in the King's presence.'

'Yes, yes, I remember those ceremonies,' Athelstan murmured. 'They were staged in Westminster Abbey, Canterbury, and other great cities.'

'On one such occasion,' Cranston continued, 'I was helping the King to divest in the sacristy. Fitzalan of Arundel came in, but young Richard snapped his fingers and indicated he should leave. Fitzalan, his cunning face twisted into a smirk, bowed mockingly and sauntered off. Once the door closed behind him, the King confided in me that he had a dream, in which Arundel took both his crown and his life. Richard truly believes Arundel wishes him ill.'

'But that's only a nightmare?'

'Brother, young Richard is deeply sensitive in nature. He is vulnerable. Think of him as a foal surrounded by wolves. They slope either side of him and they watch as they snarl at each other. Arundel is a leader of the pack. Athelstan, you must have met someone you take an immediate and intense dislike to?'

'Yes,' Athelstan smiled, 'God forgive me I have, and most of them are priests. But, you are correct, I have met people whom I dislike immediately, and never change my mind about them.'

'Well, that's our young King's attitude towards Arundel. According to Master Thibault, Richard has instructed his beloved uncle John of Gaunt to watch Arundel closely. As you can imagine, our noble regent needs little encouragement: the two lords are at daggers drawn, and wage their bitter feud at court, in Parliament and, above all, across the city.' Cranston beat his fingers against the goblet, clattering it with his nails. 'Gaunt controls gangs such as The Master of the Minions, whom you have met, Mine host at The Tavern of Lost Souls. Arundel, however, has his leash on the Flesher and his gang the Sycamores who lurk at the Devil's Oak tavern. To cut to the quick, Gaunt and his Master of Secrets Thibault want the Flesher and his power to be utterly destroyed. They believe Arundel is plotting against the Crown and intends great mischief when Parliament meets after the feast of All Hallows.'

'What!'

'They don't know for certain, but they suspect Arundel may try to overawe Parliament with the mob.'

'But that can be countered.'

'Oh, the Flesher will whistle up his rifflers and summon all their scurriers from the alleyway. But Gaunt is also very apprehensive that Arundel, who is hiring mercenaries, may try to bring liveried troops into the city and lay siege to Westminster.'

'But I thought that was strictly forbidden. You can only quarter troops in London on land which is yours. Arundel may own a house along the riverside, as do many of the lords, but these residences are not extensive enough for troops to pitch camp. Sir John, you told me this yourself, did you not?'

'Yes, yes. I did.' Cranston scratched his chin. 'Nevertheless, I am certain that Arundel and the Flesher are plotting some mischief; something to do with the coming Parliament, though God knows what. And so we come to the Sicarius.'

'The dagger man? It was apparent that you and Raquin had a bitter feud over him. Who is he?'

'Eudo Ingersol,' Cranston replied, grasping his wine cup and making himself more comfortable on the settle. He paused at the shouting and yelling from outside, followed by the strident wail of bagpipes and the blowing of horns. 'They are taking a group of whores down to the stocks,' Cranston murmured, 'to be ridiculed until sunset. Now, Brother, the Sicarius, the dagger man.' Cranston paused to collect his thoughts. 'Master Thibault and I have grown deeply concerned at the growth and the power of the riffler gangs throughout London. They are a plague that spreads and taints everything. We decided in secret council to confront and destroy the greatest . . .'

'The Flesher and his so-called Sycamores?'

'Brother, in a word, yes. We recognise that Master Makepeace has a fearsome reputation as the Flesher. He is a killer to the bone and a vile abuser. We know he has slaughtered prostitutes for his own pleasure and barbarously removed any threat to himself or his interests. We decided to suborn his hideous coven by stealth rather than open attack.'

'Why now?'

'Why not?' Cranston testily retorted, then grimaced his apology. 'It's a matter which infuriates me, Athelstan. I would love to invoke the law against the Flesher and his coven. But, if I take him to court, what evidence can I bring? Whilst he will hire the sharpest lawyers to be found in the Inns of Court, they would swoop like a host of ravens on any indictment we lay against the Flesher. So, Master Thibault and I prayed for an opening, a secret way into the Flesher's world of wickedness. Brother, I have lit candles and tapers before the lady altar in many London churches with one prayer: let me send the Flesher to judgement. The good Lord did not let me down. On the eve of the feast of the Assumption, I was sitting here in this solar when I had a visitor. He slipped through that door, a swift shadow, cowled and masked, hidden by a heavy military cloak from chin to toe. He took this off and sat down opposite me. A youngish man, well educated – a mailed clerk, no less. He had served in the King's army and worked for a while in the chancery offices of one of the guilds. About five years ago, life changed dramatically when he entered the Flesher's household.'

'No!'

'Oh yes. Eudo Ingersol, otherwise known as the Sicarius, was one of the Flesher's leading henchmen. A very valuable retainer, a man of experience, schooled in the halls of Oxford as well as on the battlefields of France. A soul who knew many of the Flesher's secrets and, to put it bluntly, where the corpses were buried.'

'What did he want?'

'A free pardon for all crimes, certain monies and licences for himself and one other, yet to be named, to go abroad under the protection of the Crown.'

'So he wanted to betray the Flesher?'

'Yes, he was willing to sell his master and be admitted with honour into the King's peace.'

'And the other person?'

'We do not know and, perhaps, never will.'

'So why did this sinner seek repentance?'

'Oh, he cited the Flesher's cruelty, as well as his own desire for peace. I think he meant it. He wanted to escape, as he put it, the world of the knife and the garrotte. Ingersol was also brutally honest. He believed the Flesher's days were numbered, that the riffler leader had overstretched himself and was ripe for a fall. In the end, he promised to bring the Flesher and his ilk to due process of law, but he would do so gradually. He would not turn King's approver, but weaken the Flesher as much as he could from within by providing valuable information. He also believed the Flesher and Arundel were deep in some mischief, though he could tell us little about that. However, the information he did provide about robberies, housebreakings and assaults on different persons proved to be priceless and helped us frustrate him. Our bailiffs could never finger the Flesher's collar, or those of his henchmen, but a good number of Sycamores are either rotting in Newgate or hanging from the gallows.'

'Sir John, why did he have the name Sicarius?'

'Because he was a dagger man, a very skilful one. He carried a rather unique weapon, daggers especially fashioned in Italy. A craftsman in Rome created something quite unique for him.' Cranston turned and drew out his own dagger with its ornamented hilt and Toledo steel blade. 'Brother, what you see is obvious, a dagger, a knife. The Sicarius carried what looked like a small, black ivory rod. Press the hidden catch, however, and a deeply embedded blade sprang out – long, deadly, pointed and serrated on each side, sharp as a polished razor. He sat in this solar and showed me it. You could actually hide it in your hand; perhaps tuck it under the cuff of your jerkin. You wouldn't know he had it until the blade appeared. Moreover, the Sicarius was very fast, swift and skilful.' Cranston grinned. 'Even I became wary of him.'

'Could such a dagger have been used in the slayings at St Benet's?'

Cranston shrugged. 'Perhaps. The wounds were deep slits. Ingersol, however, never let that dagger out of his sight.'

'Could he be responsible for the killings?'

'A very remote possibility. In the end, Ingersol did betray the Flesher. He provided us with names and places, all the secret chambers and hidden dens along Hell's buttery. We netted many a rogue, seized malefactors and, as I have said, fingered wicked collars. It was harvest time for us; we were doing great damage to the Flesher and his coven. Then about ten days ago, everything ended. Nothing. No further information.' Cranston blinked, his face now solemn. 'I feel . . .'

'What, Sir John?'

'I don't think Ingersol was responsible for the murders at St Benet's. I have a feeling he is dead. Do you know, Athelstan, I truly liked him. Oh, he was a rogue, a true dagger man but

he had a soul. He felt guilty about what he'd done. He wanted
forgiveness. Above all, he wanted to start a new life. We would
meet in shadowy ruins, places where no one could follow
either of us, no spy, no eavesdropper. We would talk. I liked
him. We also agreed that if something went truly wrong, he
must come here to the Lamb of God, cloaked and hooded.
Mine hostess would send one of her spit boys for me. But that
never happened . . .' Cranston wiped his eyes. 'God have
mercy on him. I am sure the Sicarius has been murdered, and
cruelly so, either in the Flesher's Mansion of Murder, or in
the gloomy vaults of the Devil's Oak.'

'So he must have been discovered or betrayed?'

'No, he probably made a mistake. The Flesher may look
like Flaxwith's Samson, but his mind twists and turns as any
rat in the sewer and his wits are razor sharp; that's why he's
survived for so long.' He paused. 'Ingersol was giving us
information. We were inflicting great damage on the Flesher
and his coven. Now, we always prayed that the Flesher would
put this down to circumstances. I know he plays hazard. He
must have seen the cup cast the wrong dice but, on reflection,
he and Raquin must have realised a traitor lurked deep in their
household. If they did, and Ingersol made a mistake, that
precious pair would close the trap and kill him. He would be
shown no mercy, given no second chance. In the end they
must have done, that's why Raquin was baiting me.'

Cranston cooled his face with a scented napkin. 'The Fisher
of Men came to Queenhithe at my request. I am making
discreet enquires. I want to discover if the mangled corpse of
a fairly young man has been found floating in the river or
along its banks, but there's nothing. Flaxwith has questioned
the collectors of corpses, but again, nothing.' Cranston rose
and stretched. Athelstan could detect the tension in his great
friend's soul. 'I am going to settle scores,' the coroner hissed.
'I swear on all that's holy, I am going to settle with the Flesher
and his kindred spirit, his filthy familiar Raquin. So, friar, we
might as well begin now. I think we'll visit the Mansion of
Murder and the Devil's Oak.'

Athelstan hid his disquiet. Cranston had a fiery temper, and
the friar was worried about his present mood: the coroner

could be easily provoked to do something stupid. 'You have warrants?' Athelstan asked.

Cranston strapped on his warbelt, fastened the buckle and tapped the hilt of his sword. 'This is my warrant. Listen, little friar, if I approached the justices at the Guildhall and asked for warrants to be sworn out, the Flesher would know within the hour. He has a myriad of spies, clerks, scriveners – yes, perhaps even justices. As far as the Flesher is concerned, the walls do have ears, and eyes as well. No, we will surprise him. And you will come with me?'

'Most reluctantly,' Athelstan agreed, getting to his feet. Secretly he prayed that Cranston's temper would dissipate and his common sense prevail. The friar shook his robe and picked up his chancery satchel. 'I am in all things, Sir John, your faithful scribe, but I would like you to reflect and use your sharp wit, not your hot temper. First, let us go back to St Benet's. I need to view that place of murder. I am sure there is something amiss, a morsel of evidence I can discover and, above all, I need to revisit that church, scrutinise the corpses and question our leading parishioners.'

They left the Lamb of God, battling their way through the surging crowd. The day had drawn on. The trading along the broad swathe of Cheapside was now totally frenetic. Traders were desperate to move goods and make a profit before the market bell tolled to mark the end of business. Stalls had been totally uncovered to display all their wares. Journeymen stood on boxes, shouting a description of their goods and the prices 'much reduced'. Apprentices slipped like lurchers through the crowd, snatching at sleeves, belts or cloaks to compel would-be customers closer to their masters' stalls. Dung carts tried to clear the stinking midden heaps where children scrambled, screaming as they chased the dogs and cats which haunted that place. The stiffening breeze carried all the flavour of this great trading area: the salty reek of fresh blood from the slaughter pens; the stench of innards dragged out from the slit bellies of poultry and other stock. All these mingled with the fragrances of the perfume sellers, as well as the sweet flavours of the cook shops and the strong fumes drifting from the countless ale houses in whose doorways the orange-wigged whores clustered to solicit for custom. Tale tellers and relic sellers touted for business. A wild-eyed, sunburnt preacher held up a bottle with a red-painted stopper. He claimed that the swarm of flies buzzing angrily inside were in fact a host of demons he'd captured under a gallows on the Oxford road. Funeral processions with bell, book and candle jostled alongside wedding marches. Two such cortèges, its members much the worse for drink, had now merged together, with the bride sitting on top of the coffin, held by a line of laughing mourners and wedding guests. Bailiffs led a line of chained prisoners, most of them in rags, down to different stocks, thews, pillories and compters. Cranston was recognised, but the coroner ignored both the greetings and the insults, except for two grotesques who, faces hidden behind garish visors, began to dance in front of them. Cranston half drew his sword and both tormentors disappeared.

They turned off the busy thoroughfare and along the needle-thin alleyways into Queenhithe. They followed the trackways which twisted into Hell's buttery, strangely silent and desolate, though Athelstan was aware of figures swiftly disappearing at their approach, as well as hollow-sounding cries and shouts which proclaimed who was passing by. Cranston apparently was tolerated; no abuse was offered, nor did he suffer the rain of missiles which would greet many a city official. At last they reached St Benet's Woodwharf and began striding across the concourse towards the church. Flaxwith had left his bailiffs on guard just within the main doorway. These assured Cranston that the corpses had been removed to the death house. One bailiff escorted them across the cemetery, whilst another was despatched to fetch the people Athelstan wished to question, the friar adding that he would meet these in the priest's house.

St Benet's mortuary chamber was a long, dismal building. Its outside whitewashed walls were smeared with dirt, its tiled roof patched, whilst the windows were roughly hewn squares with shutters pushed between the wooden frames. The painted double door hung off its latch. Athelstan pulled this open and walked into the dank, cold mortuary room. This was no better than the outside: dismal and rather squalid; a dirt-packed floor with tables standing at either side and – on the two end walls

– black, wooden crucifixes, no more than pieces of wood nailed together. The rusting, corroding braziers had been lit, and the herbs strewn above the crackling charcoal did something to offset the horrid reek of corruption.

Daventry and Parson Reynaud lay naked on two of the tables. Cranston, at Athelstan's request, took a tinder and lit the tallow corpse candles. Athelstan used these to inspect both cadavers, studying the dead flesh from chin to crutch, in particular the death wounds on each of the victims.

'You see, Sir John,' Athelstan pointed to the wound in the left side of Daventry's chest, 'a blow direct to the heart. The wound is now congealed but look at its shape, like that of a leaf. The entry is a mere slit, but then the blade was pushed in and twisted up. I suspect the killer knelt before both of his victims, or just to their side. Now with Parson Reynaud I would understand that, if the assassin was pretending to be a penitent wanting to be shrived, but why kneel next to Daventry?'

'Unless he wished to whisper something.'

'In a deserted church, Sir John?'

'True, but that brings us to the problem of who was where and when? Were Daventry and Reynaud together in the church? Did the assassin creep from one victim to another, or did the killer deal with Parson Reynaud, then wait for Daventry to arrive and kill him?'

'My friend, all this is speculation, but both men must have been dead before their assassin removed the corpse of that old lady, unlocked the arca and stole its contents.' Athelstan paused. 'But as you say, it is speculation. Let us recite what happened, as if it is a mummer's play. So, Sir John, why should anyone steal that old woman's corpse?'

'First, she was the only person the Flesher loved. Isabelle Makepeace reigned at the Devil's Oak like an empress and, if the gossip is true, Isabella Makepeace was as cruel and as vicious as her son.'

'So she would have enemies?'

'Does a dog have fleas?'

'And secondly?'

'Profit. A demand has been made, a veritable treasure to

have the corpse returned. However,' Cranston brushed some crumbs from his cloak, 'that means our assassin must reveal something of himself, which would be extremely dangerous, dealing with the likes of the Flesher.' Cranston peered at his companion, who was lost in thought. 'There is something else, Athelstan?'

'Yes, yes, Sir John, but at the moment I cannot place it. It was something I saw on the corpses.' Athelstan shrugged. 'Or was it something else? Anyway, for the moment let us put those matters aside and return to the church.'

They left the death house and took the winding, weed-strewn path, which cut like a twisting snake through the sprawling, neglected cemetery. The ground was peppered with funeral stones and requiem crosses, nothing more than a tangle of decaying wood and stone, most of it hidden by the sprouting briar and bramble. Athelstan paused and stared across the cemetery, noting the neglect, the crumbling burial mounds and half-dug pits.

'Sir John, what is happening here?'

'I have asked the same. According to Flaxwith, who has had words with Sexton Spurnel, Parson Reynaud was keen to clear the cemetery, empty as many graves as possible and so start anew.'

'Why? I mean Parson Reynaud, God rest him, seemed more interested in his comfortable house, amenable whores, his expensive robes and jewellery than God's Acre. Indeed I do wonder, Sir John, if Parson Reynaud went into the church yesterday evening not so much to shrive a penitent but meet someone, a person he did not want others to see.'

'Such as?'

'Sir John, for the time being, that's mere speculation. So let us begin. Now,' Athelstan turned and pointed back to the death house, 'yesterday afternoon, Isabella Makepeace's corpse was taken by the sexton and others to be churched in St Benet's, the Flesher and possibly his henchmen being present for the ceremony?'

'According to Sexton Spurnel, yes. But by then,' Cranston continued, 'the coffin was sealed. They brought it through here.' Cranston reached the shattered devil's door and he helped

Athelstan step over the debris which still littered the entrance. They entered the damp, chilly nave. Athelstan opened the candle chest just within the entrance. They took out and lit the squat, tallow tapers, as well as others fixed on their spigots in the Lady Chapel and elsewhere. The candlelight glowed, casting circles of golden warmth in what Athelstan now regarded as one of the most eerie churches he had ever entered. The nave seemed to create its own darkness, a presence with a life of its own. The silence was oppressive, as if it housed beings of the night who'd gathered to watch and, if necessary, intervene to provoke nameless fears. Athelstan tried to shrug off this chilling of the soul as he stood before the empty coffin.

'So, Sir John, we have the problem.' Athelstan just wished his voice did not have that sepulchral echo. 'Yesterday afternoon, this coffin, with Isabella Makepeace's corpse inside, was brought into this nave to be blessed. Later on two men entered. First Parson Reynaud, who sat in the mercy chair in the entrance to the chantry chapel, whilst his visitor Daventry, an emissary from my Lord of Arundel, also came here. We do not know Daventry's business, perhaps we never shall. Nor, at this time, do we truly know if the priest and the messenger were aware of each other. In the last resort they both came in here. They sat down quite apart. Daventry in the sexton's chair near the main door, Parson Reynaud in the entrance to that chantry chapel. I have noticed that they would not have been able to see each other. The assassin then enters; he approaches one, then the other. Both men are murdered. The coffin lid is ripped off and the old woman's corpse plucked out. How that cadaver was removed from the church is also a mystery.'

'Brother?'

'Well, it must have been dark or at least dusk. Autumn is drawing on, and to leave a church carrying an old, dead woman is fairly singular. There is the danger that the assassin might meet someone, or be seen by parishioners, or indeed anyone passing the church. Curate Cotes, Mistress Martha, Sexton Spurnel, Cripplegate, or one of the Flesher's vast retinue might visit St Benet's, though perhaps not for matters spiritual.'

Athelstan walked back, measuring his steps carefully. 'They must be gathering,' he murmured, 'perhaps when we meet we might learn more, but other mysteries remain. Sir John, the arca? A heavy, stout, reinforced money chest. It has two different locks with unique keys carried only by those who own the arca. Parson Reynaud's was still hanging about his neck when we examined his cadaver this morning. Of course, it could have been taken, used, then put back. But the Flesher was wearing his around his neck. Unless it was the Flesher who carried out the killings for his own secret purposes; that seems a logical explanation, at least superficially.'

'Yes, yes,' Cranston rubbed his hands together. 'If I empanelled a jury to sit at Westminster, they might rule there is a case to answer.'

'Precisely, Sir John.' Athelstan chuckled. 'Such an explanation sounds fine but signifies nothing.'

'Oh I know,' Cranston murmured, 'my impatience is getting the better of me.' The coroner shrugged. 'Why should the Flesher murder his own henchmen? Why should he abuse his own beloved mother's corpse then steal his own money? Finally, as God made little apples, if I summon the Flesher before any jury, he would terrorise its members, as well as turn up with a host of witnesses: they would swear the most solemn oath that yesterday evening the Flesher spent every second of his time praying in his own private chapel at the Devil's Oak. Oh no! So, back to the mysteries. How were money sacks, heavy pouches of coin removed from the church so no one can witness it being done? I cannot imagine Mistress Martha, Curate Cotes, Cripplegate or Sexton Spurnel, or indeed any other suspect, staggering through the cemetery at twilight with heavy sacks of clinking coins. And where could that be hid?'

'And of course,' Athelstan grasped Cranston by the wrist and took him back to the devil's door, 'the final mystery.'

'The doors were left locked and bolted from the inside.' Cranston waved around. 'This was broken into because, unlike the rest, it is not of solid oak but heavy panelling. According to all the witnesses, Sexton Spurnel smashed the slats and was able to stoop in to draw the bolts as well as turn the key in the lock. The evidence indicates that all the other doors were locked and bolted from within and, like this one,' Cranston pulled the door backwards and forwards, 'the keys were still in the locks. That includes every door to this church, a building with narrow windows and no secret entrances. For the love of God, Athelstan, can you imagine it? Each door has a lock and two bolts. But can an assassin pass through solid stone carrying the corpse of an old woman and heavy sacks of coin?'

'A maze of murderous mystery,' Athelstan agreed. 'Ah well, Sir John, let us meet our parish worthies and see if further light can be shed.'

They left through the devil's door and stood on the pebble-dashed path that surrounded the church. Athelstan stood kicking at this with the toe of his sandal. Many churches had such paths, and he had been advised to lay the same at St Erconwald's. Athelstan had been informed that a pebble path around the church helped to soak up and retain the rainwater when it poured down the church walls or through the gullies. Athelstan crouched and sifted through the pebbles with his fingers before he and Cranston continued their scrutiny of the entrances to St Benet's. They went round to the corpse door. Athelstan inspected its heavy, oaken frame, a thick wedge of wood hinged securely to the lintel; its bolts were slightly rusty but workable, and the friar could see they had not been inter-fered with. The same was true of the lock, its key still hung on the inside and, again, they could detect nothing amiss with the key or the large keyholes either side of the door. He and Cranston continued their way along the pebble-dashed path around the church. Again they were struck by how desolate and derelict the cemetery had become. On closer inspection, a good many of the ancient crosses and headstones had been removed; shallow graves very close to the church showed where the harrowing of the dead had taken place. Empty burial pits from where the skeletons had been plucked and flung into that great, cavernous charnel house which filled the crypt beneath the church. Athelstan felt he was walking the blighted moorlands of Hell. He truly believed the cemetery was not God's Acre. Indeed, this graveyard, together with that macabre crypt, were no more than murder pits used by the Flesher with the full connivance of a wicked priest to hide the victims of his crimes; be it whores, rivals, or anyone who dared to oppose

him. They would be slaughtered, their corpses deliberately
lost here in shallow graves, to be later dug up and hidden in
the monstrous tangle of bones beneath the church.

'A fitting home for demons,' Cranston murmured.

'I agree. Look around you, Sir John, sniff the air – to me
it reeks of wickedness. I will leave it for a while but, Sir John,
when all this is over, I intend to seek an audience with the
Bishop of London. This church should be razed to the ground,
its cemetery reconsecrated and stripped. Let the grass grow,
plant gardens. Allow this morbid, sombre place to flourish so
as to reflect God's smile.'

They walked on, pausing to scrutinise the locks on the other
doors, the main entrance, its postern gate and, finally, back to
the devil's door. Athelstan could see how the parishioners had
broken in, removing the slats before pulling at the bolts and
turning the key.

'We have seen enough,' Athelstan declared, walking back
on to the pebble-dashed path. 'Oh yes, for the moment, we
have certainly seen enough.'

Sexton Spurnel, Mistress Martha, Cripplegate and Cotes
were waiting for them in the oak-panelled solar of the priest's
house, a truly comfortable chamber with its gleaming oak
and pink plaster, whilst thick, heavy turkey rugs covered the
polished floor. Triptychs and other devotional paintings
exuded their own brightness in a wide array of vivid colours
to portray scenes from scripture. Warmed by a magnificent
dragon-mouthed hearth, as well as merrily burning braziers,
the solar was as comfortable and luxurious as any Athelstan
could recall in the great mansions of London or the bright-lit
chambers of the court. Candles glowed in silver spikes
along the rim of wheels lowered from the timber-beamed
ceiling. The air was fragranced by the sweet smell of baking
from the kitchen. A place of rest and relaxation. Athelstan
felt the cloying warmth of the house lull his wits and soothe
his humours.

The friar shook himself and sat up straight, staring about
as Sir John and all the company gathered around the solar's
polished chancery table. Mistress Martha offered ale and
freshly baked scones covered in butter and a sweet sauce.

Cranston eagerly accepted, but Athelstan shook his head and opened his chancery satchel.

'You are to question us again?' Martha asked, squeezing herself into a chair pulled close to the table. Athelstan smiled at her. He was grateful for her kindness, and intrigued by this good-looking woman who had not been Reynaud's leman or doxy. Athelstan could well understand why both the parson and his curate had lusted after such a woman.

'As Martha said, you are to question us again?' Cripplegate rested his elbows on the table. Athelstan studied the locksmith more closely. He did not look so composed or assured as he had earlier in the day. Was the locksmith innocent? A member of the guild, leader of this parish council who, like so many in life, just looked the other way? He and others had done no harm, which was as true as its hidden twin, that they had also done no good? Cripplegate held Athelstan's gaze then blinked, wetting dried lips and scratching at his grey beard. 'What more can we say?' Cripplegate's voice held a hint of desperation.

'I have certainly nothing to add.' The curate had apparently not changed his clothes and looked as bleary-eyed and sottish with drink as he had earlier.

'I have thought and thought again,' Sexton Spurnel waved a hand. 'I cannot recall anything amiss.'

'Is that true?' Cranston retorted. 'Two men murdered, one corpse stolen and a treasure chest robbed, and you still can recall nothing out of place?'

Athelstan felt a twinge of cramp. He murmured his apologies, stood up and walked around the solar, going into the small buttery, a pantry chamber where jugs of wine and water were held. Athelstan filled a beaker and drank the water greedily. He glanced around and marvelled at the small tuns of Bordeaux which he recognised as the best, the kind Prior Anselm served royal guests. He also noticed the altar wine casks, which had been removed from the sacristy, all six of them lined up against the wall. Athelstan went over, each of them was empty, waiting for the next purveyance cart. He went back into the solar and smiled at the company who were staring fixedly at him.

'I am sorry,' he declared. 'Mistress Martha, your ale is very tasty, but I find water is best for my thirst. Tell me something, have you searched the church and this house, not to mention the mortuary and cemetery for any sign of a corpse or the stolen monies?'

'We have searched.' The sexton gestured at Cripplegate and Cotes. 'And of course Master Makepeace has sent down his men as well, but we can find no trace. As Mistress Martha declared those responsible are hardly going to hide what they have stolen under our very noses.'

'Very well.' Athelstan retook his seat and rapped the table top. 'Let us quickly recall what happened yesterday evening.' He smiled around. 'A long enough day, whatever that means in St Benet's. Isabella Makepeace is placed in a coffin in the death house, her son Simon is present and places a bouquet of red roses in the casket, which is then sealed. The coffin is lowered on to a sled and carted over to St Benet's, where it is placed before the rood screen, blessed and churched.' Athelstan shrugged. 'And so on and so on.' Everyone murmured their agreement. 'Once the reception of the corpse is completed, Compline is chanted by Parson Reynaud and Curate Cotes. Parson Reynaud adjourns to his house, Curate Cotes leaves to visit certain parishioners before arriving at the Devil's Oak. Yes?' Again there was agreement. 'Parson Reynaud, according to you, Martha, meets Daventry in his chancery chamber here in the priest's house. God knows what they talked about or what messages Daventry brought. According to you, Sexton Spurnel, both men were seen walking towards the church; that's the only proof we have that they entered it together.' Athelstan pulled a face. 'After that, darkness falls in the full sense of the word. Night passes. Uneventful in itself, except for the dreadful happenings in St Benet's. Mistress Martha, you awake the following morning, you find neither Parson Reynaud nor the curate in their beds, so you hurry down to the devil's door carrying its key. You are joined by Masters Spurnel, Cripplegate and Cotes. You break in through the devil's door, only to find a true hall of abomination.' Athelstan paused. 'Oh, by the way, Parson Reynaud's papers, manuscripts and chancery coffers?'

'Master Makepeace has already taken those – or rather his familiar Copping has,' Martha replied.

'Of course they have,' Athelstan murmured. 'I am sure that anything that was written down has now vanished, so we will make little progress in that quarter.'

'Brother Athelstan,' Martha smiled, 'even if certain manuscripts hadn't been taken away, and my companions can vouch for this: the Flesher and Parson Reynaud were loath to put anything in writing.'

'So they kept everything in the dark, concealed?'

'What do you mean?' Cripplegate demanded.

'I mean, we mean,' Cranston brought his hand down on the table, 'that this church and its dead priest were involved in all kinds of iniquity.'

'Sir John, that is not fair,' the curate protested.

'Master Cotes, that's the truth,' Cranston riposted.

Athelstan sat back in his chair. He agreed with Cranston: these worthies needed to be confronted with the truth they had ignored over the years.

'Why,' Athelstan demanded, 'was the cemetery being cleared? Why has it not been properly fenced off? Why does the crypt lie open? I shall answer my own questions.' Athelstan got to his feet, one hand raised, as if taking an oath. 'I agree with the Lord High Coroner, all kinds of wickedness were carried out in St Benet's, positioned so close both to the river and the Devil's Oak tavern: smuggling, the purchasing and selling of whores in both this kingdom and abroad, the handling of stolen goods, the protection of felons fleeing from the law and the murder of those the Flesher grew tired of. This is not a parish,' Athelstan's voice rose, 'it's nothing but a house of sin.'

'How dare you!' Cripplegate rose.

'He dares and so do I.' Cranston got swiftly to his feet, half-drawing his sword in a rasp of glittering steel.

'This is not true,' Cripplegate shouted, retaking his seat.

'I am a priest here too,' the curate yelled.

'And shame on you for that,' Cranston retorted. 'You followed one line from scripture?'

'Which is?'

'You certainly looked the other way.'

The shouting and the protests continued. Athelstan waited till the hubbub had died; only then did he retake his seat.

'He is right. The friar speaks the truth,' Martha declared, her voice harsh and carrying. 'Why should we defend Parson Reynaud? We may not have done anything wrong, but did we do anything right?' She let her question hang in the air as she stared around at her companions.

'Oh yes.' Cripplegate gave a deep sigh. 'What's the use? Martha is correct, we all know she is. Sir John, Brother Athelstan,' Cripplegate held up his hand, forefingers intertwined, 'you know it's the truth. Parson Reynaud and the Flesher were—'

'Thick as thieves,' the curate jibed.

'Yes they were,' Cripplegate declared. 'What could we do? We accept they are sinners to the core, but what they did was simply a matter of much suspected and nothing proved. Moreover, Sir John, the people grouped around this table are indebted to the Flesher: he loaned me money when I left the company of the Tower archers. I used that to finance my progress from an apprentice to journeyman, to full member of the locksmith guild.' Cripplegate spread his hands. 'The same could be said—'

'Of me and Sexton Spurnel,' Cotes interjected. 'And I am glad you've raised it, Nathaniel, aren't you?' The curate turned to the sexton.

'Yes, yes,' Spurnel whispered, 'it's time we summoned up the ghosts.'

PART FOUR

Psalm-singer (**Old English**): an informant

A deep silence descended on the solar. Athelstan felt a shiver as he looked at their faces, Cranston included. He sensed the past was breaking through.

'We have to speak about it,' Cranston murmured. 'Eighteen years since that night on board *The Song of the Sword*. The Twelve Apostles and the Rose Casket mysteriously taken. Good comrades slaughtered. Somebody betrayed us, yes?' A wall of silence greeted his question. 'Yes,' Cranston roared, slamming the table with his fist.

'Yes, yes, yes,' Cotes conceded. 'But who? Eighteen years on and we all ask the same question. And yes,' the curate now became quite heated, 'unlike you, Sir John, we were trapped by what happened. The old King and his son the Black Prince excused you, they pardoned you, they did not hold you to account, but we were summarily dismissed from the Tower guard. We are Queenhithe's men. Who could we turn to? Like others, we were swept into the Flesher's bloody embrace. He gave us money, smoothed the way here and smoothed the way there. He helped us – and I know why.' The curate stopped, breathing heavily.

'Why?' Athelstan asked softly.

'The Rose Casket, the Twelve Apostles,' Cotes blurted out. 'I am sure the Flesher helped us so as to keep us under close watch. The Flesher suspects that the precious stones are still in London, hence he watches us just in case we know something about their disappearance. Such scrutiny is not difficult,' he added bitterly. 'Spurnel, your post gives you a house, food on your table and, like me, enough to drink. Cripplegate, you are now a member of a guild but you are also in the Flesher's debt. You are a man with skills and knowledge he finds useful.'

'Yes, yes,' Cripplegate shrugged, 'I accept what you say.'

'And I am what you see,' the curate continued mockingly, 'a man who entered the church because he had nowhere else to go. I was given a benefice here because no other parish priest would accept me.'

'And you, Mistress?' Athelstan turned to Martha, who still sat serenely staring at the wall.

'I am what you see, Brother,' she replied. 'A widow, forced to accept the kindness and patronage of the Flesher, Parson Reynaud and their ilk. But I have no complaint. I sit, wait, watch and pray,' she smiled thinly, 'that the new parson, even if it's you, Curate Cotes, will allow me to continue in the post I have held for so many years.'

Athelstan smiled understandingly, though he quietly promised himself to interview the housekeeper separately. Such a sharp-witted, keen-eyed woman may know more than she had revealed.

'Brother,' Martha had her head down, playing with the bracelets on her wrists, 'so far I have not told anyone about this, but when you met the Flesher earlier today, three of his bullyboys were outside. Apparently they'd been with Lawyer Copping down to the execution scaffold at the Elms. Afterwards they visited St Bartholomew's Hospital and talked to its keeper, Brother Philippe.'

Athelstan caught his breath. 'And?'

'They mentioned something about a precious jewel, how it had been sold by Brother Philippe to a Cheapside goldsmith; that's all I could learn. However, once the Flesher was informed, he became deeply excited.'

'In God's name, I can see why!' Cranston exclaimed.

The others lost their sullen looks, all attentive, the years now rolling back as the great mystery which both bound them together, and yet divided them so bitterly, re-emerged from the darkness of the past.

'The Twelve Apostles!' Sexton Spurnel exclaimed. 'Impossible! It cannot be! They are back after eighteen years. So they were stolen and hidden! The person with one must have the others.' Spurnel paused and glanced sideways at Cripplegate and Cotes.

'God help anybody,' Cripplegate murmured, 'who the

Flesher suspects holds that casket. Sir John, Brother Athelstan, I give you good counsel: the Flesher will tear London apart to find that treasure; he will kill and kill again.'

'You seem to know a great deal about what the Flesher will do?' Athelstan retorted.

'Brother Athelstan, over the years I have studied the Flesher. I have never mentioned the Twelve Apostles to him, nor he to me, yet I tell you this.' Cripplegate leaned closer. 'Firstly, if the Flesher discovers who killed Parson Reynaud, abused his mother's coffin, killed Daventry and broke into that arca, then that person will take days to die. Secondly, anyone who prevents the Flesher seizing the Rose Casket and its precious contents will perish just as miserably.'

'But none of you,' Athelstan demanded, 'has heard anything about the whereabouts of these jewels since that fateful night?'

'Not until now,' Cripplegate replied.

'I often wonder,' Sexton Spurnel murmured, 'when I am deep in my cups, who betrayed us.'

'You say all this,' Athelstan countered, 'yet you still ally yourself to the likes of the Flesher, the very felon who could have organised the attack on the royal barge *The Song of the Sword*?'

'Oh for God's sake,' Cripplegate retorted, 'he helps us and he terrifies us. He treats us like he does his ferocious dogs. As long as we obey him and humour his whims, we are kept safe.'

'We have already explained our situation,' Cotes sneered. 'What choice do any of us here have? Oh, by the way,' Cotes's voice turned mocking, 'Sir John, you are the Lord High Coroner of London. The Flesher is a dyed-in-the-wool villain. Why has his collar never been fingered by you?'

'We grow old,' Cripplegate declared. 'Sir John, Brother Athelstan, we really have no choice about who we deal with. We are the little men. We have our narrow houses, a few treasures but,' he snapped his fingers, 'who would mourn for me if the Flesher decided that I should go? Curate Cotes is correct, if the King's coroner in London cannot check the Flesher – what chance do we have?'

Athelstan nodded understandingly. Deep in his heart, he felt sorry for these people: they were trapped. He could sense their intense dislike, even hatred, for the Flesher, but they were caught in his malignant web. 'Tell me,' Athelstan took a deep breath, 'does the name Grenel mean anything to you?'

'Of course,' Sexton Spurnel replied. 'You know it does. The Grenels were also Tower archers. They were killed, probably drowned, when *The Song of the Sword* capsized during the attack.' Sexton Spurnel's face was now flushed, and Athelstan suspected the sexton had been drinking for most of the day.

'And,' Athelstan demanded, 'what were they like? Good comrades?'

'Father and son,' Curate Cotes retorted. 'Decent men, skilled archers. They kept to themselves. I mean, we hailed from Queenhithe, they were from Southwark.' The curate narrowed his eyes. 'In fact, I think they were in your parish of St Erconwald's?'

'Long before my time.'

'As I said, they kept to themselves. The father was married to some local woman. Walter, the son, was a bachelor. One day whilst practising at the butts I asked Walter if he had a sweetheart. The lad just grinned and replied how he had found happiness in the House of Bethany – that's all he said.'

'Bethany, what's that?'

'Brother, this was years ago. Perhaps it was some brothel or house of pleasure, but more than that . . .' Cotes's voice trailed away.

'Let's return to the matter in hand,' Cranston demanded. Athelstan looked towards the mullioned glass window, a small square of light now darkening as dusk set in. Athelstan pulled his chancery satchel closer. It had been a long day; it was time to return to his parish. He was curious to find out about Brother Philippe and that precious stone. Athelstan again wondered about the cellar beneath Margo's house and those two mummified corpses.

'And Daventry?' Cranston asked. 'Do you know why Arundel's man came here?'

'Sir John,' Martha replied, 'I have told you: Daventry was closeted with Parson Reynaud. I know nothing of what passed between them, and that is true of all of us.' A murmur of agreement echoed her words. Athelstan could see that the three men were still distracted about the possibility that the Twelve Apostles had reappeared in London.

'And Ingersol, the Flesher's henchman commonly known as the Sicarius, the dagger man?'

'Oh yes, we glimpsed him coming and going between here and the Devil's Oak.' Cotes replied. 'A secretive soul. A man of the shadows.'

Martha shook her head as she repressed a shiver. 'God forgive me,' she whispered, 'but I felt like a mouse that lived constantly in the shadow of the cat. Ingersol was a dangerous man; he gave me that impression. A constant visitor here, the go-between used by the Flesher to bring messages to and from Parson Reynaud. He rarely spoke or met your eye. He dressed most soberly. You would think he was a priest more than an assassin, a true thief of the night. Brother Athelstan, Ingersol would come and go, one menacing shadow flitting amongst the rest.'

'Do you think he brought messages about the cemetery outside, its clearance, the work being done? Was that the decision of Parson Reynaud, the Flesher or both?'

'Sir John,' Sexton Spurnel shook his head, 'I – we – cannot say.' He blew his cheeks out. 'The dagger man came and went. A forbidding enough character; in fact I haven't seen him for the last two weeks or so.'

Athelstan sat in silence as the parishioners scraped back their chairs, whispering to each other. The friar was baffled by the fog of mysteries which swirled about this parish and its church: murder, theft, sacrilege. Athelstan rubbed his face and lifted his head.

'Master Cripplegate?'

'Yes, Brother?'

'We have touched on this before. I ask you not because I accuse you, I am just deeply curious.'

'Brother?'

'The arca.' Athelstan pointed at the coroner. 'I want that empty arca taken to Sir John's chamber in the Guildhall.'

'Why?'

'Because I am the Lord High Coroner and I want it so,' Cranston snapped.

'Very good, Sir John.' Cripplegate turned back to the friar. 'So, Brother, your question – though I can hazard a guess.'

'Can the keys to the parish arca, whether they be the work of a craftsman or not, be copied precisely and accurately?'

'The blunt answer is yes. Sir John, Brother Athelstan, there's not a key under heaven which cannot be copied accurately and most skilfully.'

'And how?'

'Ideally, a piece of pure Castilian soap. It captures every little twist and cast of a key pressed into it. I have seen it done. A cast is made of both sides of the key, particular attention being paid to what we call the teeth, which fit snugly into the lock to turn it. Of course,' Cripplegate spread his hands, 'I am sure the Fl . . .' He caught himself in time and smiled. 'Master Makepeace, like Parson Reynaud, never let that key out of sight.'

'We'd all swear to that,' Spurnel added.

'And Isabella Makepeace? Mistress Martha, we have spoken of this before, but I would value your opinion.'

'The truth? Isabella Makepeace was of the same evil substance as her son.' Martha's voice trilled with hatred. 'No one will gainsay me.' She paused and stared around. 'Brother, Sir John, I speak honestly, Isabella Makepeace was hated. She ruled from her chamber in the Devil's Oak like any tyrant. Ask anyone who had dealings with her.'

'I have,' Cranston interjected.

'Then you will know all about her.' Martha half smiled. 'Oh, Mistress Makepeace could act the part of the great lady but, when she wanted to, she would cruelly inflict her anger on some poor unfortunate.'

'As she did to many, including myself,' the curate declared. 'The wrong word, the awkward glance, the failure to jump when she whistled were, in her eyes and her son's, heinous crimes. But Sir John, Brother Athelstan, the day draws on, the hour is late. I am sure I speak for the rest, but I have no more to say.'

Cranston glanced at Athelstan who nodded. The meeting ended, though the friar beckoned to Martha and asked her to stay for a while. They waited until the steps of the rest faded and the main door closed.

'Brother?' Martha sat on the chair closest to him. He could smell her fragrance, a sweet herbal essence.

'You do not like the Flesher or his mother?'

'Nobody does or did.'

'And you can cast no light on these mysteries?'

'Brother Athelstan,' she glanced across at Cranston, 'Sir John, you heard the Flesher's filthy remark to me this morning. Like many in St Benet's parish, I have to tolerate insults because I have no choice.' She paused, glancing down at the table top, and when she lifted her head, tears brimmed in her eyes.

'I married very young, my husband was sickly. He'd hardly made any profit from his work and, when he died, he left a mountain of debts. I buried my husband here, Brother Athelstan, and three months later found myself in the House of Delights. It was either that or whoring along the streets of Queenhithe, pandering to the sailors or working in the sweatshops of the squalid stews along the river. In the House of Delights the Flesher provided me with a chamber, food, clothes and a few coins. I was careful about who I went with.' She shrugged prettily. 'Brother Athelstan, Sir John, go through this city tonight and you will find many a woman with a similar tale.'

'Yes, yes,' Cranston agreed. 'What you say is true. You had no kin?'

'I had no kin and I had no choice,' she replied fiercely, 'until you can create that choice. I was most prudent with my monies. I counted and hoarded the coins and eventually I bought myself out.' She dabbed at her sweat-soaked brow. 'At the House of Delights I had entertained Parson Reynaud. I approached him after he made it obvious that he wanted a housekeeper. I replied that I would serve him as a good housekeeper, but I made it very clear that this would be in his house and not in his bed.'

'And he agreed?'

'Brother Athelstan,' she grinned, 'he had to. I am an excellent cook. I am also discreet, clean, and I knew Parson Reynaud in every sense of the word.' She waved a hand. 'So here I am and, if God is good, here I stay. You would think I might know of all Parson Reynaud's dealings – after all, I did share the

same house as him. The blunt answer is no! I served him and
his sinister, shadowy visitors their food and drink. I ran errands
and delivered messages, but Brother Athelstan, I am not a fool.
I was accepted, even favoured, because I knew my place. I
did not want to know what was going on. I made no attempt
to find out, to spy, to eavesdrop – in fact the opposite. Brother
Athelstan, that is how you survive in the Flesher's world. Keep
to the straight and narrow, and all will be well. Make a mistake
and you pay dearly for it. You can put me on oath; you can
go through Parson Reynaud's manuscripts,' she pulled a face,
'though the Flesher or his lawyer Master Copping have
collected these, for what they are worth. However, if you
scrutinise Parson Reynaud's world, you will find that I was
his housekeeper – nothing more, nothing less . . .'

A short while later, Cranston and Athelstan left St Benet's
and stood in the empty concourse before the church. The friar
stared up at the ancient stone front of St Benet's and wondered
how such a house of prayer could become a mansion of murder.

'Sir John, Sir John?'

Athelstan turned as Tiptoft slipped out of the darkness.

'Sir John, Brother Athelstan.' He hastened across the
cobbles, wiping the sweat from his face. 'A thousand pardons,
but I bear urgent messages from Brother Philippe and
Benedicta, not to mention Mauger and the rest. You must return
to St Erconwald's.'

'Why, what has happened?'

'Rifflers attempted to rob your cottage and that of Margo.
Benedicta was threatened—'

'No injury surely?' Athelstan clutched his stomach at a
spasm of cold fear.

'Oh no, all are safe, but they wrecked your house, or tried
to, and they dug up poor Margo's coffin. Anyway, all are safe.
Brother Philippe has closely examined the corpses.' Tiptoft
scratched his spiky red hair, 'Although I am not too sure what
that means, but that's what Benedicta said: that he has examined the corpses and has much to say. Brother Philippe hasn't
returned back across the river. Benedicta has lodged him in
the Piebald. Mine host Jocelyn says he will look after him
until our good brother returns.'

'Sir John, we should . . .'

Cranston, however had walked away, staring at the mouth of an alleyway across the concourse, one of those thread-thin ribbons of utter darkness where the night-walkers swarmed ready for the hunt.

'I am sure I heard the clatter of steel,' the coroner murmured. 'Oh heaven and all its angels, Tiptoft, Athelstan!'

The friar stared in horror as figures carrying cresset torches, their leaping flames glittering in an array of drawn steel, debouched out of the alleyway. Athelstan counted at least seven in all, each hooded and visored. They carried sword and dagger, whilst an eighth trailing behind them had a powerful arbalest, primed and ready to loose. Cranston threw his cloak back and whistled shrilly, hoping that Flaxwith or some of his bailiffs were still in the vicinity.

'*Pax et bonum.*' The leading figure placed his sword and dagger on the cobbles and held up both hands. 'Sir John, Brother Athelstan, I repeat, *pax et bonum*. We wish you no ill but we need to converse.'

'French,' Athelstan whispered, 'he has the tongue of Paris.'

'I repeat,' the man called, 'we wish you well.'

'You choose your time and place unwisely,' Cranston shouted back. 'Couldn't we meet in the full light of day in my chambers at the Guildhall?'

'That may suit you, Sir John.' The stranger gestured at his company to stay where they were whilst he, hands outstretched, walked slowly towards Cranston and Athelstan. 'I agree, Sir John, but there are some things which are best said in the dark rather than in the brightness of God's day.'

'Dark, light, day and night mean nothing here in Hell's buttery. Indeed,' Cranston continued, 'in this valley of sin the night has both eyes and ears and, at times, even hands which carry sword, dagger and every other weapon known to man.'

'Be that as it may . . .' The stranger pulled back his hood and lowered the visor concealing the bottom half of his face. 'Time passes,' the stranger murmured, 'the hours flit. I need to speak to you urgently,' he turned to the friar, 'Brother Athelstan especially.'

'And you are?' Athelstan demanded.

'Wait.' Cranston held a hand up and turned back to where Tiptoft stood. 'Search out Flaxwith and my bailiffs. Tell them to find me wherever I go.' The coroner pointed at the alleyways. 'There will be people watching who, for a coin, will lead Flaxwith through that hellish maze. Now sir,' Cranston turned back to the Frenchman, 'you are?'

The stranger scratched his black, tousled hair, his cheerful face breaking into a grin, his eyes wrinkling in amusement. A mailed clerk, Athelstan concluded, educated in the chancery and the tiltyard. Skilled in weaponry, with a sharp mind and a keen wit.

'I am Hugh Levigne.'

'And who is Hugh Levigne?' Cranston mocked.

'I am the Candlelight-Master. My companions are members of a cohort known as the Luciferi. We lodge with the French ambassador, Monseigneur Derais, in his house—'

'La Maison Parisienne.' Cranston finished his sentence. 'The official residence of the French King's principal envoy to the English court.'

'And a close friend of your King Richard,' Levigne added quickly. 'Who, I understand,' he grinned, 'adores everything French.'

'As did his father and grandfather,' Cranston retorted. 'They certainly took enough armies to France to seize and hold it as their own.'

Levigne elegantly raised a gauntleted hand. 'Those days are over. We now talk peace to each other. Heart speaks to heart. King Richard, my Lord of Gaunt and Monseigneur Thibault, your regent's Master of Secrets, all seek amity and reconciliation – Monseigneur Thibault in particular.'

'A truly delightful man,' Cranston declared drily. 'I wondered if he would appear in the masque now being staged.' Cranston tapped his warbelt. 'A very murderous play,' he murmured.

'Sir John?'

'The Twelve Apostles,' Cranston declared. 'I have more than a feeling that this is about the Twelve Apostles.'

'Sharp as sharp can be,' Levigne declared. 'More cutting than the hydra's tooth. Bluff old Jack is never what he seems to be.' Levigne, head to one side, studied Cranston from head to toe before his gaze shifted to Athelstan. 'And your constant little shadow.'

'Some shadow,' Cranston retorted.

'Bluff Jack, merry Jack,' Levigne leaned closer, 'please, I shall resheath my sword and dagger, then let us talk.' He gestured around. 'There are taverns enough here?'

'Taverns indeed, hostelries and alehouses,' Cranston declared, then paused at a whistle which cut sharply across the concourse. Athelstan glanced over his shoulder as Flaxwith and his cohort of bailiffs walked out of the darkness around St Benet's.

'We fashioned a few torches and were looking in the crypt behind the church,' Flaxwith called out. 'We have also been watching your visitors.'

'Not visitors, but friends yes?' the Candlelight-Master called out.

Cranston turned back and smiled at Levigne. 'Oh yes, our new-found friends. So Master Hugh, pick up and put away your weapons; the same goes for your companions. Once I am satisfied that they have done as I ask, we shall adjourn to a hostelry I have always wanted to visit, the Devil's Oak.'

'Sir John,' Athelstan warned, even as he noticed how Levigne was also taken aback.

'Why not?' The coroner chuckled. 'I want to show the Flesher that the King's law, the King's peace and the King's Lord High Coroner cannot be checked, curtailed or controlled but, like the spirit, we can go where and when we will. I want to visit the Devil's Oak, and now is as good a time as any. So, my friend, tell your company to follow close behind Master Flaxwith. Tiptoft,' he bellowed, 'you too stay close. Right, my beloveds, let's go sup with demons.'

The Devil's Oak was, despite its age and use, still a magnificent, if malevolent, hostelry, boasting three gables, sloping red-tiled roofs, protuberant chimney stacks and walls of ashlar stone. The front of the tavern spread out behind a porticoed entrance, its columns of pure oak painted and picked out in brilliantly garish colours; these caught the light of the many sconce torches flickering in their cressets. The entire tavern was surrounded by a battlemented wall and entered through a fortified double gateway, where some of the Flesher's liveried retainers stood on guard. They tried to stop Cranston, but the coroner yelled at them to be damned, and swept into the large cobbled bailey which stretched either side of the gateway. This great stabling yard echoed with noise and tumult: people shouted, sang, cursed and yelled; horses neighed shrilly as they kicked at their stalls behind the tavern; dogs barked. A sow, which had escaped from the piggery, lumbered into the yard, where it was swiftly slaughtered by a cleaver, its massive head split clean as an apple, the rich-red blood spouting out to bring in the kennel dogs eager to lap, wary of the fists and boots of the slaughter boys. Numerous carts loaded with provisions stood about. Travelling tinkers, chapmen and all kinds of river people made their way up through the grand entrance into the welcoming warmth of the spacious taproom. On either side of the steps perched two long arrow chests. Each contained a corpse, black as soot from head to toe, though some effort had been made to cleanse their faces. One of the Flesher's henchmen, his jerkin displaying the Sycamore insignia, proclaimed how these two corpses were those of thieves; malefactors who had tried to burgle the house of one of Lord Makepeace's friends by breaking through a chimney stack. Both felons had been trapped and killed by crossbow bolts, so anyone who recognised them should say so now under pain of forfeiture. The customers simply averted their gaze from the gruesome sight of the barbs, still deeply embedded in the dead men's bellies, and hurried on.

Cranston's arrival in the courtyard soon made itself felt. The noise subsided. People turned, hands going for knives and daggers, or they picked up cudgels close to the arrow chest. A horn brayed and a door to the side of the main entrance opened in a gust of steam, which carried the reek of burning oil and other cooking smells. The Flesher appeared, flanked by Raquin and Copping. The riffler leader hurried down the steps, his ugly face twisted in a smile, though he was clearly surprised to see the coroner grace his premises.

'Sir John, Sir John,' he blustered, 'you are most welcome. You have news of my beloved mother, Master Daventry—'

'And your gold and silver?'

'My rightful property.'

'No news, Master Makepeace; my apologies but no news.' Cranston stepped back, as if surveying the Devil's Oak from the top of its pointed gable to the pricks of light just above the ground, the soft glow of candles and torches burning in the cellars beneath the tavern. 'Do you know something, Master Makepeace? One of these days I am going to come back here, perhaps even tonight, and do a truly thorough search.'

'For what?' Raquin demanded.

'For whatever I find.'

'And this evening, Sir John?' The Flesher peered over Cranston's shoulder at Levigne. 'The Candlelight-Master, the Luciferi,' he murmured. 'You keep strange company, Sir John.'

'Bearing in mind who I am now talking to, that's probably the most truthful thing you've said in decades, Master Makepeace.' Cranston clapped his hands. 'But enough of the pleasantries. I want my retinue here entertained in your taproom. I also need a secure chamber, one of your best, guarded by Master Flaxwith and two of my good friend's escort. So,' Cranston again clapped his hands. The Flesher glanced at Raquin, shrugged, and led Cranston and his party up the steps and into the spacious taproom.

Athelstan gazed around in silent wonderment. If any chamber was heavily tainted with sin, this one certainly was. A yawning, cavernous place, the taproom had a high-beamed ceiling; its floorboards were covered in sawdust stained by food, drink and, Athelstan peered at one large blotch, what looked like congealed blood. The noise was raucous and never-ending: singing; carousing bagpipes wailed and trumpets blared. Two drunks, naked except for their muddy boots, danced grotesquely to the merriment of other customers. Three women tied to each other were boxing and wrestling whilst the onlookers laid wagers. A young whore disported herself on a mattress in one corner whilst her companions tried to persuade a sottish city fop to join them in the darkness beneath the stairs. Smells of cooking billowed from the kitchen behind the great serving board. Cries, moans, calls and shrieks of pleasure and pain echoed on all sides. A rat pit, built just beneath one of the shuttered windows, was being prepared for the usual slaughter and the betting which accompanied it. Close by, wiry-haired dogs, eager to be at their prey, threw themselves against their cages. Levigne swore loudly. Cranston just turned and clapped the Frenchman on the shoulder.

'I've seen worse – a rare event, but I have seen worse.'

The Flesher took them up on to the first gallery and showed them into a chamber warmed by braziers and well lit with candles placed along the oaken polished table and the broad windowsill. Herb branches hung from the rafter beams to perfume the air. The floorboards, polished and gleaming, were covered in soft black turkey rugs, whilst leather-backed cushioned chairs were placed around the long table; this sported a small, silver nef which glowed in the dancing light. The Flesher bowed mockingly and left, saying he would send up a carafe of wine, fresh bread and platters of minced pork. Cranston thanked him, shouting in a sarcastic tone that all expenses and bills should be sent to the Exchequer at Westminster for payment, before slamming the door shut. He gestured at Levigne and Athelstan to sit down, but then he tiptoed back to the door, swiftly opened it, looked out and closed it with a sigh.

'Good,' he murmured. 'Flaxwith and two of your company, Monseigneur Levigne, will guard the gallery. I believe these walls are solid enough, there is no room on either side whilst,' the coroner peered up at the ceiling, 'all above seems safe enough . . .' He broke off at a tap on the door and Tiptoft pushed his head through.

'Sir John, do I stay?'

'No.' The coroner sat down on a chair, beckoning the messenger in. 'Go to Southwark, yes Brother?' Cranston didn't wait for an answer. 'Ask Brother Philippe the physician to stay in the parish until Athelstan and I return. Good, good.' Cranston ushered Tiptoft out and they all waited while the cheeky-eyed slattern came in to serve both wine and food. Cranston ate as if starved, Levigne picked at his platter, whilst Athelstan, lost in his own thoughts, sipped at his wine and wondered what the Frenchman really wanted. The friar rose and walked across to stare at the wall paintings. On their way up to this room, the Flesher had offhandedly referred to it as 'the devil's chancery', and the crudely painted wall paintings reflected this: vigorous depictions of Hell which recalled the Hangman of Rochester's work. On this particular wall the Archangel Ariel scourged the wicked across face and eyes, driving them across a meadow where black smoke curled, shot through with fire. Next to it, a cohort of demons hunted the damned, chasing them across red-hot flagstones to a bubbling, black lake.

'We are ready,' Cranston murmured.

Athelstan returned to his seat opposite Levigne, who raised his head.

'Sir John, Brother Athelstan, we should begin. I do not like this place much.'

'I agree.' Cranston put his horn spoon away. 'Brother Athelstan, let me formally introduce Hugh Levigne, Candlelight-Master and leader of the Luciferi – the Light Bearers who are information gatherers for His Catholic Majesty the King of France and Monseigneur Derias, his envoy to England. They all reside in La Maison Parisienne, the Paris House, in Lothbury. They collect information, but also work quietly and secretly to advance their master's cause.' Cranston pushed his platter away. 'Sometimes they are our enemies; sometimes they are our allies. On the rare occasion, they could even be our friends. So,' the coroner turned to Levigne, 'what is it this time?'

'Your friend, Sir John. Let me be precise and to the point. Eighteen years ago, the French Crown, much against its better judgement, though at the time it had little choice, handed over to the English court so-called reparation for war damages.' Levigne shrugged and spread his hands. 'It was really a bribe to keep Edward of England and his brood of falcons out of France. We had no choice but to surrender the Twelve Apostles, exquisitely beautiful jewels, in their container, the Rose Casket. This coffer was regarded as equally costly, fashioned out of rare wood with golden, silver-stemmed roses.' Levigne sipped at his wine. 'At the time the French Crown was determined, as it still is, to recover this unique sacred treasure. The Rose Casket and all it contained was handed over to the Hanseatic merchants to be taken to Queenhithe on one of their ships,

The Glory of Bremen. We kept our word and stayed out of the proceedings; then we heard about the attack on you, Sir John, and your war barge, *The Song of the Sword.*' Levigne toasted Cranston with his goblet. 'We also learnt you had been injured and pulled from the river, but that the Rose Casket and the Twelve Apostles had vanished. Like the English Crown, we thought it was only a matter of time before such a gorgeous casket, with its truly precious stones, emerged on the London market or, indeed, anywhere else.' He paused. 'And yet, nothing. We know that your King's ministers searched high and low, and we certainly did. Time passes, but the Luciferi do not forget. We pay for those who act as our eyes and ears along the thoroughfares and waterfronts of your city. We are always interested in what is being offered for sale, be it a secret or a sapphire.' Levigne cleared his throat. 'Then, about two months ago – yes, about the feast of the Magdalene, we heard a most curious story. A woman, fairly old, poor and decidedly unwell, had approached London merchants, cabinet-makers and casket craftsmen. She was offering the most beautiful coffer for sale. From the description given, we realised it was the Rose Casket, but who the woman was remained a mystery until now.' Athelstan glanced warningly at Cranston to remain silent on what they already knew. 'No matter, Brother,' Levigne leaned across the table and gripped Athelstan's wrist, 'we have learnt a great deal and – how do you put it? – we are ahead of the game. We understood that a woman from your parish took a precious stone to the keeper of St Bartholomew's Hospital. She apparently offered it in return for treatment. We believe the keeper did not realise what he had received and sold it to the Cheapside merchant Blundel.' Levigne, his face all excited, leaned across the table. 'Brother, what is important is that the Twelve Apostles and the Rose Casket have reap-peared. It seems that this woman of your parish first offered the Rose Casket for sale and then one of its precious stones.' He held a hand up. 'Before you ask, she failed to sell the casket. From the little we gleaned, the woman became deeply concerned at the keen interest shown in the casket. She must have realised that no one would accept it was some family heirloom but part of a treasure stolen from a royal barge. We know that the London merchants were given a description of the casket and its contents eighteen years ago.' He shrugged. 'Merchants never forget, especially when they have received a warning from the Crown and, correct me if I am wrong Sir John, but anyone caught handling that casket, be it a seller or a customer, could face a charge of high treason?'

'Correct.' Cranston wiped his mouth on a napkin. 'Monseigneur Levigne, we know a little about what has happened. We are now hastening back to St Erconwald's. I concede that you have learnt a great deal; indeed you must also realise that the owner of this hostelry, Master Makepeace, popularly known as the Flesher, may have had a hand, and I suspect he did, in the attack on the royal barge when the Rose Casket was stolen.'

'Yes, yes, I accept that.'

'And you must also accept that the Rose Casket and the Twelve Apostles are the legitimate property of the English Crown?'

'Ah yes.' Levigne opened the buttoned pocket of his doublet and handed a cream-coloured scroll of costly parchment to Cranston, who broke the seal, read its contents, sighed dramatically and passed it to Athelstan. The message written in the clerkly hand of Thibault's Secret Chancery, asked Cranston and his '*nobilis secretarius*' Brother Athelstan 'to cooperate fully with Monseigneur Levigne in the discovery and seizure of the Twelve Apostles and their coffer the Rose Casket, feloniously taken by an act of the most heinous treason.'

Athelstan studied the signature and seal of Thibault, Gaunt's enigmatic Master of Secrets, then tapped it with his fingernails. 'Thibault,' he declared slowly, 'wants these precious stones, but he also wants to give them back to the French Crown, that is obvious.' Athelstan smiled at Levigne. 'Otherwise he wouldn't ask us to cooperate with you. In return for what, Monseigneur?'

'Gold,' Cranston whispered. 'French gold, French troops, French assistance if needed here in this kingdom. Young Richard is famous for his love of all things French and it is equally well known that the English Exchequer is empty.'

'What you say may well be correct.' Levigne rose. 'But

now you know why we have and will continue to take a great interest in you, Sir John, and the worthy Athelstan. Now we must go.'

They all left the Devil's Oak. The tavern was, as the hour grew late, the true home of all creatures of the dark. Athelstan felt wary as he followed Cranston through the throng of garishly dressed night-walkers, be it the tribe of thieves or the world of the whore. The noise was raucous in the extreme. The rough music strident. The air perfumed with all kinds of smells, both rank and sweet. Cranston did not bother to clasp the Flesher's hand but brushed it aside as he led his group out across the yard and through the massive double gates. Here Levigne and his cohort made their swift farewells and left. Cranston turned, leading Athelstan, Flaxwith and his comitatus of bailiffs along the waterfront towards London Bridge. The coroner had decided that crossing the Thames by barge was too dangerous. Athelstan agreed. The night was pitch dark, whilst a stiff easterly wind buffeted the river, making any crossing extremely perilous. Conversation was difficult. Cranston and Flaxwith were also very wary. They might well be King's men, buckled for war and vigilant, but they were, as the coroner remarked, in the kingdom of the damned. Here human wolves sloped through the darkness and demons crouched on rooftops behind sills and in the filthy enclaves, their knives sharp, eyes bright, and wits ready for any mischief which might bring them profit or the twisted merriment of hurting another soul. Eerie chanting and echoing cries cut the night air. Shouts and curses dinned the ear. They passed through the occasional pool of light, thrown by crossroads lanterns, or by bonfires where the city rubbish was burnt. The dispossessed flocked to these to warm themselves, as well as to cook the food they'd filched earlier in the day from the butchers' bins and bakers' trays. Dogs fought the feral cats and both confronted the long, grey rats that infested the alleyways leading down to the river. They passed gallows and gibbets well stocked with the ripening flesh of malefactors hanged earlier that day. Occasionally they would glimpse a furtive funeral party, pushing a corpse in a barrow to one of the many cemeteries, and Athelstan recalled that bleak wasteland around

St Benet's. The friar was even more convinced that the grave-yard and crypt of that sinister church had been used by the Flesher to hide the victims of his murderous rage. Athelstan just wondered how many corpses lay there unknown, and why the Flesher and Parson Reynaud were so intent on clearing God's Acre – for what?

At last they reached the approaches to London Bridge, where Cranston made his farewells of Flaxwith, telling his chief bailiff to inform the Lady Maude where he was going and that he would return to her on the morrow. The coroner then used his passes and seal to gain entrance, through the postern door and on to the moon-washed strip which cut across the bridge, with houses, storerooms and warehouses built on either side. The bridge lay silent, doors and shutters had been pulled closed and locked. Here and there, patches of candle glow or lantern light broke the darkness. All sound was hidden by the constant thunder of the river now in fast flow, hurling itself against the struts and starlings below, whilst the fish-tainted breeze whipped away any words he or Cranston tried to exchange. They hastened past the ancient, small chapel dedicated to St Thomas a Becket, towards the towering mass of Southwark gatehouse: here its keeper Burdon and his ever-growing brood of children kept close watch over the severed heads of traitors brought to be tarred and poled above the railings of the bridge. At last they reached the other side. They passed through the wicket gate, across the execution yard, where the corpses of malefactors still dangled either at the end of a gallows rope or gibbeted in a metal cage. Athelstan murmured a hasty prayer, then they were through, on to the alleyway leading up to St Erconwald's. Athelstan paused to bless both himself and Cranston in thanksgiving for being safely home.

'Excellent oatmeal,' Cranston declared to the agreement of others gathered around Athelstan's great table in the stone-flagged kitchen of his priest's house. Athelstan smiled, gesturing in welcome at those who'd joined him and Cranston to break their fast; Brother Philippe, Benedicta and Mauger. Sir John had lodged at the Piebald in the chamber next to Brother Philippe's and enjoyed a good night's rest. Both the coroner and the physician had risen early and attended Athelstan's Jesus Mass just after dawn. Once Athelstan was finished in the church, they'd assembled here in the priest's house to feast, as Cranston put it, on the sweetest oatmeal, the freshest bread and creamiest butter from Merryleg's pie shop.

Athelstan stared around the kitchen. On his return the previous evening he'd become very angry when he had learnt about the attack on his house, the desecration of Margo's grave and, above all, the nasty threats issued to Benedicta. Nevertheless, all had been put right. Margo rested peacefully in her coffin. Benedicta assured Athelstan that she was fully recovered, and took great pride in how other parishioners, Crispin the carpenter especially, had gathered to put matters right so even the marks of the break-in could scarcely be detected.

'Once again,' Athelstan picked up his tankard of light ale and toasted Benedicta's lovely smiling face, 'once again my profound thanks. But let us move swiftly to what brings us here.'

'It would appear, Athelstan,' Brother Philippe broke in, 'before you continue any further, well . . .' The physician scratched his cheek and blinked. 'I am sorry, but I am a little bit confused. I know from Benedicta about the conclusions you may have reached, about the two corpses found in that cellar. However, I urge you first to inspect them as I have my own theories.'

'Then let us finish eating,' Cranston urged. 'I do want to see this.'

Once the meal was over, cloaks were collected and they hurried out into the cold, misty morning, down the path, through the lychgate and across God's Acre. Here the wisps of a thick river fog, which had rolled in the previous evening, now thinned, parting and shifting like ghostly curtains. Godbless was standing outside his cottage and greeted them all before proclaiming how the demons were back. Fluttering figures, shadowy people shrouded in knotted glass; how these stalkers of the sky walked the wind and rode the clouds. Athelstan stopped to bless both beggar man and goat, then they hurried on. Mauger went ahead to unlock the death house, a grim, cold place despite the glowing braziers, the nosegays hanging from the rafters and the bowls of crushed aromatic herbs placed around that long, cold, barn-like chamber with its whitewashed walls and earth-beaten floor. Two of the mortuary tables were covered with coffin cloths. Mauger pulled these back so Brother Philippe, standing between the tables, could explain his conclusions. Athelstan stared pityingly at the two cadavers, father and son locked in their mysterious deaths. The bearded faces looked at peace, eyes and mouths closed, arms across their chests, legs together. The skin of both corpses now exuded a strange, glossy, yellow-white tinge, and Athelstan glimpsed the horrid, purple-red cuts to the chest, belly and, when he moved both corpses, the lower back.

'Death wounds,' Brother Philippe explained. 'Very serious injuries. I suspect both men were attacked by assailants carrying both sword and dagger. The victims were standing close together. They were struck from behind, they turned to face their attackers and received further wounds to the front.'

'Would they have been killed immediately?'

'No, Athelstan, Sir John will be my witness. Men in battle can and do sustain savage injuries yet still fight on. Yes, my Lord Coroner?'

Cranston stood, eyes closed, rocking backwards and forwards on his booted feet. Athelstan sensed he was going back in time. 'The attack,' Cranston murmured, 'was ferocious and swift. They overran *The Song of the Sword*, our men were struck; I saw some of them stagger about, archers going overboard—'

'Tell me,' Athelstan asked, 'where were you exactly? Were you off Southwark side?'

'Yes, yes we were. I remember glimpsing the beacon light in the steeple of St Mary Overy. The captain of our barge had moved his craft across river to confuse anyone who might be following us. *The Song of the Sword* went backwards and forwards. Eventually the captain pronounced himself satisfied and so he turned, aiming like an arrow for the north bank of the Thames. I recall the river fog parting and the wolves were upon us.'

'You were knocked unconscious?' Athelstan asked. 'You fell overboard and were fished out of the river?'

'In a word, yes.'

'And so let us move forward eighteen years,' Athelstan declared, 'and what do we have? Fat Margo, Margaret Grenel, widow of this parish, falls ill. She apparently held a great treasure. We suspect she tried to sell the Rose Casket but became frightened at the reaction of those she offered it to; that is most understandable but then matters moved on.'

'Margaret had a grievous, morbid sickness upon her,' Brother Philippe declared. 'She crossed the Thames and was admitted to the great hall at St Bartholomew's. We can only do what we have the time and money for.' The physician paused. 'So many come,' he whispered, 'one after the other. I need money, good coin to buy medicines, powders, potions and philtres. Margaret Grenel was part of the throng until she approached me. Now, I was honest with her. I could do little to assuage the humours in her belly, but she wanted opiates to control the pain and these are costly. I agreed and she gave me a jewel. Ah well,' Brother Philippe shrugged, 'I am a physician, a Benedictine monk. I know nothing about amethysts or such costly items. I took the precious stone Margo offered me in full payment for all treatment. Naturally, I wanted to be rid of it, to exchange the item for good pounds sterling, so I took it to Merchant Blundel. Looking back,' he added ruefully, 'I suppose Blundel must have been truly delighted to secure such a treasure for such a petty sum. It simply proves, as the good Lord says, that the children of this world are more astute in their dealings with their own kind than the children of the light.' He smiled. 'I am not saying I am a child of the light, just that I work for them.' The physician pulled his ave beads out of a pouch and began to sift them through his fingers. 'Athelstan,' he continued, 'what you told us this morning before Mass is truly fascinating. How the amethyst Margo Grenel gave me is part of a long-lost treasure hoard, a king's ransom now being sought by all the great, the good and the ghastly. So what will happen next?'

Cranston explained how he would visit Merchant Blundel, demand the amethyst be returned and tell the goldsmith to seek redress at the Exchequer. Athelstan let himself relax and the conversation swirl around him as he tried to impose order on his own tumbling thoughts. He and Cranston had met Brother Philippe, Benedicta and Mauger in the sacristy before mass. In hushed tones Athelstan had informed them about the history of the Twelve Apostles, the attack on the royal barge eighteen years ago, the involvement of the Flesher and their meeting with the Candlelight-Master and the Luciferi the previous evening. Both Benedicta and Mauger had explained how strangers had certainly been seen in and around St Erconwald's, on the approaches to London Bridge as well as near Haceldema, the Field of Blood, a stretch of wasteland beyond the cemetery. However, neither Benedicta nor Mauger could say if these were the Flesher's henchmen or those of the Candlelight-Master.

'We are finished here,' Athelstan declared absent-mindedly. He picked up one of the coffin sheets and draped it over the younger man's corpse. Benedicta and Mauger did the same for the other cadaver and Athelstan declared they should return to the priest's house. 'Oh,' he paused, 'where are the clothing and other effects of these two corpses? I suspect Margo must have dressed them in fresh garb and burnt what they wore on the barge.'

'Over there!' Mauger pointed to a barrel in the corner. Athelstan and Cranston walked over to this. They picked out the paltry belongings: hose, jerkin, boots, belts and other items. Cranston held up the mailed wrist guard and stared sadly at it.

'All Tower archers were given one of these,' he declared. 'Once they'd been inducted, it was a badge of office. Ah well . . .'

They left the mortuary. Mauger abruptly broke away from the group, hurrying across the burial ground, shouting and waving his hands. Athelstan glimpsed a flash of colour from behind a rather large tombstone, then Cecily the courtesan and her sister Clarissa stood up, like rabbits all alert. Athelstan was sure he glimpsed a man clad in brown and green fustian, the usual garb of a travelling chapman, scampering away as fast as he could. The chapman's swift flight was shielded by the two sisters who, all pert and dainty, blocked Mauger's rush.

'Good morning, Father,' Cecily waved. 'We were just saying farewell to one of our friends who,' she held up a tawdry necklace of white stone, 'has sold us this.'

'At this time in the morning,' Mauger scoffed, 'in God's Acre?'

'Well it's quiet here,' Clarissa retorted.

'And good for business,' Benedicta whispered.

Athelstan gestured at her and the rest to stay quiet. The friar knew from previous encounters how Cecily and Clarissa, if provoked, could give as good as they received. They could act like young ladies but, once they lost their temper, their language was extremely ripe and their tantrums uncontrollable. Mauger, however, wouldn't let the matter rest.

'What business,' he taunted, 'and how much do you charge?'

'Not as much as we would ask for you, Mauger,' Clarissa yelled. 'Not now, when you no longer have that poor widow woman kneeling before you. Gone to rest, she has, from all her troubles, and from you.'

Mauger simply waved his hand and strolled back, muttering curses to cover his deep embarrassment at Clarissa's outburst.

'Let's wash our hands,' Athelstan declared, eager to divert his companions, 'and have some more bread, honey and ale.'

Once they had gathered around the great kitchen table and the friar had served the meagre food, Cranston, who had been as fascinated as Athelstan by the sharp altercation between Mauger and the two sisters, raised his tankard in a toast. 'So, we have made some progress, yes?'

'It would seem,' Brother Philippe declared, 'that those two men, father and son, whose corpses we have just viewed were on your barge, Sir John. Grievously wounded, they both fell overboard and, I suggest, somehow reached the Southwark shore, probably not far from here. Local men, they would know the swiftest route to their house where Margo Grenel was waiting.'

'Loyal archers,' Cranston declared, 'men who took the oath and believed in it. They must have seized the casket and taken it with them.'

'I agree,' Athelstan declared. 'Margo must have learnt what had happened. She would certainly realise her menfolk were grievously wounded. She would tend their injuries but there was nothing she could really do. Both father and son died. Margo Grenel was confronted with caring for the corpses of the two men she dearly loved. She was also the most reluctant possessor of the Rose Casket and the Twelve Apostles. If she went to the Crown or any of its officers, God knows what might have happened. Would the finger of suspicion be pointed at her and her menfolk? She might be accused of high treason, of being an accomplice.'

'But surely,' Benedicta demanded, 'both men were wounded in the service of the King: they tried to save the royal casket?'

'No, no.' Athelstan shook his head. 'Sir John, you'd agree with me? The Crown lawyers would be looking for a scapegoat. They might argue that all three Grenels, or at least the bowmen, were part of a conspiracy. The two archers had betrayed the secret of *The Song of the Sword* and all the details of the treasure it held. How they had planned to steal it and simply been injured.' Athelstan paused. 'Margo might have escaped punishment, but the corpses of her beloved husband and son would have been seized, even gibbeted.'

'I would agree,' Cranston replied. 'I remember how things were after the robbery. Even I, though I nearly drowned, was closely investigated. Now,' Cranston spread his hands, 'I am a royal knight, I have influence, I am skilled in law. How could poor Margo Grenel plead? She would soon become flustered. No, no, what she did was both understandable and logical.'

Athelstan played with the crumbs on his platter. He kept thinking of Mauger, who sat with his head down; the bell clerk had not touched either drink or his food. Athelstan recalled what had happened when this business first came to light.

'Athelstan?' Cranston queried.

'For the moment we should leave the various theories which might be spun of a woman holding a king's treasure, stolen with violence, during the theft of which royal retainers were slaughtered.'

'Margo Grenel would have realised that,' Brother Philippe

offered. 'Before they died, her menfolk must have told her what had happened. After their deaths, what could she do with their corpses? If she revealed what had happened, she would bring a whole torrent of troubles down upon herself.'

'Any other woman,' Athelstan declared, 'would have panicked, tried to hide the corpses but, of course, Margo had the unique skill of being a corpse-dresser – and a very good one. She also had the cottage to herself, so she embalmed both cadavers and kept them hidden in that dry cellar beneath her house. To all intents and purposes, her menfolk had left on Crown business and never returned. Go around Southwark and you will find such a story is common. Young men, fathers, brothers,' he glanced quickly at Mauger, 'who go across the Narrow Seas and never return, not even heard of again. Those in authority, such as Sir John, who helped organise *The Song of the Sword* and its clandestine business, would conclude that both archers had been killed, drowned in the Thames. They would have no reason to think otherwise. The Twelve Apostles disappeared forever and, with no sight or sign of the Grenels, who could even suspect what had truly happened? Time soon dims memories, and so it did until Margo Grenel fell ill. I suspect the poor woman knew enough about the body to conclude that what she suffered from was deeply malignant. She had kept the Rose Casket and the Twelve Apostles well hidden. But she now decided it was time she profited from the treasure and the evil which it had brought. She tried to sell the coffer, but became frightened by the interest shown. Margo, God bless her, became truly ill. What did it matter? She took the amethyst from the chest, settled her affairs in Southwark and moved across to St Bartholomew's.' Athelstan shrugged. 'The rest we know. Interest in the Twelve Apostles would probably be quickened by the reappearance of the Rose Casket. Merchant Blundel's purchase and Roslin's attempt to steal it only proclaimed that an eighteen-year-old mystery had emerged from the darkness and the great treasure was still to be had.'

'And that's it.' Benedicta spoke up. 'That's the true problem. Where is the Rose Casket and its precious treasure now? Where could it be? Margo must have hidden it somewhere, in the church, God's Acre or elsewhere? Mauger, what do you think?'

But the bell clerk just shrugged, lost in his own thoughts. Athelstan again wondered why Mauger's confrontation with the two sisters seemed to have greatly subdued him.

'Brother Philippe,' Cranston asked, 'did Margo ever say anything about the amethyst or its origins?'

'No, no, far from it. The poor woman was very ill. She became delirious; she talked about the parish here. She mentioned you, Athelstan, on a number of occasions. She also talked about the bell and, strangely enough, how Arthur would come again.'

'Bell?' Benedicta asked. 'We have no church bells here, and who on earth is Arthur?'

'The once and future King,' Brother Philippe murmured. 'Yes, she repeated that about the bell but it was all disjointed, the utterings and mutterings of a very frenetic mind. Sometimes she would talk about her husband and son, about secrets, and she asked me if her sins would be forgiven, so I reminded her about the mercy of Christ.' Brother Philippe spread his hands. 'More than that I cannot say. Brother Athelstan, Sir John, I truly must leave.'

The meeting ended. Mauger seemed eager to be gone and slipped out of the house. Cranston and Brother Philippe made their farewells. The coroner declared he intended to visit Merchant Blundel and collect the amethyst. The physician said he would accompany the coroner as a witness. Athelstan and Benedicta watched them leave arm in arm, then returned to the priest's house. They were immediately joined by the great one-eyed tomcat Bonaventure, who strolled imperiously over to the hearth, hungrily lapped the offered bowl of milk, then threw himself down as Athelstan said, like any Roman emperor fresh from the battlefield. Benedicta and Athelstan quickly cleared the table and scrubbed the pots, tankards and platters. The widow woman asked what was to be done with the two corpses?

'We will bury them quietly tomorrow after the Jesus Mass,' Athelstan declared softly. 'Tell Mauger to prepare a grave close to Margo's. If anyone asks, tell them you are taking care of nameless corpses being buried here as an act of mercy.'

Benedicta promised she would, and left telling Athelstan not to brood too long by himself. Athelstan absent-mindedly nodded and sat on a stool before the hearth, warming himself while stroking Bonaventure, patting the great tomcat as he reflected on all that he had seen and heard. 'It's like being in a maze, Bonaventure. You twist and turn but you cannot find a path which will lead to the centre, to the heart of the mystery, though you know that path is there.' The great tomcat's response was a long, drawn-out purr of contentment. 'Quite, quite,' Athelstan whispered. 'Keep warm, my old friend, the days are closing in and the weather turns colder. I think we will have a river mist tonight, so it will be an early bed for both of us. No climbing to the top of the church tower to study the stars. The sky will be clouded, the breeze too strong and cold.' Athelstan repressed a shiver. 'Talking of church towers, my friend, I wonder what Margo meant by the bell? Even more so, the reference to King Arthur – what has that got to do with her?'

Athelstan chewed the corner of his lip. Once those two corpses were quietly buried and the grave blessed, he intended to organise a most thorough search of that cottage, as well as the parish death house where Margo had worked. Athelstan crossed himself, rose, and walked over to the lectern where his psalter was opened for the office of the day. He read the psalms, his attention caught by the words of Antiphon:

'Blessed be the Lord, my rock, who prepares my arms for battle, and readies my hands for war.'

'Do so.' Athelstan closed his eyes and fervently prayed. 'Do so now.'

Curate Cotes struggled to wake in his narrow bedchamber in the priest's house at St Benet's Woodwharf; his head pounded as if a tambour was being loudly beaten close to him; his eyes were filled with mucus, his stomach pitched with sharp, short pains. The curate felt heavy-limbed, his throat dry as dust. He heard a sound, rolled over, and stared in astonishment at the blond-haired, lissom young man, naked as he was born, pulling himself up. Curate Cotes swung himself off the bed and stared at his own clothes strewn across the floor. He heard a cough and glanced in horror at the Flesher squatting like a toad on a stool just within the doorway. This hung open and, despite his bleary eyes, Cotes glimpsed Martha, Cripplegate and the sexton staring fixedly in at him.

'Naughty, naughty boys,' the Flesher sneered. 'Curate Cotes, you are a sodomite. You visited the Devil's Oak yesterday evening and left with young Marcel here.' The Flesher assumed a mock, pious look. 'I never guessed at the truth of it till I visited St Benet's this morning.' He spread his hands. 'And so here we are.' The Flesher stooped down, picked up a heap of clothing and threw it at the young catamite. 'Swift as you can, Marcel. Dress and be gone, you naughty boy. Curate Cotes, make yourself as decent as you can and meet us all downstairs.'

Curate Cotes, now dressed in a dark nightgown, slid on to the stool in the buttery and glared at the Flesher sitting so self-satisfied and smug at the top of the table. Martha sat opposite the curate, staring in open-mouthed astonishment at him. Cripplegate and Spurnel also grouped around the table, looked highly nervous and refusing to meet his eye. The Flesher picked up his tankard of morning ale and mockingly toasted what he called, 'his guests'. Cotes grabbed his own tankard, eager to slake his burning thirst.

'I am not a sodomite,' he blurted out. 'I was drinking in the Devil's Oak, talking to people, then I staggered back here by myself. That's the last thing I remember.'

'Well, well, well,' the Flesher jibed, 'we've all seen what we saw. According to at least five witnesses, and that includes young Marcel, you, Curate Cotes, are a sodomite and, priest or not, you could face humiliation and the full rigour of the law. Being burned alive at Smithfield is a gruesome prospect, though you might die in good company because your two friends here, Cripplegate and Sexton Spurnel, certainly share your predilection for smooth-skinned youths. Don't you, gentlemen?'

'This is preposterous,' Cripplegate retorted. 'Master Makepeace, what is this all about?'

'Do not act the outraged, virtuous locksmith,' the Flesher snarled. 'You and Spurnel also visit certain houses which the mayor and his bailiffs would dearly love to raid – to search and seize the likes of you – but enough of that. You act all innocent but I, and others will agree with me, believe that the three of you must know something of the truth about the horrid events in our church.' He turned and pointed at Martha. 'I suggest, Mistress, you entertain similar suspicions?'

The housekeeper, who looked terrified, just opened and closed her mouth, then shook her head slightly. The Flesher, elbows on the table, jabbed a finger at all three men. 'I suspect you had a hand in the killing of Daventry and Parson Reynaud. I also believe that you stole my beloved mother's corpse and robbed that arca of my silver and gold.'

'You have no proof,' Cripplegate spluttered.

'I do not need proof,' the Flesher snapped. 'But if we are going to go down that path, then why did you tell fat Jack Cranston and his furtive little friar that you and the sexton were at home,' he smirked, 'in your respective beds? You weren't.'

'I was in the Devil's Oak,' Cotes declared.

'Later that night you were but, correct me if I am wrong, all three of you met in the Prospect of Jerusalem, close to St Andrews-by-the-Wardrobe? You were in a closeted window seat overlooking the tavern garden. You ate and drank till late in the evening then left. Hours later, Curate Cotes, you came to the Devil's Oak. So tell me, what did you talk about?' The Flesher moved his gauntlets, lying on the table before him, and used his stubby fingers to emphasise his points. 'It would take three to kill Daventry and Parson Reynaud. At least one of you to distract, the other to strike. And you, Master Cripplegate, did you fashion keys for that arca?'

'As the angels are my witness, how and when would I even get the opportunity to make a cast?'

'You met one of my henchmen, a fellow I truly trusted till I discovered he was a Judas. You knew him well, Ingersol; popularly known as the Sicarius.'

'I never—'

'You must have met him. He would come to St Benet's with messages from members of my household. I know, for God's sake, because I sent him. He would visit Parson Reynaud in his house. Isn't that right, Martha?'

'Yes, yes,' she whispered, 'but when he came in I left. I was very frightened of him. A dark man. He would be closeted with Parson Reynaud and, if they wished, I would serve them some refreshment.'

'Of course, of course.' The Flesher stroked Martha's hand, gripped it, then let it go.

'And Ingersol would linger to talk here, yes?'

'To me and others,' Cripplegate stuttered.

'So you did meet him?'

'Well of course but—'

'Never mind.' The Flesher was now becoming heated, his face even more flushed, the veins on his thick neck bulging in fury. No one dared move. The Flesher's hand had fallen beneath the table; his eyes – more pig-like than ever – glared at those around him who knew the Flesher's fingers were not far from the hilt of his flat-bladed cleaver. The Flesher's 'guests' also realised that all he had to do was shout, and the rifflers, who undoubtedly stood around the priest's house, would burst in with sword and mace.

'My mother's corpse, my money.' The Flesher fought back the tears of fury welling in his red-rimmed eyes. 'You would need more than one person to do all that mischief. All three of you,' the Flesher waved a hand, 'ingrates, helped by me in the past, bear some responsibility for what has happened here. Fat Jack Cranston is no help but,' the Flesher shook a fist at those seated around him, 'I want my mother's corpse as well as my money returned to me by All Hallows or, by all that you hold sacred, you shall pay for it either in the Devil's Oak or one of my other dwellings. Perhaps,' he flailed a hand, 'I should let fat Jack parade you on the public gallows at Smithfield. All three of you remember, by All Hallows or else!'

PART FIVE

Cramp Abbey (**Old English**): Newgate Prison

A thelstan sat at his kitchen table staring into the flames of the fire leaping merrily in the hearth. The day was drawing on and the friar felt slightly drowsy. The parish now lay quiet. Athelstan had walked its bounds and assured himself that all was well. The menfolk were at work, the women busy in their cottages involved in a wide variety of tasks. They always impressed Athelstan with their skill, be it the stitching of a torn cloth, the management of a spinning wheel, their expertise with the churn or the baking of different breads or pastries. He had unlocked the sacristy and checked on both the parish chest as well as the arca in its secret hole beneath the floor. He had also opened St Erconwald's chancery coffer, where important parish charters and documents were carefully stored. Once he'd satisfied himself, he moved into the sanctuary and found all was well, the Sacrament light glowing a bright red in the gathering gloom. Athelstan was scrupulous in his inspection, scrutinising the pyx, the altar, the cruets and the sanctuary furniture. The empty nave had been carefully swept, its benches, stools and leaning rods carefully stacked against either wall. The chantry chapel of St Erconwald's was Athelstan's pride and joy, a delight to sit in: its large window was filled with painted glass, and when the light poured through, it created a breath-taking vision of lovely colours. Dark blue turkey rugs softened the tread. The altar, celebrant's chair, stool and bench were of the same polished oak wood as the trellised screen which closed off the chantry chapel from the rest of the church. Athelstan just loved to sit inside, lean back in the chair and contemplate the cross of San Damiano which hung above the altar. The chantry altar was majestic, a thing of beauty covered in its royal blue coping, which protected the pure white linen cloths, the best

of Cambrai, used during Mass. To the left of the altar, next to
the window, hung a brilliant triptych, which recounted scenes
from the life of St Erconwald, a useful foil for Athelstan when
he tried to educate his parishioners on the virtues of their
patron saint.

Athelstan had also tried to find Judith the mummer, after
rumours he'd heard about a possible quarrel between some of
the parish women over the play being prepared. However,
when Athelstan visited the Piebald and nearby cook shop,
neither Jocelyn nor Merrylegs knew anything about the quarrel
or Judith's whereabouts. Athelstan sensed they were being
parsimonious with the truth but decided to leave it for a while.
He believed the play was becoming increasingly divisive, and
already the tensions were making themselves felt in other
ways. The Hangman of Rochester, the parish painter, had
decided to begin a fresco illustrating the ascent of the soul
from purgatory to the gates of heaven. Each soul was depicted
as a golden globe, full of light, with a little figure inside, rising
through the swirling murk of smoke and flames. Nearby, dark-
garbed demons crouched on burning rocks to watch the souls
ascend. To the right of this was another scene depicting the
souls' family and friends in life. These were divided into
those who were saved and those who had sinned grievously.
The hangman, out of sheer mischief, and greatly encouraged
by the likes of Watkin and Pike, was placing members of the
parish in one of these two groups: the identity of each person
being revealed by some sign or symbol, be it Mauger with
his bell or Pike the ditcher with a mattock and hoe. Parishioners
were soon discovering where they would be placed and tempers
were running high.

Athelstan stared down at the notes he had made as he tried
to map a path through the mysterious murk of murder
confronting him and Cranston. He idly wondered what the
coroner was doing and quietly prayed that Sir John did not
give way to the anger seething inside him and return to the
Devil's Oak for a further confrontation with the Flesher or
Raquin. Sir John had not forgotten that fateful night eighteen
years ago, and wished to bring matters to a close. Nevertheless,
the Flesher was a most vicious opponent, a powerful lord of

London's seedy underworld. More importantly, the Flesher was patronised by Fitzalan of Arundel who, by his own admission, or so Cranston reported, didn't give a fig about King or Crown, or indeed the Lord High Coroner.

'Please God keep Cranston away,' Athelstan murmured. 'Don't let him go down to the Devil's Oak.' Athelstan joined his hands, closed his eyes and quietly prayed. After all, Cranston would not be the first law officer to be provoked into a quarrel, stabbed to death and have his assailants later plead, with a host of perjured witnesses, that it was all done in self-defence.

Athelstan opened his eyes and glanced again at the memoranda. He'd tried to distance himself from the mysteries which teased and taunted his wits, and the best way to do that was to concentrate on his priestly duties. He'd continued to walk the parish bounds, returning to the church for the Angelus. After this had been recited and Mauger had rung his bell, the children of the parish gathered in the lady chapel for their religious instruction. 'His beloved scholars', as Athelstan called them, had proved to be particularly lively. Athelstan secretly compared them to a horde of busy grasshoppers, and wondered why certain children, who should go nowhere near a naked flame, being a clear danger to themselves and others, seemed to have an irresistible compulsion to light candles. The friar had been relieved to be joined by Imelda, Pike the ditcher's sharp-tongued wife. She was of valuable assistance with the children, even though she kept up a monologue about the shortcomings of her own brood. Athelstan had pointed at the statue of the Virgin and exhorted Imelda to pray for help; after all, the friar pointed out, Mary had been a mother and raised a son.

'Ah yes, Father,' Imelda had retorted tartly, 'she certainly had a boy, but she never had daughters. Now daughters, rather than sons, are hard work . . .'

Athelstan only half listened. At last the children quietened as Athelstan instructed them in the 'Ave Maria', using both the statue of Our Lady of Walsingham as well as the vivid wall paintings in the lady chapel to illustrate his lesson. He then made the children recite the 'Ave' in Latin, making them laugh at the strange sounds. Once the lesson was over, Athelstan had distributed some sweetmeats and asked the children if they had anything to tell him? Harold Hairlip, one of Hig the pigman's children, stood up and announced in his strange voice how he had seen strangers in the parish.

'Some men, Father, with a cart on the far side of the cemetery.'

'In which case, keep well away from there,' Athelstan warned. 'It's a very lonely, desolate stretch of land. God knows who wanders such a place. All right?' Athelstan stared around. 'Nobody wants to say any more?' He lifted a hand in blessing. 'Then go in peace.'

The children had fled the church back to their cottages. Most of them were under strict instruction to do so. The days were drawing in. Autumn was making itself felt and many families in the parish had to use the daylight hours to complete work both in their homes as well as their different trades – be it sewing, weaving, clearing the soil, planting vegetables or herbs, not to mention cooking and baking in the common ovens at the Piebald or Merrylegs' cook shop.

Athelstan made sure all the children had left the church, then returned to the priest's house. He'd laid out a scroll of vellum and once again began to organise what he and Cranston had discovered so far. Item: Athelstan wrote carefully, then paused to sharpen the fine quill-pen Cranston had given him from the Guildhall chancery. Item: Simon Makepeace, also known as the Flesher. A true sinner in every sense of the word. A master of mischief, a killer and a thief, who presided like an emperor over an empire of like-minded souls. Sir John was correct, the Flesher was responsible for a whole host of crimes; in particular, the attempted theft of those precious stones, the Twelve Apostles in their Rose Casket some eighteen years ago. The Flesher controlled the parish of St Benet's Woodwharf, its priest Parson Reynaud and others on the parish council: Cripplegate, its leader, Cotes the curate and Sexton Spurnel. In turn the Flesher was the cat's-paw of Fitzalan of Arundel. According to the evidence available, both of these, probably with the connivance of the parish priest, had been plotting some future mischief. In the main, the Flesher appeared to have left the church of St Benet's alone, except for the crypt and cemetery, which he had freely used to hide the victims of his macabre murders, either at the Devil's Oak or that forbidding mansion of murder.

Item: Sir John Cranston had been fervently against the Flesher and his ilk for years. Accordingly the cororner had been delighted to be approached by the Sicarius, one of the Flesher's leading henchmen, who offered to betray his master for a pardon. Athelstan lifted his head and stared at the crucifix above the hearth. God knows why the Sicarius made his decision but, there again, Athelstan reflected, he had sat in the mercy seat at the shriving pew and, over the years, listened to confessions from hundreds of people. One thing constantly surprised him. How people can change, usually due to other people: that was interesting because in his discussions with Cranston, the Sicarius had demanded a pardon not only for himself but for another – a comrade? Was it this which had changed the Sicarius, or something else?

The Flesher is as arrogant as Lucifer. Such men always overreach themselves. Was the Flesher's empire beginning to crack? Had the fear and terror he had instilled in others begun to curdle? Was an opposition forming to the nightmare he had created? Was that the reason his henchman and Parson Reynaud had been murdered, the arca plundered and Isabella Makepeace's corpse stolen? Perhaps this was not an attempt to steal the treasure or to hold a corpse for ransom, but public mockery of the Flesher? After all, the news must have seeped along the dark runnels of Queenhithe and elsewhere. The Flesher was no longer invincible. There would be hidden laughter and quiet enjoyment at the deep discomfiture and insult inflicted upon this self-proclaimed Prince of rifflers. Athelstan returned to his memorandum.

Item. The Sicarius had proved to be a man of his word: he had certainly inflicted damage on London's most notorious wolfshead. The Sicarius had supplied Cranston with a stream of invaluable information about all kinds of mischief being plotted; this had continued until about two weeks ago when the Sicarius had disappeared, making no attempt to contact Cranston or anybody else. There could only be one possible conclusion: Ingersol had been trapped by the Flesher and brutally murdered. Cranston's informant had been unable to tell the coroner what secret mayhem the Flesher and Arundel were plotting; however, that was a loose strand Athelstan could do nothing about, unless someone else decided to betray the Flesher.

Athelstan dipped his quill pen into the inkpot and continued writing. Item: the Twelve Apostles. Eighteen years ago this treasure had been taken from a Hanse ship *The Glory of Bremen*, sealed in a chancery bag and placed on board a royal barge, *The Song of the Sword*, under the command of Cranston. The barge had been attacked by two other craft as it made its way along the river on a dark, fog-bound night. Sir John had been wounded; he'd fallen overboard only to be miraculously plucked from the water. The barge had been manned by Tower archers, skilled bowmen patronised and favoured by the Crown. They included men from Queenhithe and, in particular, parishioners of St Benet's: Cripplegate, Cotes and Spurnel. Like Cranston, they had survived. Of course all three had incurred royal anger, fury and suspicion over the robbery. All three parishioners had had no choice but to accept the help of the Flesher after their dismissal from the Tower cohort. Athelstan paused. Of course, he continued writing, all three men would have fallen under suspicion not only by the Crown but the Flesher. After all, the treasure had disappeared. Had any of these been involved in its theft? According to the evidence, they had not. A clearer picture was now emerging, the real suspects being the Grenels, father and son. Both had been sorely wounded. However, during the attack on the royal barge, they must have plucked up the chancery satchel containing the treasure and either jumped or been pushed overboard. They reached Southwark shore and somehow made their way back to their own home. Both men had eventually died of their wounds. Margo, distracted by grief, was also faced with the worry of what to do with the mortal remains of her beloved menfolk, who had disappeared in such mysterious circumstances along with the royal treasure. How could she explain all that away? Margo's next decision was logical. She used her undoubted skill and experience to lovingly embalm both cadavers, turning that cellar into a family shrine. As the months and years passed, Margo would become accustomed to, and even like, the arrangement. She could take her own food down there and talk to the dead. Athelstan did not consider himself a man of sorrows, but he was acquainted with grief both as a person and as a father confessor. Occasionally, on top of the church tower or in the privacy of St Erconwald's chantry chapel, he would talk to his dead brother. He had met others who did the same. God's Acre outside was often visited: tombs, graves, headstones and crosses being carefully tended and adorned with fresh flowers or coloured ribbons. He had seen the living kneel beside the dead and speak to them. Margo Grenel would be no different. More importantly, where had she stored the Rose Casket and its precious stones? Margo must have hidden them away in some place known only to her. She would probably have left them there, but the years passed and Margo needed medical care, good physic for her malignancy. A poor woman, she had little money, so she tried to sell the Rose Casket but became deeply flustered by the keen interest shown, so she withdrew it. Margo's ill humours worsened. Now desperate, she took one of the Twelve Apostles, the amethyst, across to St Bartholomew's to buy good treatment.

'And she met,' Athelstan murmured, 'my friend Brother Philippe, who knows as little about precious stones as I do.'

The physician, a true innocent and totally unaware of what wealth or riches are, accepted the amethyst in payment, and took it down to a reputable goldsmith who would have realised its worth immediately. Perhaps that's where the rumour started; it would account for Roslin the robber breaking into Master Blundel's shop. During that affray, the amethyst becomes even more public, glimpsed by the Flesher's henchmen. 'And so,' Athelstan whispered, 'the banner is raised.' The Flesher and others, Levigne, even Master Thibault must have soon realised that if the amethyst was being sold, the Twelve Apostles must have reappeared on the London market, and so their fingers would have itched with greed. The Flesher undoubtedly sent his rifflers to search Athelstan's house, Margo's cottage and the poor woman's grave. They had discovered nothing. So where are the Twelve Apostles? Margo had left little clue, though whilst in the hospital at St Bartholomew's she had sunk into delirium and gabbled about Arthur the once and future King. But what did that mean? Was it some reference to the whereabouts of the treasure? Did her menfolk leave any hint about what they had taken from the royal barge, *The Song of the Sword*? Apart from how they died, what else was known about Henry and Walter Grenel? Good men? Skilled archers? Margo and her husband seemed an ordinary God-fearing family, though Margo never came to be shriven, even at Easter or thereabouts. Well, certainly not at St Erconwald's. Little was known about her son, Walter, except that he had been sweet on 'a woman from the House of Bethany', but what did that mean? All three Grenels were now dead, as were so many who had been involved in the transport of that treasure eighteen years ago. Sir John believed Raquin had led the attack, yet the coroner still did not know who had betrayed them. And who could that be?

Athelstan closed his eyes and tried to imagine that fateful evening, *The Glory of Bremen* berthed at Queenhithe, the barge coming down from the Tower. A spy on the quayside would soon see it approach and watch the barge's departure. The spy would then alert, if Cranston was right, the Flesher, and those two pirate craft would prepare their ambuscade. But who was that spy who had told the Flesher? One logical conclusion was that it could not have been anyone on board *The Song of the Sword*. In the middle of a fog-bound, pitch-black freezing night on the Thames, it would be very difficult, if not impossible, to distinguish between friend and foe. Moreover, Cranston was no fool and neither was the Flesher. In the weeks, months, even years following the attack, they would keep a sharp eye on the markets to see if the Rose Casket or the Twelve Apostles were offered for sale, but that did not happen. Moreover, nobody on board that barge had profited from the attack; far from it. Cotes, Sexton Spurnel and Cripplegate could not be described as being particularly wealthy. Athelstan opened his eyes and put his pen down, his mind going back to Margo mumbling about Arthur and the bell – was that a reference to Mauger? And what about the confrontation between the bell clerk and those two sisters? Perhaps it was time to question Mauger.

Athelstan sat back and dozed, only to be woken by a sharp knock on the door. He started and turned as the door was flung open and Crim the altar boy led a hooded, visored figure, garbed in black from head to toe, into the kitchen. The altar boy looked terrified, head turning against the sharp, serrated knife held against the side of his neck. Athelstan rose slowly, trying to wet his throat and lips, abruptly dry with fear.

'You must come priest! You must come now!' The voice behind the mask was low and guttural. 'Go on boy.' He shook Crim. 'Tell him.'

'They have Benedicta, Godbless and Thaddeus.'

'Where?'

'Haceldema.' The wolfshead tripped over the word. 'What you call the Field of Blood, where those hanged on the Southwark side of London Bridge are buried. You know it. Come priest!'

'Who sent you?'

'No questions, come!'

Athelstan dried his sweat-soaked hands on his robe, grabbed his cloak and keys and followed the sinister figure, one hand firmly on Crim's shoulder, out of the priest's house.

'Let him go,' Athelstan pleaded. 'He is only a child.'

'Who can run and raise the alarm. Now come before my knife slips.'

The wolfshead led Athelstan out into the cemetery. Daylight was beginning to die, the weak sun hidden by gathering clouds. The long grass and gorse, which sprouted between the gravestones and crosses, bent under a piercing cold breeze. Athelstan was now ordered to lead the way and he hurried in front. The friar anxiously peered from left to right, desperate to glimpse any parishioner who might have wandered in on some pretext or other, but there was no one. Athelstan prayed that help would be sent. They were heading for a very lonely, desolate place. Haceldema was regarded as blighted and haunted. A stretch of wasteland peppered with stinking morasses and clumps of rough gorse, the last resting place for a legion of malefactors hanged near the bridge. Athelstan's parishioners

firmly believed that it was a murky, macabre hosting ground
for the ghosts of those executed and the demons who herded
them.

At last they reached the wicket gate on the far side of God's
Acre and followed the narrow coffin path which twisted past
the wild hedges on to the wasteland bounded by a thick copse
of trees. Athelstan crossed himself and again prayed for help.
This place was rarely visited; it was even devoid of birdsong.
Only wild pigs came to snout for the acorns from the ancient
oaks, the branches of which curled up to tangle with each other.
Athelstan, however, only had eyes for the two dark-clad wolfsheads, cowled and masked, who suddenly appeared from behind
one of the thick bushes. Each carried a crossbow. They beckoned
at Benedicta, who cradled Bonaventure, to leave her hiding
place. She was followed by a terrified Godbless, one hand on
Thaddeus's neck, the other holding the goat's shabby leather
leash. Both beggar and goat looked truly terrified. Godbless,
like Benedicta, kept staring at the fringe of trees. Athelstan
followed their gaze and glimpsed movement. Two more wolfsheads emerged from the copse. Each of these led on a leash a
ferocious war dog; huge mastiffs with bulbous heads, they were
long-legged, their short-haired, tawny coats rippling with
muscle. The mastiffs walked slowly but Athelstan recognised
that deliberate pacing as highly dangerous. He had seen the
King's great cats in their cages at the Tower; they too had that
menacing stalk. The hounds were tightly muzzled yet they
strained against the chained leash attached to the spiked collars
around their bulging necks. Savage animals, these two strained
forward, eyes blazing with fury, eager to attack. Thaddeus's and
Godbless's agitation was heart-rending. Clad in his flapping
rags of cloth and leather, the beggar man was now hugging the
goat, which whimpered, eyes rolling back in terror.

'In God's name . . .' Athelstan stepped forward; he tried
not to flinch as both war dogs lunged towards him.

'In God's name,' one of the wolfsheads mocked. 'Then
tell us?'

'What?'

'The whereabouts of the Rose Casket and the Twelve
Apostles.'

'I don't know.' Athelstan gestured at the mastiffs. 'What are these dogs called; why are they here?'

'They have no name, clever priest.'

'The Flesher, Master Simon Makepeace.' Athelstan was desperate to delay matters as long as possible. 'He sent you from the Devil's Oak, didn't he?'

'We know of no such person or place.' The harsh voice remained flat and incisive. 'The Rose Casket, the jewels, priest – where are they?'

'Were you involved in the attack eighteen years ago?'

'The jewels, the Rose Casket, where are they?'

Soaked in sweat, Athelstan gazed up at the grey, lowering sky. He took out his ave beads and tried to avoid Benedicta's gaze. She just stood, Crim next to her, cradling Bonaventure. The tomcat had gone strangely silent and submissive; whether he was frightened of the dogs or preparing to flee, Athelstan could not say. He stared around this sombre, god-forsaken field – well named, he bitterly thought. Would this truly become a Field of Blood?

'Priest, I asked you a question?'

Athelstan held up the ave beads. 'And I swear by the cross, I don't know where they are, and for God's sake, show mercy.' He gestured at his parishioners. 'An old man out of his wits, a poor widow woman and a child.'

'And a goat and a cat,' the wolfshead added, to guffaws of laughter from his companions. He walked over to Benedicta who was cradling Bonaventure. He grabbed the cat and pushed her away, only to scream and jump back as Bonaventure, swift as light, twisted abruptly, his front paws lashing the wolfshead's face, who promptly dropped the cat. Bonaventure, like an arrow from the bow, shot across the grass into the undergrowth. The war dogs strained forward, their handlers cursing and shouting. Athelstan stood tense, Benedicta and Crim likewise, but the beggar man jumped to his feet shouting, 'God bless Bonaventure! God bless Thaddeus!'

'The goat!' the scarred wolfshead exclaimed, nursing the deep weals on his face. 'The goat!' he repeated. One of his companions put down the crossbow, hurried over, knocked Godbless aside, seized the goat's leash and smacked it hard

on the rump. Unlike Bonaventure, Thaddeus, stricken with
fear, raced blindly toward the trees. Athelstan now realised
why the hounds had been taken there, to cast about, to recognise the terrain. Now released, they hurtled after the fleeing
goat. Godbless was screaming. Crim tried to break free of
Benedicta; both were sobbing frantically. Athelstan watched
in horror. The hounds racing either side of the goat soon caught
Thaddeus. One knocked it, the goat stumbled, and the other
hound ripped the poor creature's throat, shredding the flesh as
the blood gushed out. Godbless, now hysterical with fear,
threw himself at one of the attackers, who clubbed him on the
side of the head, knocking the beggar unconscious to the
ground. Athelstan hurried over to Benedicta. She cradled Crim
in her arms so the boy couldn't see the hounds savaging the
mangled remains of the goat, nothing more than a tangle of
skin and bone swimming in a thick puddle of blood. Athelstan
stood in front of both Benedicta and Crim, doing his best to
shield them from this gruesome sight. The hounds nosed the
remains. Now and again one of them would turn its great
bulbous head, huge jaws frothing blood and smeared with
gore. They would glare at Athelstan before returning to burrow
their massive heads into the gruesome remains.

'Perhaps the boy next, priest.' The self-appointed leader of
the wolfsheads swaggered over to Benedicta and tried to snatch
Crim from her embrace. She lunged at him, striking out with
the small knife she kept hidden in her gown; a thin, pointed,
razor-sharp blade which slashed the wolfshead's sword arm.
He screamed, staggering back to trip over the now prostate
and unconscious Godbless. The wolfshead lurched to his feet,
clutching his bloodied arm, his companions, swords and
daggers out, hurried across. Again Benedicta lunged, scything
the air with the knife, only to have this knocked aside and to
be pulled by the hair away from the screaming, terrified Crim.
Athelstan felt the red mist descend. A roaring in his ears, an
uncontrollable fury which made him shake. He screamed
and threw himself at the malefactors. The friar no longer
cared about anything but killing his opponent. Desperate to
defend Benedicta and Crim from further harm, he was shoved
and pushed back. A dagger blade cut the air. Athelstan

glimpsed this, he moved to one side and, as he did so, the wielder of the knife screamed and staggered back. The man's face seemed to collapse into a bloody pulp as the crossbow bolt struck him deep in the forehead. Other voices were raised and Athelstan wondered at the cries of 'Saint Denis, Saint Denis!' Shaken and confused, Athelstan realised the struggle had abruptly changed. He stood, sweat-soaked, trying to clear his head. Benedicta and Crim crouched on the ground beside him, hugging each other.

'In God's name,' Athelstan whispered, 'what on earth, what on earth?' He glimpsed the two great mastiffs, both killed, sprawled on the ground, massive jaws half-open, eyes all glazed, their corpses stiffening in widening puddles of blood. The five wolfsheads had suffered a similar fate; crossbow bolts had smashed into faces, necks, bellies and chests. Benedicta's assassin sat half sprawled, quietly moaning. One of the shadowy, cowled figures, who had abruptly appeared in Haceldema and were milling around them, walked over, yanked the wolfshead back by the hair and slit his throat. Athelstan felt both hot and cold. He was trembling, fearful that he might faint. Desperate to control his breathing, he moved slowly, hands out, staring at his saviours. Athelstan reckoned there were about eight in number.

'Who are you?' he called. 'Who are you?'

One of the strangers hurried forward, pulling back his hood, and Athelstan stared into the smiling face of Hugh Levigne the Candlelight-Master. '*Benedicat te Dominus*. May the Lord bless you, Brother Athelstan.'

'And may the Lord bless you too, Monseigneur.' Athelstan clasped the Frenchman's hand.

'God sent you,' he murmured, moving over to join Benedicta; she and Crim were now trying to help an injured, confused Godbless. The widow woman had taken one of the dead malefactors' cloaks and covered the pathetic remains of Thaddeus. 'Evil men,' Athelstan whispered. 'Yet the Lord delivered us. How come such deliverance occurred?'

Levigne stood watching his men move from one corpse to another. 'Brother Athelstan, we know what happened to the Twelve Apostles. Like your good friend Sir John, we strongly suspect that the attack on him eighteen years ago was planned, plotted and perpetrated by the Flesher. Now we know him by reputation. Over the years, we have kept close watch on him.'

'Of course,' Athelstan breathed, 'Sir John told me how the mayor of Rouen fixed a price on the Flesher's head for the atrocities he committed in France.'

'I have seen the indictment, Brother. It is a litany of cruelty and horror. You wouldn't think any human soul could inflict such suffering on so many innocents. Once we knew that the Twelve Apostles had emerged on the London market and that you were somehow involved in it, we decided to mount a discreet but careful watch. The Flesher is not as intelligent as he thinks. We know all about his use of war mastiffs in his Mansion of Murder.'

'So you watched the bridge?'

'We watched the Devil's Oak and the bridge.' The Candlelight-Master nodded towards the trees. 'I am sure we will find the cart with two cages and all the necessary paraphernalia for the keeping of two war dogs. We saw them arrive earlier. We had to make sure. Of course I am sorry we could not save the goat but, at least and most importantly, we have saved you, the woman and the boy. Brother Athelstan, whether you like it or not, we will continue to keep you under close watch.'

'And thank God for that, Monseigneur. So come, let's go to my house.'

Sir John Cranston stood, booted feet apart, and stared down at the corpses. 'Five men, two beasts!' he exclaimed.

'Seven beasts in all,' Athelstan remarked, standing next to the coroner.

Cranston pulled his beaver hat further down on his head and threw back his cloak to reveal his resplendent warbelt; he then glanced over his shoulder at the parishioners who'd crowded into Haceldema to see the effects of the gruesome slaughter which had occurred yesterday. Indeed their priest had done nothing to prevent them. Once Athelstan had recovered his wits and shared a deep-bowled goblet of wine with Levigne, he'd thanked the Frenchman and asked him to mount guard over the corpses until the parish watch was summoned. Levigne quickly agreed. The Luciferi searched the dead men's wallets and purses. They stripped the cadavers completely, keeping the clothes, weapons and any coins for their own use. The Frenchmen were thorough. They also found the cart and cages as well as a dray horse, hidden away deep in the copse of trees. Athelstan ruefully reflected that he should have paid more attention to what young Harold Hairlip had told him – strangers in St Erconwald's parish usually meant trouble. The parish watch was eventually organised just before Compline. Athelstan briefly explained what had happened and how they would have to set up a watch until the following morning when Sir John Cranston would decide what to do with the dead. Levigne came and made his farewells late in the evening. Athelstan was resting with Benedicta and Crim, Godbless being fast asleep in the bedloft. Levigne assured the friar that he and his retainers had searched all the attackers' belongings. They could not find a shred of evidence about who they were or who had sent them which, Cranston now declared, was a sure mark of the Flesher.

'He hides his tracks very well,' the coroner declared. 'Cunning, subtle and devious he is. Now you know, Brother, why he has never been fingered.'

Most of the parishioners believed all five wolfsheads had been despatched by the Flesher. They'd heard rumours about their little priest being involved in that heinous business at St Benet's Woodwharf, and how he had visited the Flesher's lair at the Devil's Oak. There were also whispers about a certain treasure being found, though such wild stories often ran rife throughout the parish. They'd certainly heard about the attack on Godbless and the utter destruction of Thaddeus. The mauled remnants of that four-legged parishioner had been wrapped in a coffin cloth and taken to the death house. After the Jesus Mass, just before dawn that morning, Athelstan had given a pithy description of the attack and, despite all the suspicions being voiced, he refused to name who could have been respon-sible for such wickedness. Athelstan had certainly glimpsed Watkin and Pike out of the corner of his eye, deep in discus-sion. Both of these parish worthies stood just inside the rood screen, immersed in an argument which seemed to have lasted throughout morning Mass. Watkin appeared to want to have words with his priest, but Pike tugged at the dung-collector's sleeve and led him down the nave, whispering heatedly at him. Athelstan wondered what the issue was but then became distracted when he learnt that Sir John Cranston had arrived and had been taken straight to Haceldema, where the parish watch, under Beadle Bladdersmith, had set up guard. Athelstan joined them and immediately informed Cranston about exactly what had happened the previous day.

'Yes, that's all logical,' the coroner murmured. 'A fine example of Makepeace's malevolence. Do you know, Athelstan, sometimes I feel like kidnapping the Flesher, putting him aboard a war cog and taking him to Rouen myself to watch the bastard hang.'

'Oh, he'll hang all right.'

'Do you want his death, Athelstan?'

'No, Sir John, God does.' Athelstan struck his breast. 'I have a feeling here, deep in my heart, that the Flesher's cup of wickedness is brimming over. Somewhere beyond the veil, the books are being opened and a court is being set up. The sheer terror and horror he has inflicted upon total innocents must be paid for.' Athelstan gestured at the corpses. 'This is only the beginning. I have given the dead a simple blessing. I cannot see my way to delivering absolution for sinners intent on such sheer malice.'

'And Bonaventure?' Cranston asked.

'Hale and hearty, Sir John. He did what damage he could and fled, cunning cat.'

'Very well,' Cranston whispered. 'But, Brother, let us dispense with the audience.' Cranston turned and walked back to the parishioners. 'I need to have words with your priest,' he bellowed, 'so apart from Master Flaxwith and his bailiffs,' Cranston pointed across Haceldema, where his henchmen had gathered, 'it's time all of you went about your lawful business. Master Joceyln, Master Merrylegs, I give you an invitation. All upright members of this parish may break their fast at your worthy establishments. The Guildhall Exchequer will honour all reasonable bills.' Athelstan had rarely seen his

parishioners move so fast. Joceyln and Merrylegs, delighted
at the prospect of such profit, led the charge from Haceldema,
streaming across God's Acre to feast on fresh bread, spiced
meats and strong ale. Cranston and Athelstan watched them
go. The friar then turned back and stared at the corpses, as
well as those of the mastiffs brought low by crossbow bolts
to their heads. Athelstan felt a pang of sorrow at the pathetic
sight.

'Magnificent beasts,' he whispered, 'abused by wicked men
for their own evil purposes.' He shifted his gaze to the dirty,
white corpses which, naked as they were born, sprawled gruesomely, their purple-red death wounds clear to see.

'Who would have thought,' Athelstan exclaimed, 'the death
of poor Margo would provoke such murderous fury?'

'The Flesher is responsible.' Cranston's face and voice was
sullen and, tired though he was, Athelstan felt a prickle of
cold agitation.

'Sir John,' he warned, '*tace atque vide*: stay silent and
watch. We do not have a shred of evidence to place these
horrors at the Flesher's blood-soaked feet, even though we
know he is the *fons et origo*.'

'Oh, he certainly is the fount and origin of all this wickedness,' Cranston intervened. 'God knows he is, yet even the
heaviest stones crack.' Cranston gestured at the corpses. 'When
I received your message last night, I ordered Flaxwith to seize
the remains of both man and beast. They can be exposed on
the steps of St Benet's, with a proclamation pinned to the
church door as well as at the cross in St Paul's churchyard.
Anyone who recognises any or all of these corpses should
immediately present themselves before me and my fellow
justices at the Guildhall.'

Athelstan clutched Cranston's arm. 'My friend, I understand
your anger but, again I repeat, do not do anything imprudent.
I have been thinking, reflecting, puzzling: there are other paths
to be followed.'

'Such as?'

'A visit to the House of the Delight. Oh, by the way, talking
of visiting, have you dealt with Merchant Blundel?'

'Oh yes. He demonstrated all protest and outraged

righteousness, yet Merchant Blundel knows he cannot keep
the property of the Crown. He also is fully aware of the
ordinances of the city council and his own guild.'

'And where is the amethyst now?'

'In my arca at the Guildhall.'

'Which brings us back to the question of the arca at
St Benet's.' Athelstan patted Cranston on the arm. 'A thought
has occurred to me, but first I need to deal with our bell clerk.'

They found Mauger busy in the death house. At Athelstan's
instructions he, helped by Watkin and Pike, also sworn to
silence, had quietly and secretly buried the Grenels in a grave
close to Margo's. Now he was tidying up before hurrying off
to join the rest breaking their fast free of charge at the Piebald
and the adjoining cook shop. Athelstan closed the door to the
death house behind him and, beckoning at Cranston, walked
over to where Mauger was washing down one of the corpse
tables. Athelstan always insisted that this take place once a
cadaver was removed, whilst Mauger was well paid for such
services. The friar stood at the head of the table. Mauger kept
scrubbing, although Athelstan could see that the bell clerk was
so agitated he was almost scrubbing the table with his eyes
closed. At last Mauger threw the brush down on to the ground
and went over to sit on a three-legged stool in the corner. He
put his face in his hands and began to quietly sob.

'Satan's tits,' Cranston breathed. 'What is wrong with the
man?'

Athelstan went to crouch by Mauger. He gently prised away
the bell clerk's hands. 'Look at me, Mauger.' The man raised
his long, tear-streaked face. 'Now,' Athelstan brought across
another of the mortuary stools and sat as close as he could to
the bell clerk, aware of Cranston standing just behind him. 'I
shall tell you what I think, Mauger, then you can tell me if
I have spoken the truth. Very well?' Mauger nodded.

'When the facts behind Margo Grenel's secret life began to
emerge,' Athelstan continued, 'on the morning of her funeral,
I noticed you were most attentive to where both Benedicta
and I went that day. Benedicta had discovered the secret of
Margot Grenel's cellar and came to fetch me from the church.

Now Benedicta did not wish for the hue and cry to be raised, for shouts of "Harrow! Harrow!" to rouse the parish watch. No, Benedicta is prudent. She came to me discreetly, even secretly. But, of course, you were watching and waiting most attentively. You followed us to Margo's house and, acting all innocent, stumbled in, as if as surprised as anyone else. You blurted out the story about the Grenels joining the royal array on a chevauchée across the Narrow Seas, some military expedition under the old King. Of course, that's utter nonsense. Even at the time, I thought it came too glib, too fast, too polished, as if you had been preparing it for some time. Now,' Athelstan paused, 'before I continue, Mauger, do you know anything about the whereabouts of the Rose Casket or the precious stones known as Twelve Apostles?'

'No, no, no,' Mauger mumbled, 'no I don't. Brother Athelstan,' he moaned, 'do not judge me harshly.'

'You are the bell clerk at St Erconwald's, Mauger: you have access to the parish chest where Margo left her keys before going across to St Bartholomew's. You took these. You searched that poor woman's house. What were you looking for? The treasure?'

'I found nothing. I took nothing, please believe me.'

'I do and I am grateful, Mauger, that you have not challenged me. I thought your explanation was too glib. Then we had Margo's ramblings when she was in a delirium, sleeping under the influence of an opiate in St Bartholomew's. She muttered disjointedly about a bell. Now, we do not have a church bell in the steeple, but we do have you, Mauger, our bell clerk. Why should she mention you? What was your true relationship with that dead woman? What did Cecily and Clarissa mean about Margo kneeling before you? What did she do for you, Mauger, and why?'

'Yes, why?' Cranston echoed.

'Come on,' Athelstan urged, 'your intervention on the morning of Margo's burial? What did those two sisters see? Clarissa and Cecily have their own peculiar trade, they carry it out in the most hidden places, which is why they are in the cemetery almost as often as you are. That's where you met Margo, wasn't it?'

Mauger nodded.

'So, Mauger, how did that come about? Why should Margo – and she did – perform sexual favours for you, with her mouth or her hands? I am sure that's what Cecily and Clarissa were referring to. Yet Margo was a respectable widow with a good name in the parish.' Athelstan sighed and tapped his feet. 'Of course, Mauger,' he breathed, 'you could meet Margo in the cemetery but, bearing in mind your parish duties as well as Margo's, you would have every excuse to be seen together, even in her cottage.' Athelstan looked around, 'Or even in here, the death house.'

'And those two doxies,' Cranston observed, 'are experts at peering through keyholes or cracks. So tell us, clerk, how did this situation come about?'

'Eighteen years ago . . .' The bell clerk straightened up, resting his hands on his knees as if he were a minstrel or troubadour sitting in the inglenook to recite a poem or story. 'Eighteen years ago,' he repeated, 'I was not a bell clerk, but a watchman like Beadle Bladdersmith is, but better,' he added warningly. Mauger half closed his eyes. 'A bitterly cold night. A river mist had rolled in like the thickest steam, hiding everything in sight and dulling all sound. I was trying to keep warm, sheltering in an enclave against the bitterness, when I glimpsed lights along the river and muffled sounds. Then I heard a crack carry across the water. Yes, that's it, a sharp, horrid crack of something deadly, followed by the cries of men in mortal agony and the blood-chilling shrill of battle, of sword against sword, knife against knife. Only then did I realise some bloody affray was raging along the Thames. I wondered if the French had brought their galleys up, but there again, those were the stirring days where no enemy would dare bait the old King.' He paused. 'Even an angel from heaven couldn't have guided St Peter up the Thames in such weather; a thick, cloying mist hung over the water. I then thought it might be pirates.'

'Didn't you think of raising the alarm?'

'Of course, Sir John. There was the crack, the cries and the clash of steel, but then it all faded away. You must remember the season. I even wondered if I'd heard the echoes of some ghastly conflict from a long time ago, ghosts from the past, a haunting over the Thames. Strange things do happen along the river.'

'They certainly do,' Athelstan remarked. 'But you realised it was no ghostly conflict because of the Grenels, Henry and Walter. They came staggering ashore, one of them carrying a blue and red chancery bag. Mauger, you said you were standing in an enclave. You were a watchman. You were carrying a lanternhorn, weren't you?'

'Brother, Brother,' Mauger held up a hand, 'of course I carried a shuttered lantern and I used that – the notion of some haunting was just a passing thought. I left the enclave, climbed the barrier wall and walked across the shale. I saw two men, helping each other, crawl out of the water. They were soaked, shivering, finding it hard to keep upright. I raised my lantern and realised they were dressed in the garb of Tower archers; the royal insignia decorated their right shoulders. As I drew closer, I recognised Henry and Walter Grenel.' The bell man paused, eyes closed, breathing noisily through his nose. 'The Grenels.' He murmured. 'I'd greeted them in the parish and along the quayside. I was shocked to see them wounded so grievously. Henry carried a bag sodden with blood. They were on the point of collapse. I am not too sure if they recognised me but, to cut the quick, I helped them back to their cottage. Margo was beside herself.' Mauger lifted a hand. 'Sir John, Brother Athelstan, I swear I did not realise at the time what that chancery satchel contained. It just looked stained, soaked in both blood and river water.' He paused.

'Continue,' Athelstan gently insisted, 'tell us the truth. I can guess what it is, but we need you to describe what actually happened, to confirm our suspicions.'

'Brother, both men were mortally wounded. I had nothing to do with their deaths. Margo begged me to help her. I did, but there was little even the most skilled physician could achieve.' He sniffed noisily. 'I have served in the King's array. My duty was to help the leeches and the physicians of the royal army in the hospital tents. I can recognise a deadly wound when I see it. Henry and Walter Grenel had sustained hideous injury. They were dead within the day. When I met you that morning, I intimated that perhaps Margo had killed her husband and son; that was very wrong of me. A pernicious lie. I must put that right. Henry and Walter died because of wounds inflicted by others. Both Margo and I did our very best to help them but there was nothing we could do.'

Athelstan stared at Mauger and realised the bell clerk was probably terrified of being indicted for murder. The friar stretched out and clasped the man's mittened hands. 'Mauger, I believe you but, before those men died, did they speak?'

'Henry gasped about being attacked on the river, of dark shapes hurtling through the night. How he and Walter had grabbed the chancery satchel and fought their way through, only to be surrounded and receive grievous wounds. Henry was in deep pain. I believe Margo fed both husband and son heavy wine soaked with opiate.' Mauger wiped his face. 'As I said, they were dead within the day.'

'And after that?'

'Well, over the weeks following, rumour ran rife along the riverside about a furious night battle on the Thames. Apparently a great slaughter had taken place—'

'It certainly did,' Cranston interjected. 'I was there.'

'Corpses, weapons and clothing were swept ashore. Only then did I realise what had truly happened. I returned to question Margo but she had become tight-lipped, obdurate: she refused to talk about what had happened or what she'd done that fateful evening. The weeks passed. Stories about a treasure being stolen during the affray were repeated in the alehouses and taverns along both banks of the Thames, especially in Queenhithe. People wondered if the Flesher had had a hand in that hideous mischief.'

'And then?'

Mauger swiftly crossed himself. 'Father, I am a sinner. I always did like Margo. In her prime she was plump and comely. As Scripture says, I lusted after her in my mind's eye. I am a lonely man, Father. My woman died decades ago. I have been with Cecily and Clarissa but . . .' He shook his head.

'You threatened Margo, didn't you?' Athelstan insisted. 'That's what those two sisters were referring to, sexual favours in return for your silence. You wore her down. Margo may remain obdurate but, as time passed, she realised that she could never allow anyone into that cellar, and God help her if the Twelve Apostles and the Rose Casket were found upon her. Margo was a working woman. She had dressed enough corpses for burial, including those executed. Little wonder that she gave in to you and offered sexual favours in return for your silence.'

Mauger just nodded.

'And, of course,' Athelstan continued, 'that's why she would not come to be shrived at the mercy pew. She could not come to confession, at least not here. She was ashamed, frightened that I might recognise her voice. More importantly, it might make me wonder with whom she was consorting. If she had confessed, I might well have asked her, or she might have given me the name freely. She would also have to confess that she was being forced and that might lead to the reasons why. God rest the poor woman.' Athelstan smiled thinly. 'So many souls whisper their sorrow and pain to me. I cannot, I do not and I never shall remember or recall what is confessed to me at the shriving stall, whilst the seal of confession is the most solemn and sacred in our church.' Athelstan leaned over and gently nudged Mauger. 'Bell clerk, you must be shriven very soon yourself. You must confess and be absolved by me or another priest. You do understand? So, to return to that evening when the royal barge was attacked. You were in Margo's cottage with those two dying men, Henry and Walter? You must have heard what they said.'

'Henry was the clearest. His son Walter seemed to be in a delirium, a fever. He kept babbling about the House of Bethany and, like Lazarus, he must go there. Margo did her best to soothe him. Both men fell unconscious and drifted away.' The bell clerk flapped a hand. 'Brother Athelstan, Sir John, more than that I cannot say, I am sorry.'

Athelstan stared hard at this solemn, morose man, steeped deep in his shame. 'Come, Mauger,' Athelstan patted the bell clerk gently on the arm, 'when you are ready, you may come back and talk to me. In the meantime, here is your penance.' Mauger raised his head. 'Go into the church, spend an hour there, just sit in the warmth of the chantry chapel and pray for the souls of all three Grenels. And, when you have finished, present yourself before the lady altar and light a candle for each of them, a prayer that their journey into the light be peaceful.'

'I will, Father.' Mauger got to his feet, clearly relieved. 'But do you know, I have been thinking about what young Walter said. I mean, about Lazarus: didn't he come back from the dead? Isn't that what happened in the Scriptures?'

'Yes, yes,' Athelstan agreed. 'And we also have the story about Lazarus the poor man; that when he died he went to heaven, whilst the rich man Dives was buried in Hell because of his lack of care. But go, Mauger, we are finished here.'

Once the bell clerk had left, Athelstan closed and bolted the door behind him. He took out another tallow candle from the chest and handed it to the coroner to light.

'Brother?'

'Think, my fine friend,' the friar urged, 'you are Margo Grenel. You hold a great treasure which makes the world itch when it hears about it. She has to hide it. A coffer with twelve beautiful, precious stones. Now, where would she conceal it? Where are those places people do not want to go?'

Cranston held the candle up, admiring the flame. 'Well, she is not going to hide it in her cottage, is she? We have already seen what happened, and Margo would have recognised the danger. I understand she dressed corpses for burial, so she could hide those jewels amongst the dead, but that's dangerous. She has to wait for a certain funeral and there is always the risk of being discovered. She could conceal it in a privy, jakes or sewer but, there again, these are cleaned and swilled – though not as often as I would wish.' Cranston stamped his foot on the earth-beaten floor. 'You think she could have hidden it here, in the death house, a place everyone avoids?'

'Precisely,' Athelstan agreed. 'Sir John, let's search this place as carefully as we can.'

Both coroner and friar did. Athelstan scrutinised the ground, especially where it met the wall, but he could find no trace, no evidence which would suggest a treasure had been buried or concealed in the mortuary.

'So if it's not here, where?' Athelstan murmured. 'Sir John, let us leave this for the moment. We have certain ladies we must talk to.'

Cranston and Athelstan left the death house and were making their way through the cemetery when Benedicta called their names and hurried out of Godbless's cottage. The widow woman was followed by Bonaventure, the great tomcat walking proudly, as if a victor in a tournament; as Athelstan remarked, 'Not a whit the worse for his brush with savage death the previous day . . . Cunning, cunning cat,' Athelstan declared, and sketched a blessing over his constant dining companion before turning to Benedicta, who looked pale and drawn.

'You should rest.' Athelstan grasped her hands; they felt cold. He gently squeezed her fingers. 'Sleep,' he urged. She smiled and gestured with her head back at Godbless's cottage.

'Our poor friend sleeps, thank God. I gave him some wine mixed with a little poppy powder. He wants Thaddeus's remains, pathetic and as few as they are, to be buried in the sacred soil of God's Acre. Godbless insists on this. He claims it is only right – after all, the previous priest buried a bear here.'

'A bear?'

'Yes,' she smiled. 'A bear called Tori.' She stumbled over the name. 'I think it was that. Anyway, I was a mere slip of a girl. A dancing bear, and its keeper visited the parish one May Day and joined in our festivities. Oh yes,' Benedicta's smile widened, 'that bear could dance a merry jig, and he did until he fell sick and died. The parish priest at the time was petitioned by the council, on one of the few occasions when he wasn't drunk. Anyway, he agreed, and the poor animal was buried here. I am sure a headstone was erected in its memory. I hope so; after all, it truly was a merry dancer. Now Father, Godbless?'

'Benedicta, please take him to your cottage. Cast around the parish, see if you can find, purchase or borrow a baby kid, a young goat.' He answered Benedicta's quizzical look. 'Let us see if we can find Thaddeus the Younger. Right, Sir John . . .' Athelstan watched Benedicta hurry back along the coffin path to Godbless's cottage.

'Where to now, Brother?'

'Not the Devil's Oak, my Lord Coroner, oh no! I suggest we visit the House of Delights in Grape Lane. I'll tell Benedicta where we are going and then we will be gone.'

Athelstan was genuinely surprised when he and Cranston stopped before the glossy, painted door of the narrow three-storey house in Grape Lane. He glimpsed the bell under its coping, on which a bronze angel nestled all coy, its wings decently covering its breast. The door and its latch were highly polished, its white-stone steps scrubbed clean. When he stepped back and stared up, Athelstan could see how the windows were filled with painted glass rather than horn, whilst all the shutters, neatly thrown back, were painted to gleaming.

'A true place of joy,' Cranston murmured. 'There's a number of these houses across the city and, unless you thought otherwise, you would think they were rich, comfortable nunneries.' Cranston rubbed his hands gleefully, icy blue eyes full of mischief. 'So, Monk?'

'Friar, Sir John.'

'Brace yourself against a tide of beauty, my little ferret.' Cranston pulled on the bell and, within a few heartbeats, the door swung back on its well-greased hinges. A young woman stepped out. She was dressed soberly in a brown gown from neck to foot, with white bands at cuff and neck; the maid's raven-black hair was pinned neatly under a white gauze veil, her pretty face framed by a starched wimple. She stood on the threshold and looked them up and down from head to toe; she grinned, stepped back, and beckoned them in with a cheeky wink at Cranston.

'Enough of that, young Ursula,' the coroner growled. 'Just let me clap eyes on the domina of the house, the Lady Beatrice.'

'I am here, Jack Cranston.' A voice further along the passageway, behind the maid, called mockingly. 'Come in Jack, the weather is turning cold.' Ursula ushered Athelstan and Cranston into a well-furnished, opulently decorated waiting room, just inside the front entrance. Athelstan was aware of comfortable turkey rugs on the polished floor, perfume pots in wall niches, candles with their darting flames illuminating the carefully etched frescoes. Both coroner and friar sat on a comfortable settle as Lady Beatrice swept in. The domina was garbed like Ursula. She was old, lean and sinewy, her good-looking face marred by a cynical twist to what was now faded beauty. She eased herself on to a chair opposite them, Ursula standing beside her. Beatrice carefully folded back the cuffs of her gown, lifted her head and smiled at Cranston.

'So, Jack, this is an official visit?'

'As it always was and always will be, Mistress Beatrice. You know that. You also know that I, Jack Cranston, have more than a soft spot for you because our pasts are closely entwined.' The domina blushed and glanced away. 'The Flesher,' Cranston abruptly declared. 'Simon Makepeace. Does he come here?'

On their journey across the river, Cranston and Athelstan had discussed what path they would follow during their investigation at the House of Delights. The friar had insisted that they seek confirmation of a growing suspicion he had carefully nourished.

'The Flesher?' Cranston repeated gently. 'What does he do here? How does he act? Where does he go? I need answers to these questions.'

'And so you shall.' The Lady Beatrice was trying hard to control the fury seething within her. 'Jack, I can see you and the redoubtable Brother Athelstan are here about a man I loathe. I appreciate you are in a hurry.' She smiled dazzlingly at Athelstan, who realised that – in her youth – this domina must have been a truly beautiful woman.

'Lady Beatrice,' Cranston declared, 'you are correct, we are in a hurry.'

'I will only say this in your presence and yours alone.' Beatrice's face became drawn and fierce. 'I truly detest the Flesher. He repels me. He is a devil incarnate. I hate him, his coven and all that he does. I would do anything, pay any sum, to bring him down.' She leaned closer; her voice now hissed with a deadly rancour. 'Jack, I sit here like a cloistered nun but, as Ursula will tell you, I listen carefully to all the chatter and gossip which trickles through London's underworld like filth seeps along a sewer. I keep an eye on the Flesher and his horde of rats at the Devil's Oak. I am of the mind that the

Flesher is riding for a fall. Oh yes, in my green and salad days, I studied the classics. The ancient Greeks talk of "hubris", an arrogance which contains the seeds of its own hideous destruction. The Flesher is guilty of great hubris. He is as saturated in this as he is in the blood of others . . .' She wiped spittle from her lips. Despite the heavy brown robe, Athelstan could see Beatrice's body tense in spasms of violent anger.

'Lady Beatrice?'

She took a deep breath, then glanced up, all pretty and pert. 'Yes, Brother?'

'Martha Ashby, housekeeper to Parson Reynaud – or Parson Reynaud that was. In her green and salad days she worked here in the House of Delights?'

'Oh, sweet Martha,' Lady Beatrice smiled, 'she certainly did work here, but only for a short while. She was very popular and, consequently, very expensive.'

'What do you mean? I don't understand.'

'Brother Athelstan, have you ever heard about the triple crown of Venus?' Beatrice and Ursula grinned whilst Cranston coughed self-consciously. Athelstan, colouring slightly, shook his head, even as he half suspected what he was about to be told.

'The triple crown of Venus? Well,' the domina was clearly enjoying herself, 'in the act of love, as described by the Roman poet Ovid, in his *Ars Amandi, The Art of Loving*, some women just use their bodies, a few their hands and, fewer still, their lips, all with the greatest skill. This is the triple crown of Venus worn by only a few women. Young Martha was certainly one of these. If you want,' she added impishly, 'Ursula here can demonstrate what I mean.'

'And if you want,' Athelstan countered, 'I am prepared to lead you in reciting fifteen decades of the rosary on your knees on the cobbles outside.' Beatrice and Ursula laughed, both raising their fingers coquettishly to cover their mouths. 'Seriously, and this is serious,' Athelstan's smile faded, 'why did Martha leave; I mean, if she was so skilled?'

Beatrice replied: 'Sir John here is, I understand, a superb swordsman, but only when he has to be. So it was with Martha. For a time she had to but, when she no longer had to, she left. Brother Athelstan, I have heard of you and your work amongst the poor. You know this world and how it is if you are a woman alone in this city, you are highly vulnerable. Visit the nunneries, be it in Farringdon ward or Queenhithe, you'll find these houses throng with young women who are there not because they wish to serve God, but because they are desperate to escape the cruel world of men. If a woman has money or, better still, wealth and menfolk, she is safe. If she is cloistered by Holy Mother Church, she is protected. But, as for the rest, they are lambs wandering through the wolf pack.'

Athelstan closed his eyes. For a brief moment he recalled poor Thaddeus being torn to pieces by those war mastiffs.

'Why are you interested in Martha?' Ursula asked. 'We have all heard what happened at St Benet's.'

'I suspect Martha knows more than she has told us,' Athelstan replied. 'She is a good woman but prudent. I think she is very much afraid of the Flesher. Now, listen, when she stayed here, did the Flesher frequent her?'

'Yes, but Martha often pleaded to be excused. She was quick to seize on any pretext, be it her monthly courses or some malignancy in her humours. She did not like him, as many of our girls did not and do not like him.'

'He is violent?'

'Sir John, you speak the truth, very violent. I am also afraid of him, yet I have had occasion to warn him. My ladies are not the doxies and common whores to be found along Queenhithe quayside. I have heard the rumours about what he does to them. Oh yes, the stories are rife about young women who disappear and whose remains are hidden in that great catacomb at St Benet's.'

'And when the Flesher comes here?'

'Oh, the Flesher wants to bathe. He just loves hot, fragranced water. He strips naked and wallows like a pig in the mud. He climbs into our large, iron-bound tub with small tables just within reach so he can help himself to wine, sweetmeat, napkins and anything else he needs.' She shrugged. 'Of course, he is joined by two or three of our ladies, naked except for their headdresses.'

'Headdresses!'

'That's what he wants. Strange sight, Sir John, a young

woman like Ursula naked except for her wimple and headdress. I have heard stories about what he did at a nunnery outside Rouen; he made the good sisters parade naked except for their veils. The Flesher is a man who likes to humiliate women at every turn and twist. But, of course, you would be surprised, Brother, at what our customers demand.'

'I am sure I would, though I have heard a number of interesting confessions. Now tell me, the Flesher, when he stripped off naked: did he take off the key which hung on a chain around his fat neck?'

'Oh yes. He took it off. He was concerned that during his water frolics with our young maids, the chain would snap and the key might fall off. Oh no, he undid the chain and stepped into the tub, naked as he was born.'

'And the key?' Cranston demanded.

'Let me guess,' Athelstan declared, 'he took it off and left it with his clothing, warbelt and purse in a small antechamber just within sight of the bath? These belongings were guarded by one of his leading henchmen, the creature Raquin or a man called Ingersol, popularly known as the Sicarius.'

'Brother Athelstan, you have the second sight!'

'No, just a student of what is possible, so I can work out what is certainly probable. I will go even further. Recently the Flesher has changed, has he not? He has taken to keeping his key and chain under the most careful scrutiny. Am I right?'

'Brother Athelstan, you are correct. Until a short while ago, a few weeks at the very most, the Flesher would strip and climb into the tub. This abruptly changed. The Flesher insisted on putting the chain and key on one of the tables close to the bathtub.'

'And at the same time,' Athelstan declared, 'Ingersol the Sicarius has completely vanished; he is no longer in the Flesher's retinue?'

'In a word, Brother Athelstan, yes.'

'What did you think of the Sicarius?'

'A shadow, a dark presence, much trusted by the Flesher. He would stand guard while his master went about his frolics. As I said, his job was to guard the devil's property.' She shrugged. 'Ingersol disappeared and the Flesher took to guarding his own precious items.'

'Tell me, Mistress, you have Castilian soap here?'

'Yes, and it is very expensive. Small tablets bought from a merchant on Cheapside. He imports them from Spain, a very profitable trade.'

'Lady Beatrice,' Athelstan took out his ave beads and sifted them through his fingers, 'you want to bring the Flesher down, that is most obvious. I also recognise that you are in considerable danger. If the Flesher knew what you are telling us, he would exact a terrible revenge.'

'Brother Athelstan, I trust you and Sir John, but you will find others are becoming tired of the Flesher and his wicked ways.'

'Tell me,' Cranston intervened, 'did Parson Reynaud come here?'

'Not as often as he used to, Jack – age can take care of a man's lusts.'

'And Daventry, Arundel's man. He visited St Benet's to meet the parson and was murdered there?'

'Yes, so I have heard. Daventry came here on one occasion. He was a mailed clerk, a man who kept close counsel; the lady he hired claimed he spent most of his time studying a chart depicting all the streets and alleyways of Queenhithe.'

'And the others?' Athelstan asked. 'Master Cripplegate, Sexton Spurnel, Curate Cotes?' Lady Beatrice's head went down and Athelstan could see she was smiling. 'Mistress?' She raised her head.

'Brother Athelstan, Cripplegate may have been married but his wife had no children. From the little I know, all three men prefer a different meal from that which we serve here.'

'You mean they like other men, or should I say lust for other men?'

'Brother Athelstan, so the rumour goes. But you asked about Castilian soap?'

'Yes, I did. Lady Beatrice I will take you into my confidence, as even Sir John must be wondering where this path is leading. The arca at St Benet's was opened and robbed. I am sure you can appreciate the mystery. The arca had two distinct locks,

each with a unique key. One was held by Parson Reynaud and
the other by the Flesher. Now we found Parson Reynaud's,
but the Flesher, according to reports, never lets that key out
of his sight. That must be wrong. Somebody got hold of that
key, just for a short while, and made an impression. I reflected
where and when would this great lecher take off that chain
and key? And then I asked where and when could a replica
of it be cast?' Athelstan spread his hands. 'And so here we
are, and that's why I am asking you to bring me a tablet of
Castilian soap.'

'Of course!' Ursula left the chamber and Lady Beatrice began
to chat with Sir John about mutual acquaintances in the city
and court: who was rising, who was falling, all the petty scandals
and gossip. Listening carefully, Athelstan realised that this
woman had once been part of the merry dance Cranston had
led as a young man, long before he met the Lady Maude.

Ursula returned with a small cake of purest Castilian. The
fragrance was so sweet it filled the antechamber, its colour
like that of the purest alabaster. Athelstan carefully picked the
soap out of its silver dish and smiled at the Lady Beatrice.
'Can I trouble you further? Do you have a coffer key?' He
held up a hand, 'I just want to make an impression. I shall do
it here and give both soap and key back to you.'

Again Ursula was despatched and returned with a small
casket key, which Athelstan carefully scrutinised. He pulled
back the sleeves of his gown, positioned the soap in its silver
dish and pressed the key gently in it. He left it for a while
then, with a thin-tipped chancery knife, carefully extracted
the key from the soap. Both he and Cranston examined the
makeshift cast made, especially the fine copy of the teeth at
the end of the coffer key.

'But what then?' Cranston asked.

'Sir John?'

'I understand your argument. You would have us believe
Ingersol took the Flesher's key, along with a fine piece of
Castilian soap, and a cast was made.'

'Once he'd done that, he would have to put the key back
as well as the . . .' Cranston grinned and shook his head. 'My
apologies, my wits are not as sharp as they should be. Of

course,' he turned to Lady Beatrice, 'the Sicarius would be in the antechamber guarding the Flesher's belongings, including the key.'

'Yes. He wouldn't use your soap,' Cranston chewed the corner of his lip, 'but his own.'

'Or some wax,' Athelstan interjected. 'You have candles burning, Mistress, of course you have. A piece of pure beeswax could provide excellent material for a cast, as it soon melts and then quickly hardens. It would keep the cast in all its detail. After all, it's the teeth of the key which matter. Mistress, Sir John and I are openly debating a matter which, if the Flesher learnt about, could place you and yours in great danger, not to mention ourselves. Sir John and I are hunting the Flesher, as we are the assassin who committed those horrors at St Benet's Woodwharf. So what we debate here is strictly *sub rosa* – a secret protected by the King's writ.'

'Yes, Brother.'

'So I ask you, from what you have heard and seen of the Flesher, his visits here, the way he trusted the Sicarius. Do you think the Sicarius had the time to make a cast of that key to the arca, the only occasion we believe the Flesher ever became separated from it?'

'Yes, Brother Athelstan, it is possible, even probable because—'

'Because what?'

'Because a few weeks ago, the Sicarius disappeared, and has never been seen since, at least not by us here in this house. Naturally, I was curious. I asked the Flesher where the Sicarius was. All I received back in reply was the most repulsive scowl. Raquin, who was with him at the time, laughed as he always does, high and piercing, like the neigh of a prancing palfrey. Moreover, I'd heard the rumours – even the Flesher himself had mentioned this – that there could be a traitor in his comitatus.' She shrugged prettily. 'And it would appear that perhaps the Sicarius was the guilty one, hence his disappearance. After all, that's what happens when you offend, alienate or obstruct the Flesher: you simply disappear. But at the end of the day, I might be wrong. Jack, I do what I am and I am what I do.' She waved a hand. 'People dismiss me as a common whore, but I have a sharp wit and a keen mind. I watch the filthy politic of the Flesher. His world repels me but it's a world which taints mine.'

'And the Sicarius?'

'As I have said, a brooding, dark presence. Fairly handsome, taciturn and watchful. He rarely talked and, when he did, he was a man of few words. A strange, eerie character. Sometimes I'd catch him staring at me sadly.'

'Why do you call him strange?' Cranston leaned over and grasped Lady Beatrice's hands and kissed the tip of her fingers. She immediately acted all coy, eyelids fluttering, hand beating gently against her chest.

'Oh Jack,' she whispered, 'we have seen the days.'

Athelstan fought to keep his face straight and impassive.

'We certainly have, my lady,' Cranston retorted. 'And so I trust your judgement about men, be it the Flesher or Ingersol. What was strange about him? Why was he sad?'

'In a word, Jack, he seemed to be a man deeply uncomfortable in his own skin.'

'And?'

'As I've said, Jack, the Flesher is riding for a fall. Perhaps Ingersol was the traitor. Perhaps he was just one of many who are beginning to grow tired of the filthy, treacherous, murderous world of Master Simon Makepeace.' Lady Beatrice smoothed her long white fingers down her gown and glanced up sharply. 'Do you think the same?' she asked.

'What I suspect,' Athelstan told her, 'is that weeks ago the Flesher came here with the Sicarius, his personal retainer and henchman. We now know the Sicarius had decided to betray the Flesher.' He smiled thinly at Lady Beatrice. 'That too is a secret, but one that will not help the poor man who has probably paid with his blood for his change of mind. Now I suggest that Ingersol was intent on a killing blow against his murderous master. He would break into the Flesher's arca at St Benet's and steal everything. How he planned to obtain the key held by Parson Reynaud is still a mystery. Anyway, on that particular day, the Flesher comes here for his water frolics, well served by the ladies of the house. He strips in the ante-chamber and, intent only on his pleasure, takes off the key chain from around his neck. Meanwhile the Sicarius sits in a small antechamber or enclave. He is by himself.' Lady Beatrice nodded in agreement. 'He has a piece of pure beeswax or a small tablet of Castilian soap; he may well have had both. He takes an impression of the key to the arca, concentrating as we did on the teeth of the key.' Athelstan paused, eyes narrowed. 'We know very little of the provenance of the Sicarius. He styled himself the dagger man. He is silent and taciturn, of a secretive disposition. He may have been well versed in forging keys or picking locks.'

'That's true,' Cranston intervened. 'Many felons, like scholars in the schools, graduate from one profession to another. Moreover, he was a clerk, a mailed clerk. He may have had a skill for picking the locks of chancery chests.'

'He was definitely sure of himself,' Athelstan agreed. 'And I am almost certain that he knew the only time he could get to that key is when the Flesher visited the House of Delights which, of course, explains our presence here today. Now he must have been successful on that particular occasion. If the Flesher had caught him, then there would have been a rather violent confrontation between the riffler and his henchman.'

'Nothing like that ever occurred here,' Lady Beatrice intervened. 'But how did the Flesher discover Ingersol was the traitor?'

'And that's my final conclusion,' Athelstan continued. 'Even though, I concede, it is mere supposition, a theory with no hard evidence. I suspect the Sicarius made a hideous mistake. Once he had finished fashioning the cast or casts, he hid these away in his wallet and put back the key. I suggest that he never examined it carefully. The soap of Castile and beeswax candles exude a beautiful fragrance. However, when they harden, any traces become small globules, rather difficult to remove. In other words,' he sighed, 'for some reason the Flesher examined that key. He smelt it, scrutinised it and, being the cunning viper he is, reached the conclusion that someone had tried to make a cast of his key. He would also realise that the only person who could have done so was the Sicarius, here in the House of Delights. The Flesher would consult with his evil familiar, Raquin. Both men would conclude that the

Sicarius intended great mischief and was undoubtedly the traitor in the Flesher's camp. A violent confrontation must have taken place. Ingersol was then executed, his corpse hidden God knows where.' Athelstan crossed himself. 'I concede this is pure conjecture, but a logical possibility.' He smiled. 'Was it the key which led to Ingersol's downfall? If not – what? If it was—'

'The Flesher would have been alerted; he would have protected the arca better,' Cranston declared. 'Surely?'

Athelstan pulled a face. 'True, true,' he murmured. 'One thing, however, I am sure of: a cast was made of the Flesher's key here in the House of Delights – whether the Flesher realised what had happened is the hypothesis we cannot definitely prove.'

They sat in silence for a while, until Lady Beatrice leaned across and nipped Cranston's wrist. 'Jack, the hour is passing, is there anything else?'

The coroner glanced at Athelstan who just shook his head.

'In which case . . .' Lady Beatrice rose, Cranston and Athelstan likewise. They made their farewells. The friar was about to follow the coroner out of the room when his gaze was caught by one of the frescoes on the wall close to the door. Athelstan peered closer and realised the painting was an artist's impression of the heavenly constellations, each titled in Latin on a silver scroll: 'Pleiades', 'Stella Matutina', 'Magnus Artorius'. Athelstan stared at these, mouthing the words, remembering something Benedicta had told him.

'Brother?'

Athelstan kept staring at the painting as his mind began to wonder. He recalled what he'd learnt earlier that day and shook his head in surprise once again, mouthing the words quietly time and again.

'Brother?' Cranston came back to fetch him. 'Athelstan, are you well?'

'I am amongst the stars, Sir John, and a thought has occurred to me. Logic dominates our lives, whether we like it or not, yet we always have to test the conclusion. So, let us leave.'

PART SIX

Sneaksman (**Old English**): a thief

They left the House of Delights and were halfway down Grape Street when Cranston abruptly turned and strode back to the shadow-filled mouth of an alleyway.

'You'd best come out,' he shouted. 'You have been following us since we left that house, hugging the wall. Come on! Enough deceit. Either show yourselves or I will go fetch you myself.'

Two figures sloped out of the murk and hurried towards them.

'Watkin and Pike!' Athelstan exclaimed. 'In God's name what are you doing here?'

'Benedicta told us. So we hurried across and were waiting for you to leave.'

'And why did you want to know where we were going? Come on,' Athelstan urged. 'You are the leaders of my parish council. You must have good reason to follow your priest across the Thames and into this maze of alleyways. Oh, for the love of Mary.' Athelstan pointed at a shabby alehouse further down Grape Street. 'We will set up camp there and you can tell us.'

'It is important,' Pike declared, his thin, choleric face all flushed. 'Watkin and I have been in discussion about what we should do and it's time we told you. It's about the Flesher, St Benet's, and Watkin's dung cart.'

'Now that does sound interesting,' Athelstan murmured. 'But come, let's make ourselves more comfortable.'

The alehouse consisted of a long, low-beamed hall where barrels, tubs and boxes served as tables and stools. A dark place, the gloom lit by a cluster of rush lights and smelly oil lamps. The stench of burning almost masked the rank, wet odour of the bedraggled chickens that pecked at the floor, scrabbling furtively away as a rat slithered through the wet rushes, snouting for morsels or scraps. The greasy-aproned slattern ushered them to what she grandly described as 'the window seat': four overturned barrels around a trestle table under a square-cut window, its shabby shutters thrown back. Athelstan peered out at the garden with its flowerbeds, herb plots, stew ponds and grassy fringes, all gaunt and stark under the tightening grip of a cold autumn. Athelstan refused the offer of a drink. Cranston ordered ale for himself and 'his two friends', bellowing at the serving girl that he wanted the tankards clean and the ale thoroughly brewed. Once the black jacks were served, Athelstan tapped the stained barrel top.

'Gentleman,' he declared, 'you have brought us here, it must be urgent, so what?'

'The business in Haceldema,' Watkin declared, indicating with one dirty hand for Pike to remain silent. 'We believe it's the work of the Flesher and it has proved too much. Oh, we've heard stories about him before, but to witness such villainy! The savage destruction of poor Thaddeus, the grave injuries inflicted on Godbless, not to mention you, Benedicta and Crim being threatened with steel and hell-hounds – these are injuries too great to bear.' Watkin drew himself up, his broad, florid face bright with anger. 'The Flesher truly is a human dung cart, full of every kind of shit, and reeking like the filthiest midden heap. He's like the river Fleet – wherever he goes, muck and dirt follow. I confess,' Watkin was now becoming more dramatic and Athelstan hid a smile. He now realised why Judith the mummer always gave Watkin a lead role in the mystery plays. 'I confess,' Watkin repeated, 'Pike and I have been supping with wolves. It's time we left the banqueting table and made our peace. Isn't that true, Pike?'

'I agree with Watkin,' the ditcher declared. 'I would love to dig the deepest pit, throw the Flesher in and bury him beneath the reeking mess of London's filthiest lay stall.'

'Look, gentlemen,' Cranston intervened, 'your detestation of the Flesher is most laudable. But what is this all about?'

'As you know, Brother Athelstan,' Watkin told him, 'I have bought a new dung cart, thanks to a loan from the Flesher. I arranged it through family kin I have in Queenhithe. The Flesher's lawyer, Master Copping, called it an investment.'

Watkin stumbled over the word and gave a broad, gap-toothed smile. 'The Flesher loans money to people like me, so I bought that cart. From what was left of the money, I had a secret place constructed, well sealed off with oaken wood which had been heavily coated with the thickest pitch.'

'Why did you do that?'

'Brother Athelstan, that's what Master Copping told us to do. The Flesher would advance us the money, I was to buy a new cart with a secret compartment.'

'And you didn't ask why?'

'Sir John, you know full well that half the coffins carried across London often contain more smuggled goods than corpses. Taxes are high. The custom collectors are sharp and ruthless. Anyway, the Flesher has similar carts all over London. We thought we'd be involved in a little smuggling.'

'And if you are caught,' the coroner warned, 'your cart would be confiscated and you would face heavy fines. You would also be led through the city to the sound of bagpipes to stand in the Pillory of Purgatory near the Great Conduit in Cheapside.'

'Oh, we know all that. But this was different.' Pike again grinned. 'Nothing illegal – or immoral, like smuggling whores. We were simply told to bring our cart to the Devil's Oak on the eve of the feast of St Cecilia.'

'Twenty-first of November,' Athelstan exclaimed. 'Cecilia was a virgin martyr executed in Ancient Rome. She is the patron saint of church music.'

'And on her feast day, 22 November,' Cranston declared, 'Parliament has been summoned to meet at Westminster, both the Lords and the Commons. The King intends to seek formal approval for his uncle John of Gaunt to act as regent, not to mention a new tax to fill the royal coffers.' Cranston fell silent, staring across at Athelstan, his blue eyes all fierce as he pondered the possibilities. 'Do you know, Pike and Watkin, when we left the House of Delights I realised we were being followed. I thought it was the Candlelight-Master and his Luciferi. A group of Frenchmen.' He answered their puzzled look. 'They are the ones who rescued Athelstan and the others in Haceldema. I now regard them as the messengers of God, as I do you.'

'Sir John, what do you mean?'

'I just wonder, I truly do, my friends.' Cranston stared around the dirty alehouse, then he abruptly leaned forward, seizing Watkin and Pike by the front of their shabby jerkins. He pulled them forward, giving each a short shake as they protested. 'Don't worry,' he growled, 'you are my friends not my foes. Raise your right hands, go on. Raise them,' he urged. They did so, eyes all anxious. 'By the power invested in me,' Cranston intoned, 'as the King's Lord High Coroner in London, I swear you to be officers of the law and members of my comitatus within the city and beyond. You so swear?'

Both men nodded, Pike gulping back his fear, Watkin slightly trembling. Both men regarded Cranston as a most fearsome figure, who sat at the right hand of the power, whatever that was. 'Brother Athelstan,' Cranston released both men, 'you are their parish priest and you've witnessed their oath of office, so give us your most powerful blessing.'

Athelstan, biting his lip to hide his smile, did so, and both parishioners, heads bowed, crossed themselves. 'Right,' Cranston waved a stubby finger at them, 'you are to remain silent about what you have learnt and might learn in the future. You are to act as upright officers, which is why I will divulge my secrets to you.' Cranston produced the miraculous wineskin and took the most generous gulp before sharing it with Pike and Watkin; the latter went to take a second mouthful, but Cranston snatched it away.

'Fitzalan Earl of Arundel,' the coroner began.

'We've heard of him,' Pike declared.

'A fearsome lord,' Watkin added. 'Very cruel to the Upright Men, a great killer of our company and our comrades.' Watkin abruptly paused, hand over his mouth. 'I shouldn't have said that, should I?'

'Never mind.' Cranston waved a hand. 'That's in the past. I deal with the future. I suspect Fitzalan of Arundel intends to overawe the Parliament summoned to meet at Westminster on the feast of St Cecilia. Now, I know the King and his council, in particular my Lord of Gaunt and Master Thibault, also believe that. They also recognise that Arundel cannot bring troops, in this case mercenaries, either into the city or

Westminster, the latter being royal property, whilst every inch of this city is owned by someone else . . .'

'Except for St Benet's Woodwharf,' Athelstan interjected. 'A large, cavernous church with a broad, sprawling cemetery which Parson Reynaud was intent on clearing. He intended to make it into a campsite, didn't he? What with that church and that wasteland of a graveyard, Arundel could easily quarter a thousand, perhaps two thousand mercenaries there. Oh yes,' Athelstan took his ave beads from his pouch, threading them through his fingers to soothe his excitement, 'moreover, St Benet's stands close to the Thames. Can you imagine troops encamped and, when Arundel decides, a fleet of war barges could ferry these soldiers to Westminster to lay siege to the palace – the abbey as well as the great offices of the Exchequer and Chancery. But can he do that? I mean, bring troops on to church property?'

'Brother, Arundel could and will. He holds the advowson of St Benet's. He possesses all the power of a manor lord. He can appropriate buildings and assemble whomever he wants. Oh yes,' Cranston exclaimed, 'that's what Arundel intends, and he brought the Flesher into his plot. That is the secret they have been preparing; that's why Daventry was sent to Parson Reynaud, probably to push matters ahead. Arundel is plotting to turn the entire church and its land into a fortified enclave, with war barges on the Thames and a few mounted hobelars to guard the approaches. They could stable their horses in the death house. Arundel may well turn Mistress Martha out and use the priest's dwelling as his own. They will have weapons enough. The main problem will be purveyance, fresh food and water for soldiers who might be quartered there for ten to fourteen days, as long as the Parliament lasts. Now gentlemen, that is the reason why –' Cranston pointed at Athelstan's two parishioners, who sat, faces all startled, staring at the coroner like frightened rabbits – 'he needs you and others, not to mention the Flesher, whose cellars at the Devil's Oak will be crammed with purveyance ready for the arrival of the mercenaries. Remember, Athelstan, when we visited that tavern? All those provision carts in the courtyard, the casks, the barrels? Once Parliament sits, I am certain that the kitchens, butteries and bakeries at the Devil's Oak will become very busy. The tavern also owns a stew pond, not to mention a well with plenty of fresh water. And so we have it. Oh yes, most cunning! Arundel will arrive and move amongst the lords with his henchmen whilst his troops stand off Westminster. He will have one aim in mind, to compel our young King to hand over the royal council to the Fitzalans and their ilk. Once he has this, Arundel will move for the impeachment of John of Gaunt. Our noble regent will realise what is coming and take ship to foreign parts, go into exile, leaving the King, the court, the council, the city and the kingdom to Arundel and his faction. Arundel will topple Gaunt and, who knows in time, may even move against our young King.'

'Sir John, you think so?'

'Brother Athelstan, I know so.'

'So, what can be done?'

'These . . .' Cranston picked up his tankard and toasted Pike and Watkin. 'Brother Athelstan, our two companions – along with others of their kind – will be our saviours. So, Brother, look to the dung collectors from where our salvation comes. I swear that I, Sir John Cranston, will invoke something much more ancient and powerful than a manor lord's right to advowson. I shall summon up all the Crown's power and ritual surrounding the crime of murdrum.'

'Sir John?' Watkin queried.

'Murder, the unlawful slaying of another human being. Now we know that has taken place at St Benet's and, by the way, I am not talking about the killing of Parson Reynaud or Daventry. Oh no, St Benet's is a house of grievous ill-repute. We suspect that the church, its cemetery and crypt are in fact a mausoleum of murder. They contain the corpses, many of these innocents, maliciously slain, their corpses hidden away. Accordingly, I am going to issue a writ under statute law and search the entire area: church, cemetery and crypt. Sooner or later I will find victims of murder. So Watkin, Pike, as duly sworn officers of both the Crown and city council, have words with your respective guilds and fraternities, the diggers and the dung collectors of London. Tell them I am going to use the law to summon them in haste to assemble under the royal standard in the cemetery at St Benet's. Tell them that the usual writs will be issued, proclamations will be posted on the Cross at St Paul's churchyard, the Standard in Cheapside, as well as the gates to London Bridge. I expect them to be there in the next three days.'

'Sir John?'

'Yes, my little friar?'

'If Arundel is plotting to do what you say, and I think he is, is it possible that the murders of Daventry and Parson Reynaud were perpetrated to thwart this? The work of some opponent of the Fitzalans?'

'Perhaps. But we have no evidence.' Cranston again took a generous swig from the miraculous wineskin and shared it with Pike and Watkin, warning them to take only a mouthful. Cranston then leaned back, beaming at Watkin and Pike as if they were long-lost brothers. He dug into his purse and plucked out two coins, pushing these towards the ragged, mittened hands of both men. 'Go, and as Scripture says,' he intoned, 'spread the word.' Cranston clapped his hands in glee. 'Arundel and the Flesher may well try to protest but, rest assured, I have the right and the law is on my side. So,' Cranston rose, 'you gentlemen be about your business. Brother Athelstan, let us adjourn to my chantry chapel at the Lamb of God.'

The church bells of Cheapside were tolling the appeal for the members of all guilds and fraternities to remember their promises to pray and provide for the poor. A preacher standing on a barrel also reminded the crowds of Christ's words, 'The poor you will always have with you.'

'True enough,' Athelstan murmured, staring round at the horde of beggars who gathered at the mouth of different alleyways or runnels. Now and again Athelstan would pause to distribute a little from his alms pouch but, for the rest, he had to follow Cranston as the coroner pushed his way through the colourful, noisy throng. Cranston had made it very clear that he had his eagle eye on one thing and one thing only, his favourite tavern's brilliantly hued, beacon-like sign, beckoning them into the comfortable and luxurious warmth of the solar, a fitting harbour against the cold, misty autumn day. The coroner and friar dodged barrows and carts. They paused to

allow coffin cortèges make their mournful way by, wished
well to wedding parties, and walked on, trying to ignore the
apprentices tugging at their sleeves to visit this stall or that,
as well as a legion of cooks desperate to sell their pies and
potages before the market bell sounded the end of trading. At
last they approached the Lamb of God. Cranston was openly
debating whether to have chicken cooked in white wine or a
minced beef pie when he stopped, cursing volubly, as he
glimpsed Tiptoft surging through the crowd like a war barge
along the river.

'Sir John,' Tiptoft proclaimed dramatically, 'My Lord
Coroner, Brother Athelstan, you must come.'

'Where?' the friar demanded.

'St Benet's Woodwharf. Flaxwith is assembling his bailiffs.
Sir John, more murder and mayhem and,' the courier lowered
his voice to a whisper, 'the Flesher is trapped and awaits
arrest.'

Cranston and Athelstan arrived to find St Benet's Church
under siege. All the doors were locked and bolted, whilst a
strong guard of Flaxwith's cohort had set up watch on the
devil's door, still not fully repaired. Cranston's chief bailiff
had brought the corpses from Southwark. The cadavers of the
wolfsheads and the two war hounds now sprawled gruesomely
on the church steps. Athelstan took his ave beads out and
threaded them through his fingers to pray and soothe his nerves.
The public display of slain outlaws was common practice, but
Athelstan found it barbaric even though it was necessary. The
bellies of the dead were now beginning to swell and the reeking
stench of putrefaction hung heavily in the air. A garishly written
proclamation, the letters etched in red ink, had been pinned
to the church door. It declared how these malefactors were
guilty of grievous crimes, including murderous assault on
citizens as well as on an anointed priest. Accordingly, the
proclamation insisted, anyone who recognised the dead, be it
man or beast, should, under the pain of forfeiture and imprisonment, present themselves immediately before the justices at
the Guildhall.

A crowd had been drawn in by the display of the dead and
the dire words of the proclamation. They were quite certain

that the dead men were rifflers from the Devil's Oak; such cries of recognition were sudden, shouted comments, though no one came forward to state the truth. Athelstan noticed how many of the crowd either spat on the corpses or made gestures against the evil eye to protect themselves against the spirits of the dead men. Here and there, someone would step forward and kick one of the corpses with the toe of his boot. Indeed, the only mercy shown to the dead was that someone had draped dirty cloths over their private parts, whilst bailiffs armed with clubs tried to drive away the mangy street dogs eager to nose the dead, lips curled back, sharp teeth ready to tear cold flesh. Flaxwith appeared. He nodded at Cranston. The bailiff winked, tapped the side of his nose knowingly and made his way to the top step where he turned to address the crowd.

'I have sent a messenger to fetch Master Makepeace from the Devil's Oak and asked him to come here as soon as possible.' Flaxwith then pointed down to Cranston. 'However, the Lord High Coroner is now present. Rest assured all is in good order. In accordance with the law, the corpses of these outlaws and their savage dogs have been displayed and you know the reason why. If you recognise the dead, you know what you must do. Now disperse. Anyone who remains will be held and sworn as members of my comitatus and assist our guard over these corpses.'

The crowd thinned and disappeared like snow under the sun. Flaxwith, all pleased, tripped down the steps, followed by Samson, who immediately tried to lick the coroner's leg, until his master hastily tightened his collar leash, pulling the dog back and ordering him to behave. He then gestured at Cranston and Athelstan to follow him into the shadow of the church porch.

'Satan's tits,' Cranston breathed. 'Flaxwith, what is this all about?' The chief bailiff stared around, then beckoned Cranston and Athelstan to draw even closer. 'Sir John,' he whispered, 'Raquin and Copping accompanied their master to St Benet's this morning. Apparently the Flesher went into the priest's house; his two henchmen visited the church.' Flaxwith pulled a face. 'All seemed well enough, Sir John, no alarm was raised. Peace reigned, until myself and the others arrived with the carts carrying the corpses. We laid them out and I thought we should, as a courtesy, visit Mistress Martha to inform her about what we had done. When I received your instructions yesterday evening, I did send a confidential message to the housekeeper about what was planned for today. Anyway, when I reached the house, I could hear moans and groans as well as shouted curses, followed by a pounding as if someone was imprisoned in a chamber, desperate to be released. The main door was not locked or bolted. Well, you'd best see for yourself.'

Flaxwith led Cranston and Athelstan from the church, through God's Acre and up the slight rise to the priest's house. As soon as they drew close, Athelstan could hear the shouts and strident curses. They went in. Athelstan hastened to the stairs to the left of the entrance hall and stood listening to the cursing and pounding from above.

'That's the Flesher,' Flaxwith declared cheerily. 'He's locked in Mistress Martha's bedchamber. The door is of the heaviest oak. Martha has the key: the window looks out over the back of the house and is far too small to crawl through. His victim is in here.'

Flaxwith led Cranston and Athelstan into the solar. Martha, her gown bloodied, her hair hanging in a tangle down to her shoulders, sat on a stool staring into the fire. She turned, smiled wanly, and rose to meet them. Athelstan hastened forward as the woman swayed on her feet.

'God in heaven,' the friar whispered, staring at her bruised face, the weals on her shoulders, neck and chest as the torn gown she wore slipped before she pulled it up again. Again Martha tried to smile, but the corner of her mouth was bruised whilst her lips were puffy and swollen.

'Mistress?' Athelstan led her across to a chair while Cranston poured a goblet of wine, which she gratefully accepted, sipping it. Now and again she would tenderly touch one of the bruises on her face. 'What happened, Mistress?'

'A normal enough morning,' she slurred. 'I was alone. Sexton Spurnel, Cripplegate and the curate were away, busy elsewhere. I mean, that's understandable as the church is sealed.' She pointed to the hour candle on its stand in the far corner. 'They are late; they should be here already. They always come in the late afternoon to ensure all is well.'

'Where are they?'

Athelstan glanced at Flaxwith, who just shrugged.

'Go out,' Cranston ordered. 'Send some of your lovely boys to take up all three of them. But do it quietly and secretly and bring them here. If they object, arrest them. But Flaxwith,' Cranston, cradling the miraculous wineskin, lifted it as if in toast, 'you have done very well. The Flesher is imprisoned upstairs. No one knows. Yes?'

'And Copping and Raquin?' Athelstan asked.

'Sir John, Brother Athelstan, they lie slain in St Benet's.'

'In God's name!' Athelstan exclaimed.

'Satan's tits!' Cranston breathed. 'Flaxwith, you didn't tell us that.'

'Sir John, I am wary of eavesdroppers – that's why there is a strong guard on the devil's door, the only entrance to St Benet's. There's nothing we can do about those two felons. Stabbed to the heart, they are. I left them as I found them. Of course I have not sent any message to the Devil's Oak – that was just a pretence.'

'Yes, yes, I can see.' Cranston put the miraculous wineskin away. 'It must stay like that or we will have rifflers gathering here like flies on a turd. So, Flaxwith, take up those three parish worthies, they may well be arriving very soon. Tiptoft, whom I have left with the corpses, must be despatched urgently to the Tower. I want a cohort of Cheshire archers here as soon as possible.' Cranston fished in his wallet and handed Flaxwith a waxen copy of his seal. 'Tiptoft is to show that to the constable at the Tower. He is to insist that the archers are needed urgently on King's business. Once you have done that, come back.'

Cranston and Athelstan then turned to Martha, who sat leaning against the table, gently sipping at the goblet. Now and again a jab of pain would make her close her eyes.

'Mistress,' Athelstan murmured, 'I appreciate you are in great distress but, as you can imagine, we need to know what happened. We must seize your attacker and take him to a place where he can be closely guarded.'

'The perpetrator,' Cranston urged, 'is guilty of house-breaking, damage to church property and, from what I can gather, the most horrific rape. We have the proof. You are both victim and witness. Mistress, you may not know this, but such crimes are felonies which carry the death sentence. Moreover, justice is swift in these matters, so I need to lay an indictment before the King's justices as soon as possible.'

'I was busy about the house,' Martha murmured, as if she was talking to herself. 'The door was off the latch. The Flesher – yes, that beast with no soul. Anyway, he swaggered in with Raquin and Copping, his lapdogs. He said they wished to survey both church and cemetery. I just shrugged and left them to it. Sir John, I don't like him or his coven, I never have and I never will. I went up to my own chamber.' She paused as Flaxwith came back into the house. She smiled at him, then listened to the Flesher's curses. 'I was in my chamber standing near the window.' She continued with a sigh. 'I was wondering what I should do now Reynaud was dead.' She drew in a sharp breath. 'I heard voices, footsteps below. I thought the Flesher and the others had left for the church; you can still enter through the devil's door. Anyway,' she gulped from the goblet, 'I heard a sound and turned. The Flesher was in my bedchamber. He kicked the door shut, turned the key and drew the bolts close.' She blinked. 'I knew what he wanted; he was always greedy for me. I begged him not to touch me, not to hurt me. I tried to explain that those days were over.'

'So he broke in here and assaulted you?' Cranston tenderly clasped the woman's hand. 'Mistress I realise you are deeply hurt, but your remedy is in the law. I must ask you these questions and you must give me the truth as if you are on oath. Did the Flesher break into your bedchamber? Was he in any way welcome there? Did you intimate that you wanted him?'

'No, no, no,' she retorted. 'I did not want him anywhere near me. I never have and I never will.'

'And he assaulted you?'

'Yes he did.'

'And he raped you?'

'Yes he abused me.' She turned on the chair and hitched

up her gown. Athelstan saw her torn stockings, as well as the bruises and cuts along her legs. 'I could pull this up to show more injury, as well as the stain of his seed. Yes, he raped me.' She paused to let the silence deepen, until the cursing and banging in the gallery above broke out again. 'I admit I acted,' she gasped, 'once the assault began. I tried to pretend, as I used to, that I loved to be ravished. I wanted it over as quickly as possible. He spent his seed then lay back on the bed. I got up and fled the chamber. I took the key from the lock and turned it. He didn't realise what was happening. He was, as usual, like a man mawmsy with ale. I came down stairs and sat here till Flaxwith arrived.'

'Mistress, I will have you taken from here,' Athelstan declared. 'Sir John will provide an escort to accompany you to Benedicta, a widow woman in my parish at St Erconwald's. She has all the skills of a leech; she will tend to your injuries. Perhaps we should confront the Flesher . . .' Athelstan broke off as Flaxwith intervened.

'Sir John, Brother Athelstan, I do urge you to view the corpses in St Benet's. Sir John, once you have as coroner—'

'The corpses belong to me,' Cranston declared, 'and can't be removed without my permission. Yes, yes, it's time we viewed these worthies . . .'

Athelstan and Cranston, followed by Flaxwith, went into the sombre, mildewed nave of St Benet's, gloomy, cold and deeply oppressive. Athelstan wondered if all the beings of light had fled this accursed parish, a sanctuary of sin, violence, murder and now rape. Before they left the priest's house, Cranston had summoned two of Flaxwith's bailiffs to lock and bolt the priest's house behind them and mount the most careful guard over Martha and the Flesher, still trapped in the house-keeper's chamber. They had found more bailiffs guarding the devil's door, the only entrance into a church sealed shut because of the terrible sacrileges perpetrated there. Cranston urged these to be most vigilant. He quietly murmured how he hoped the cohort of Cheshire archers would arrive soon – before the rifflers who thronged the Devil's Oak realised something was wrong and came searching for their master. The coroner took out his tinder and lit three of the large tallow candles, which threw moving circles of golden light as they followed Flaxwith into the same chantry chapel where Parson Reynaud had been stabbed. Raquin's corpse lay slumped in a corner at a half-crouch. The henchman's ugly face was contorted by the sudden, violent death which had snatched his soul as swiftly as a falcon would its prey: his eyes half open in an empty, glassy stare, a bloody froth on his gaping lips, hands hanging down either side. Raquin's dagger had slipped from the fingers of his left hand, though the other still half held his sword.

'Satan's tits!' Cranston crouched down, staring at his dead enemy. 'So your soul has been seized for judgement? I thank Heaven your blood is not on my hands, nor the fate of your soul dependent on my actions. God have mercy on you, though God knows he will have a veritable litany of sin to forgive.' The coroner glanced over his shoulder at Flaxwith. 'You found him like this?'

'Yes, Sir John. I viewed both him and Copping, then I left a close guard on the devil's door. Nobody has been here. Sir John, I know of Raquin – his death will shake many trees; there will be Hell to pay.'

'But not in this life,' Cranston retorted, 'not if we are cunning enough. Athelstan, what do you think happened?'

The friar stood, eyes closed, swaying slightly on his feet. 'The Flesher,' he began, 'undoubtedly arrived at St Benet's. He decided he would have his pleasure of Martha and sent his two dogs in here. I can imagine them swaggering around. Raquin was sure of himself. Copping knew that he was protected. By the way, where is Copping's corpse?'

'In the sacristy,' Flaxwith replied.

'Raquin's killer came in here.' Athelstan squatted down beside the coroner, pulling at Raquin's jacket so he could scrutinise the soaking-wet heart wound. 'Raquin adopted the stance of a veteran street fighter. Perhaps there was more than one assailant, which is why Raquin retreated into a corner to protect his back. He draws sword and dagger but, and this is the strange thing, his weapons show no sign of inflicting a wound.' Athelstan shook his head. 'Raquin was an experienced brawler, a skilled killer. Yes?' Cranston grunted his agreement. 'Yet look around, Sir John, can you detect any sign of disturbance?'

The coroner rose, peering at the floor, walls and different pieces of chapel furniture. 'Nothing!' he exclaimed. 'Nothing to show that the most deadly confrontation took place here. Nothing except a man who drew his weapons but never used them and suffered a fatal blow to his heart.'

'And the wound itself?'

Cranston crouched down again and peered at the blood-encrusted jerkin. He loosened this and raised the sopping shirt beneath to reveal a deep, bloody slit just beneath the left breast. 'Very similar to that inflicted on Parson Reynaud and Daventry,' Athelstan observed. 'Well,' he straightened up, 'Master Flaxwith, let us view Copping's corpse.'

The bailiff led them back up the nave, across the bleak, empty sanctuary and into the sacristy. Copping lay on his back, arms flung out. He'd drawn his dagger, which lay just beyond his right hand. Again Cranston and Athelstan noticed no disturbance, nothing but a dead-eyed victim with blood crusting his mouth and congealing either side of his corpse. Cranston and Athelstan crouched down to scrutinise the wound, swiftly drawing the conclusion that Copping's death almost mirrored that of Raquin. An armed, fairly vigorous man, taken by surprise and killed by a knife thrust straight to the heart.

'A skilled dagger man,' Cranston murmured, getting up and walking slowly around the corpse. 'I do wonder if the Sicarius is truly dead. But what fascinates me, Athelstan, is how this assassin can get so close to his victim and strike so swiftly that his opponent has no chance to resist. There is no sign, as with Raquin and the rest, of even the slightest struggle,' he shrugged, 'apart from weapons being drawn by these two last victims. There is something else, Brother. Have you noticed how this church has virtually become a slaughter's yard, a butcher's pen?'

'Yes, yes I agree,' Athelstan declared. 'Does the assassin choose this church because of some macabre, sinister reason? There again, Sir John, look around, this is a hall of shadows, a place which lends itself to murder.'

'True, true.' Cranston walked to the sacristy door and stared across the sanctuary. 'In my life, Brother, I have dealt with assassins, soft footed and skilful. They move like a hunting cat. I just wonder who this one is.'

'Could it be the Flesher? Has he decided to rid himself of all his henchmen?' Athelstan murmured. 'Or those three other upright members of this parish, Cotes, Cripplegate and Spurnel. Sir John, all three served in the royal array. If they were members of the Tower cohort, they would be experienced, skilled men-at-arms. Perhaps they had formed their own confederation? But it is proof we need, yet our killer leaves very little, and that's strange . . .'

'What do you mean, Brother?'

'Well, Mistress Makepeace's corpse was brutally torn from its coffin and vanishes like smoke in the air. The person who stole it left that note saying the remains would be returned at a given time, in a given place, for a substantial sum of money.'

'And yet no demand has been made?' Cranston declared. 'Not a jot, not a tittle. What do you think, Brother?'

'At this time, in this place, Sir John, I do begin to wonder. Was the corpse stolen, not to be held for ransom but simply as a heinous insult to the Flesher? The culprit has no intention of returning the corpse. He simply wants to bait his victim, taunt him and prolong the agony. The Flesher has been condemned to wait and to receive no response. Can you imagine, Sir John, how the Flesher must feel as days turn into weeks and weeks into months? No, I suspect his mother's corpse will never be returned. Well, not until we unmask this most skilled assassin. Now, back to the matter in hand. Raquin and Copping came in here and they parted. Copping wandered into the sacristy; perhaps he was looking to see if anything precious or valuable remained. I notice how the pyx, sanctuary lamp, cruets, cloths, vestments and sacred vessels have all disappeared. The Flesher would order Cripplegate, Cotes and Spurnel to keep them under close guard before Arundel's mercenaries arrive.' Athelstan stared down at the corpse. 'Is the killer someone we don't really know? Talking of which, Sir John, I wonder where the Candlelight-Master and his Luciferi are.'

'Could they be the assassins?'

'They are certainly skilled enough and nurse a powerful grievance against the Flesher from his days in France. They also suspect he was responsible for the attack on the royal barge eighteen years ago. They have already demonstrated their skill and stealth. Did they enter this church and surprise Raquin and Copping?'

'I am not too sure, Brother, even though I know they keep careful watch but only from afar, little friar. They prefer to keep your parish under keen scrutiny. After all, that's where the Rose Casket and its precious contents emerged after eighteen years.'

'True, true,' Athelstan murmured.

'Brother?'

'Nothing for the moment, Sir John,' Athelstan declared briskly. 'So, Copping and Raquin enter here and part, their assassin or assassins strike. If there was more than one, did they deal with their victims singularly or at the same time?'

Cranston walked over to Athelstan and, pretending to be the assassin, gently pressed his fist against Athelstan's left side before gripping the surprised friar by the shoulder. 'My little friar, that's how swiftly it could happen and how quickly I have seen it done. I once watched a Florentine merchant grip his opponent's hand as if to clasp it, but then he pulled him close, driving a dagger deep into his heart. There are three wounds which are deadly. The first is to the head, usually between the eyes and into the brain. Secondly, to the throat, which severes both the breath and the blood cords, whilst the third is a direct thrust to the heart. The victim has no time to respond. He or she stands in deep shock and then collapses. I'll wager that's what happened here.'

'True, true, Sir John, but remember both men had drawn their weapons. When you approached me, I did not expect you to do what you did. But, according to the evidence, Raquin and Copping had armed themselves. So how did their assailant manage to get so close?'

'Sir John!'

Cranston and Athelstan left the sacristy. Flaxwith stood in the entrance to the rood screen. 'Cripplegate, Cotes and Spurnel have arrived, Sir John. I understand they were expected to make a visit here.'

'Take them over to the priest's house,' Cranston ordered. 'Keep them separate from Martha. And, once we leave this church, set up a close guard. No one is allowed in here.'

Flaxwith nodded and left. 'Sir John, you'd best follow him,' Athelstan declared. 'Just make sure all is well. As for me, I want to walk this macabre church. I really believe it is a hosting ground for evil spirits rather than God's own house and the Gate to Heaven.'

Cranston said he would return. Athelstan watched him go then walked down the sanctuary steps. He paused to pray for a while, before making his way along the transept, peering into the shabby chantry chapels and the shadow-filled enclaves with their crumbling sills and weather-beaten frescoes. Undoubtedly the paintings he glimpsed had been the work of some long-dead artist, who had skilfully depicted scenes from the Scriptures, especially the Gospel of St John. Now, due to water running down the walls, these were beginning to decay and flake and Athelstan wondered how much money, if any, had been spent on the maintenance of this church. He walked closer; one of the paintings caught his eye. Athelstan just stood scrutinising the fresco very carefully, trying to curb the spurt of excitement within him. What he saw in that painting matched other scraps of information he had collected, as well as the half-formed suspicions he had sifted. Athelstan crouched down and studied that particular wall painting even closer. The artist had been keen to delineate the story of Lazarus whom Christ had raised from the dead. Jesus loved to relax in the house of Lazarus and his two sisters. 'You should have realised this before, stupid friar,' Athelstan murmured to himself. 'A scene from the Gospels which you have studied many a time.'

'Athelstan, Athelstan?'

Cranston came marching down the nave. The friar left the shadowy transept to meet him.

'Come my friend,' Cranston urged. 'Master Thomas Chaucer, captain of the Cheshire archers at the Tower, has arrived with his cohort, all resplendent in their livery. They sport young Richard's personal emblem of the white hart. No mob of rifflers would dare quarrel with such lovely lads.'

They left the church; the strengthening breeze buffeted their faces. Athelstan flinched at the dirt carried from the mounds of loose soil heaped near the shallow pits. The cemetery, however, had been transformed by the arrival of the Cheshire archers, garbed in their green and brown tunics, similar to the livery of the royal foresters. They also wore tabards displaying all the rich colours of the Plantagenet royal house, red-blood and gold, whilst the King's personal emblem of the 'whyte harte couchant' decorated their right shoulder. Recruited from the Welsh Marches, these were the kingdom's most skilled bowmen. They thronged about, bow staves unstrung, with quivers of goose-filled shafts hanging down by their right side. Their captain, Thomas Chaucer, was pleasant faced and red-cheeked, like some healthy plough boy. He hurried across to introduce himself, as well as to receive Cranston's orders about deployment around the church, to guard every entrance both to that and the priest's house.

'Now for the Flesher,' Cranston declared, 'and for that, Master Chaucer, I need you and three of your finest.'

Chaucer hurried to obey and, escorted by Flaxwith and the cohort, Cranston hammered on the door of the priest's house. The bailiff inside drew the bolts and Cranston swept through into the solar, where Martha lay sleeping on a settle wrapped tightly in blankets. Cranston and Athelstan inspected her carefully, then climbed the stairs, preceded by the four archers, weapons at the ready. They reached the first gallery and Cranston was ushered towards the chamber where the Flesher was imprisoned. The coroner pushed the door open and gestured at Chaucer and his men to help Flaxwith and his bailiffs. At first all was confusion, shouts and cries, furniture kicked and thrown as the Flesher tried to resist. At last he was secured, wrists and ankles lashed with cords. The riffler was then pushed on to a high stool beneath the window, whilst Athelstan and Cranston inspected the bedchamber. The room had been wrecked: caskets and coffers overturned. Small tables and stools smashed. Drapes pulled from the wall. Blankets, coverlets and the tester from the small four-poster bed lay tossed on the floor. The chamber reeked of a fragrant perfume as a table of soaps, oils and creams had been overturned, the jars and dishes crudely stamped on. Athelstan swiftly studied everything. The Flesher, now bound and gagged, eyes bulging with fury, had wrecked the room. Nevertheless, despite all the damage, Athelstan concluded this was a true lady's chamber, with its little-fringed cushions, embroidered cloths, a delicate figurine depicting St Martha and a tray of small painted scent bottles. Athelstan noticed the other items lying around, a pair of leather gloves, a studded wrist guard, and other personal possessions. He picked up the face-cloth smeared with cream and powder, shaking away the crushed shards of the goblets and jug which had been smashed and ground underfoot, the wine snaking its way through the mess which covered the floor.

Cranston, however, was more concerned with the prisoner and, flanked by the captain of archers and one of his men, the coroner crouched down before the Flesher. Athelstan, standing behind Sir John, watched the hideous anger flare in the prisoner's face. Cranston leaned over, took the gag from the riffler's mouth, then held up a gauntleted hand.

'This chamber,' he declared, 'is not the Devil's Oak. It is now part of my court. This is where you committed your hideous crimes and, because of that, you are well and truly trapped. Do you understand?' Cranston hissed. 'You broke into this house, you ravaged and ransacked it, then raped the woman living here.'

'I was welcomed here. Copping will—'

'Copping lies slain in St Benet's, as does Raquin. Both stabbed to the heart like Parson Reynaud and Daventry.'

The Flesher's jaw fell slack and, for the first time, Athelstan glimpsed fear in the riffler's small, crafty eyes.

'How is this?' he whispered.

'Your henchmen are dead, Master Makepeace. Parson Reynaud, Daventry, Raquin and Copping, as is Ingersol.'

'Never heard of him.'

'A stupid reply,' Cranston countered. 'Ingersol was one of yours until he became one of mine. You had him murdered and now, Master Makepeace, see the archers around me, you are under arrest for divers, dire felonies. You will be indicted before the justices at the Guildhall and, believe me, retribution shall be swift.' Cranston edged a little closer. 'Flesher,' he whispered, 'when you are alone in the dungeon beneath the Guildhall, close your eyes, breathe in deeply and wait.'

'For what?'

'The ghosts, Master Makepeace! All the ghosts of those you have barbarously slain over the years. You will see them gather, cluster in the corners, or crawl along the floors and across the ceilings. Flitting dark shapes, hungry for justice to be done. I will even put a lighted candle in the cell; its flame all glowing will lose its golden ring, turning to a dark blue as fire does when the dead draw close.'

The captain of archers glanced quizzically at Athelstan, who just shook his head and raised a finger to his lips. Cranston was giving vent to eighteen years of uncontrolled fury, of a deep, curdling resentment against this devil in human flesh.

'All those ghosts, killer,' Cranston continued, 'trooping into confront you and, once they've gone, Hell's own demons, a horde of them ready to welcome you. What I hope will lead this spectral visitation are the ghosts of those good men killed on *The Song of the Sword* so many years ago.' The Flesher lunged forward, but the cords that Flaxwith's bailiffs had tied so expertly made him wince, so he fell back.

'Now,' Athelstan brought a stool and sat beside Cranston, determined to divert the coroner's rage, 'what did happen this morning? What defence can you offer?' The Flesher, trying to control his breathing, brought his head back as if he was about to spit. 'I wouldn't,' Athelstan warned. 'Tell us what happened today; in return I will do something to ease your confinement, even if it is only a goblet of wine.' The Flesher glared at the friar. 'It's the only way open to you,' Athelstan insisted softly. 'Copping and Raquin do lie dead. In a very short while, the Devil's Oak will be surrounded by royal archers, a cohort of whom now ring St Benet's, its cemetery and this house.' The Flesher's face sagged. 'Come on now,' Athelstan urged. 'Your power is finished. For the first time in your life, someone has held you to account for a great crime. I am no lawyer, but you broke into this house, you ransacked it and you raped an honourable woman, housekeeper to a priest, whatever she may have been in the past. This is someone whom you cannot frighten, silence, or despatch your killers to take care of. So?'

The Flesher took a deep breath. 'I was at the Devil's Oak,' he blurted out. 'Copping said he'd received an urgent message from some street swallow.' The Flesher wetted his lips. 'The urchins whom we hire to take news or a short message. According to him, something had been found here at St Benet's. I was to come most discreetly. The urchin had learnt it by heart. I thought something had been found in the church. So we arrived. Cripplegate, Cotes and Spurnel were not to be seen, so I came up to the house. I asked Martha what was the matter. She acted all flirtatious. She said she had no reason to send any message, that it could be the work of others, but if I wanted to wait for them I was most welcome. She was the Martha of yesteryear, all coy and simpering, and I recalled how she was always a bundle of joy in bed. When the others went across to the church, I joined Martha here in the chamber.'

'And then you raped her?'

'No, she acted all difficult and resisting as she used to when playing the game.'

'Does that include the grievous injuries, scars, weals and welts, not to mention the hideous bruises on her face, and her clothes all torn?'

The Flesher just glared back.

'And the Twelve Apostles?' Cranston grated.

'I know nothing of them or that royal barge.'

Cranston drew his hand back and, before Athelstan could intervene, struck the Flesher a stinging blow across the face. The friar seized the coroner's arm and gently squeezed. 'Yes, yes, I have had enough.' Cranston scraped back the stool. 'Master Chaucer, have the prisoner hooded and masked. He is to be taken immediately to the Guildhall dungeons, where you personally will guard him until my arrival. Oh,' Cranston picked up the gag from the floor and pointed to the Flesher, 'keep him silent, and let none of your escort speak to him or about him.'

Having taken the captain of archers' assurances that all would be as he had ordered, Cranston beckoned Athelstan to follow him down to join the three parishioners seated around the solar table, Flaxwith standing just within the door. Cranston took a generous slurp from the miraculous wineskin, offered it to Athelstan who refused, and then to the chief bailiff who drank and handed it back.

'Congratulations, Sir John.'

'Thank you, Flaxwith. Leave one of your lovely lads to keep an eye on things here. What I want you to do is wrap Mistress Martha in blankets, commandeer a barge and take the poor woman cloaked and cowled across to Benedicta at St Erconwald's. You will do that?' Flaxwith nodded and left.

'Well, gentlemen?' Cranston moved in his chair. 'I shall be blunt and you will return the compliment. Mistress Martha was attacked and raped by the Flesher. She is now being taken to a more restful, safe place. Raquin and Copping have also been despatched, but to their eternal rest. Oh yes,' Cranston nodded at their exclamations of surprise, 'both men were murdered in your church, stabbed to the heart like Parson Reynaud and Daventry. So, sirs, where were you this day?' He leaned over, poking a finger at all three. 'I asked you a question, I demand a reply.'

'We gathered in the taproom of the Golden Boy.'

'Oh, I know the place well,' Cranston grinned. 'A tavern frequented by handsome young men who are also desirous of meeting other handsome young men. And so, why were you there?'

'We were discussing what was to be done here,' Cripplegate sighed. 'And we decided there was, in truth, little we could do.'

'Except now,' Curate Cotes declared, his face all flushed with excitement as well as the after-effects of copious tankards of ale. 'The Flesher has been arrested, hasn't he? Sir John, you are going to indict him and you will need all the witnesses you can gather. Well,' the curate tapped his chest, 'I will be one. I'll take the oath and swear what a true malefactor the Flesher really is.' Cotes shook his fist. 'He's guilty of every sin listed and a few that aren't. He made a mistake, didn't he? He trapped himself. Breaking and entry, ravaging a house and raping a woman; these are felonies worthy of death.'

'Oh, you'll do more than that.'

'Sir John?'

'You will join me in my foray, together with a strong comitatus of archers, to the Devil's Oak. You will be my witnesses. It's time we informed the wolf pack that their leader is caged and bound for death, whilst his lair is about to become mine.'

Athelstan sat at his kitchen table, staring down at the memorandum he'd drawn up for his own reflection. The sudden arrest of the Flesher was now two days old and the news had swept the taverns, alehouses, brothels and stews along the Thames. Already other gang leaders, riffler chieftains such as the Master of the Minions at the Tavern of Lost Souls, were flexing their muscles. The London gangs were on the hunt, sloping through the darkness to see what pickings they could seize. The Flesher's fall had been swift and sudden.

'Like Lucifer,' Athelstan murmured to himself, 'being hurled down, never to rise again. Oh yes, like lightning which strikes in one corner of heaven and lights up the other.'

Athelstan realised that the brutal murders of Parson Reynaud, Daventry, the disappearance of Ingersol, the damage that henchman had wreaked before he was discovered, and now the brutal slayings of Copping and Raquin had greatly weakened the Flesher's mob of malefactors. Moreover, the riffler leader had been taken up and committed to the Guildhall. Any influence he had with the likes of Fitzalan of Arundel or any of the leading citizens of the city faded like snow under the sun. Nobody wished to be associated with a man bound for the gallows. Cranston had proclaimed this message when, escorted by a company of Cheshire archers, he had swept into the great stableyard at the Devil's Oak. Cranston, using all his power as Lord High Coroner, had set up court in the tavern's spacious taproom and issued his proclamations. How the Flesher had been taken up and arrested for the most heinous felonies and that he would soon be indicted before the justices at the Guildhall. Only then did Cranston loose his most deadly arrows. Standing on a stout table, booted feet apart, cloak thrown back so all could see his warbelt, Cranston had warned all and sundry that if an individual associated with the Flesher was named and proclaimed as being involved in any felonious act, he or she would also face indictment and, Cranston cheerfully added, 'a swift ride to meet the hangman at Smithfield. Indeed,' the coroner had continued, 'there was no statute of limitations. The Crown was deeply interested in any information about the treasonable attack on the royal barge *The Song of the Sword* some eighteen years previously. On the other hand,' Cranston had bellowed, 'anyone who turned King's approver and brought information against Simon Makepeace, commonly known as the Flesher, such a person would receive a full and comprehensive pardon for all crimes committed. Finally,' Cranston had paused and beamed around, 'because Simon Makepeace, also known as the Flesher, was a notorious suspect of ill-repute, all his property was now seized and sealed as forfeit to the Crown, which included the Devil's Oak and all it contains.' Cranston stamped his foot. 'Accordingly,' he bellowed, 'I will be leaving a cohort of archers in this tavern to escort everyone from the premises, as well as to ensure you take nothing but your personal property with you.'

Cranston's blunt declaration had provoked uproar, but the coroner didn't give a fig. He stood on the taproom table stamping his foot and gesturing towards the door. The rifflers, leaderless, disorganised and now very fearful, had no choice but to obey. Athelstan had watched them stream out of the tavern before joining Cranston, escorted by two archers, who began a thorough search of the cellars beneath the taproom. The search soon confirmed their suspicions about Fitzalan and the coming Parliament. The cellars were cavernous and crammed with barrels of dried pork, bags of flour, rolls of bacon all cured and spiced, sacks of oatmeal, vats of ale and tuns of wine, all in preparation for Fitzalan's troops occupying St Benet's. In more secret places they also discovered precious items: pouches and purses bulging with good coin; caskets of jewellery and canvas bags containing rolls of precious cloth. Most of these, Cranston wryly observed, were probably the ill-gotten plunder of some robber in the Flesher's pay. Documents, indentures, household books, buttery bills and taproom ledgers were seized. Cranston was almost beside himself with glee, saying he was sure he had enough evidence of crimes and felonies to hang the Flesher a hundred times over, whilst Fitzalan's great scheme, planned and plotted around St Benet's, was nothing more than smoke in the wind. The plot to overawe the November Parliament was completely frustrated. Royal troops would soon occupy St Benet's, whilst Fitzalan would be ordered to appear before the King with the smallest of escorts.

'Of course he won't come,' Cranston murmured, rubbing his hands. 'He'd be too frightened; too wary of falling into Gaunt's hands, of being trapped by Master Thibault.'

Athelstan had returned to Southwark, leaving Cranston very busy at the Guildhall. In the meantime Tiptoft kept appearing in the parish, bringing messages from Cranston. How a number of the Flesher's principal rifflers had become King's approvers, each citing a litany of horrid crimes against their master. One item, however, remained unmentioned. No one had offered even a scrap of information about the attack on *The Song of the Sword*.

'My Lord Cranston,' Tiptoft intoned, 'believes most of those involved are now dead, perhaps even silenced by the Flesher, whilst the prospect of reward and a royal pardon are not viewed as the best protection against the charge of high treason and all that entails. However, Sir John does live in hope—'

'As do I,' Athelstan murmured, pushing away the memorandum and staring at the hour candle. Athelstan was sure the Candlelight-Master and the Luciferi still kept him and his parish under close scrutiny, so what he planned to do within the next hour was fraught with some danger. He pulled across his psalter and opened up at the office of the day. Athelstan read the psalm and recited the prayers until he heard a sound outside. He stood up, crossed himself and walked to the door. Just as he opened it, Mauger appeared with a barrow containing a spade, mattock, hoe, and the pathetic remains of Thaddeus the goat, carefully sewn up in a canvas sheet soaked in pine juice. Benedicta and Crim, each carrying a capped, lighted candle, would act as mourners. Godbless had declared himself too weak and frail for the ceremony.

'Good morrow,' Athelstan smiled. 'Benedicta, how is Mistress Martha?'

'She has now bathed and tended her wounds. Tiptoft brought some fresh clothing from the house, as well as the personal items, caskets and coffers she had asked for.'

'And has she commented on the Flesher's allegations that she acted all flirtatious and coy?'

'She dismisses them as lies. She hates the Flesher and all his kind. She pointed out that Copping and Raquin went down to the church. She thought the Flesher had gone with them and went up to her chamber.'

Athelstan raised a hand. 'Very good. Thank you.' He hurriedly blessed the pathetic remains, slipped back into the house, put on a purple stole and joined the small funeral cortège. The friar led them into the cemetery, along the ancient coffin paths, into a neglected area of God's Acre. Once they'd reached this desolate spot, Athelstan walked beside Benedicta, whispering at her to remain vigilant for the Candlelight-Master or his henchmen. Nevertheless, the cemetery seemed deserted on that deeply autumnal afternoon, with its lowering grey skies, its sharp breezes whipping up the dry leaves into a frenetic dance.

'Father, I think we will deceive anyone who is watching us. We are just a small funeral party carrying out some pathetic burial, but Father, do you know where we are going?'

'I certainly do.' Athelstan urged Crim to turn right, leading them through a mess of gorse which had overgrown the narrow trackway into a small clearing. At the far end stood a grey headstone, weathered and covered in thick, green lichen; some of this had been peeled away to reveal the name 'Artorius'.

'Here we are,' Athelstan declared. Mauger positioned the wheelbarrow, took out the spade and looked at his parish priest expectantly. 'Artorius,' Athelstan repeated, 'the Latin name for a bear. In this case, a poor dancing bear who came with its master to our parish so many years ago and unfortunately died. People thought its name was "Tori"; as you did Benedicta – remember? Of course the lichen hid the full name "Artorius". I discovered this after examining the Book of the Dead, the parish record of who lies buried where.' Athelstan nodded with his head. 'I discovered the headstone, but Margo also knew of it because she spent a great deal of time in God's Acre, be it dressing corpses in the death house or helping at funerals. Of course Margo was also looking for a place to hide a certain treasure. If she chose someone's grave, there was always the danger of that grave being reopened to receive the corpse of a friend or relative. Margo had a sharp mind and a keen wit.

Our God's Acre is broad and sprawling. She did not want to bury the treasure in some unmarked spot and later find she was unable to place it. This, of course, is different.'

'Clever, clever,' Benedicta murmured.

Athelstan gripped the widow woman's arm.

'I believe,' he pointed to the overgrown crumbling earth, 'that this grave contains more than the pathetic remains of a dancing bear.' Athelstan crouched down, sifting the loose soil through his fingers. 'This has been disturbed since our poor bear was buried. Of course when Margo fell into a delirium at St Bartholomew's, she started to think about the treasure and, in her muddled way, made references to the legendary King Artorius, the Latin version of King Arthur, "The once and future King." In her fever, she must have recalled what happened eighteen years ago. Perhaps she was trying to tell us but, never mind . . .'

He got to his feet and raised his voice. 'We shall now commit the remains of poor Thaddeus to the soil and his memory to God. Mauger, start digging,' he lowered his voice to a whisper, 'and be prepared for a surprise.'

The bell clerk began to shovel at the earth, Athelstan advising him to do so most carefully, whilst Crim was ordered to blow out his candle, scamper through the grass and raise the alarm if anyone approached. Mauger sifted away the dirt, the loose soil and gravel and, as he watched, Athelstan recalled God's Acre at St Benet's, those shallow pits with their dirt and fine pebbles. Athelstan closed his eyes as he wondered how that skilled assassin must have worked, using that blighted cemetery to hide what had been done.

'Father?' Athelstan opened his eyes. Mauger was leaning on his spade. 'I've hit something hard.'

Athelstan took off his stole, put down the holy water stoup and the asperger's rod, then joined Mauger in sifting back the dirt. The friar murmured a swift ave as his fingers brushed a piece of leather. Now digging with his hands, Athelstan eagerly pulled at the rotting chancery satchel, battered and fading, the leather now chipped and peeling, its bronze clasps rotten and broken. Athelstan quickly looked inside, then put the satchel on to the wheelbarrow. He asked Mauger to swiftly bury

Thaddeus's remains, fill in the grave, cover what they had discovered and go back to the priest's house.

Once they'd arrived, Athelstan ushered them in. He ordered Mauger to place the chancery satchel on the table, whilst Benedicta made sure the door was locked and bolted. Athelstan then opened the chancery satchel to reveal an exquisitely carved casket which, even under its coating of clay, exuded a unique beauty, with its beautifully worked golden roses and finely etched silver stems. Athelstan took a deep breath and opened the casket. The purple samite cushion inside was stained and dirt-engrained, but even this did not diminish the sheer, brilliant beauty of the eleven different precious stones embedded in the cushion, each with its distinctive shape and colour. Athelstan gently moved the casket and the light piercing the shuttered window made it seem as if the coffer contained its own secret power. Mauger gasped, hand going out to touch the precious stones. Benedicta exclaimed in surprise, whilst Crim danced around the table like a march hare.

'Wealth,' Mauger hissed, 'wealth like I've never seen.'

Athelstan glimpsed the greed flare in the bell clerk's face and abruptly snapped the coffer shut. 'Mauger, on your soul's salvation, do tell anyone what you've seen. Go fetch Sir John immediately. Ask him to bring a cohort of archers. Benedicta, take Crim and ensure Mistress Martha is resting and recovering.'

'And you?'

Athelstan took the casket and placed it under his chancery chair. 'Once you have all gone, Benedicta, I am going to lock and bolt that door, secure the window shutters, sit on that chair and not move until Sir John arrives!'

Once they'd gone, and Athelstan believed he and the treasure were as safe and secure as could be, he leaned back in his chair, closed his eyes and began to meditate, forcing his mind, his heart, his very soul into that sombre, macabre church. 'May the angel who once guarded St Benet's Woodwharf,' he prayed, 'return, lift the darkness and reveal the truth.' Athelstan had written and rewritten his memorandum on the murders and, in doing so, he had fashioned what he called 'certain candles' to lead him deeper into the darkness, to drive back the encroaching gloom of that sinister church and its malevolent mysteries. In his mind's eye Athelstan drifted into St Benet's nave. 'No, no,' he murmured to himself, 'first I must look outside.'

Athelstan recalled those shallow, dirty pits on either side of the church, studying them carefully using the power of his imagination, before moving back into the nave. Athelstan had developed this method when reflecting upon the life of Christ. He would try to picture himself in Pilate's hall or Calvary, where Christ had been crucified. He tried to recreate the scene, the season of the year, the hour of the day and the people who might be present. He did the same now as he entered St Benet's nave and imagined Parson Reynaud sitting on that mercy seat waiting for some parishioner to approach the shriving stool. Or was the parson really waiting for Daventry? Why had Fitzalan's man been found murdered at the other end of the nave? Distant, apart, yet both had been killed by a deep stab wound to the heart. Was this the work of a professional assassin, a man like the Sicarius, Ingersol? What role did he really play in all this? That shadowy, enigmatic figure who drifted in and out of these mysteries as he had the parish of St Benet's? Athelstan imagined the assassin slipping into the nave and felt a shiver of excitement. Was it the Sicarius? Did he survive? Did he have a copy of the Flesher's key ready for use that night? Both that key and the one held by the parson were needed to open the arca, but how did they come together on that particular evening, at that particular time and place? And once the arca was opened, where did such a large amount of money go? How was it moved out? And the corpse of Isabella Makepeace? Again Athelstan recalled that long nave and the line of the cemetery which ran past the devil's door. He must ask Flaxwith to take his ugly mastiff Samson and walk up and down that strip of God's Acre. 'I am sure the solution is there,' Athelstan murmured to himself.

He was still sifting the possibilities when he drifted into a deep sleep, rudely woken by the arrival of a rather boisterous coroner, who swept into St Erconwald's accompanied by a group of knight bannerets of the royal household, resplendent in their gorgeous livery. They led a cohort of Cheshire archers, some Genoese mercenaries skilled in the use of the arbalest, as well as Flaxwith and his comitatus of bailiffs. Cranston, however, would allow no one but himself to enter Athelstan's small house. Athelstan let the coroner stride in then locked and bolted the door behind him. Athelstan put the Rose Casket on the table and pulled back the lid. Cranston gasped in surprise.

'Satan's tits!' he whispered, leaning over and slamming the casket shut. 'The sight of that would tempt the honesty of any man. And the first thing I must do, Athelstan, is get it out of here.'

For a while Cranston busied himself. A steel-bound arca with three intricate clasp locks was unloaded from the cart Cranston had requisitioned. The Rose Casket was placed in the arca, which was locked and sealed, the treasure chest being guarded by the royal knights. Cranston bellowed he would personally ride next to the arca whilst his war horse could trail behind. Of course the arrival of Cranston and his powerful escort turned the parish into a beehive of gossip and constant scurrying about. This was aided and abetted by Jocelyn and Merrylegs, who set up stalls in God's Acre to sell hot, highly spiced pastries and frothing tankards of St Erconwald's ale. Athelstan allowed the eating, drinking and good-natured revelling in God's Acre, though he asked Benedicta to keep a sharp eye on both that and Mistress Martha. Once the arca was loaded and chained securely, Cranston invited himself back into the house, standing by the unshuttered window so he could keep an eye on the cart and its escort. For a while the coroner just stared through the open window, as if obsessed by the arca and all it contained. Athelstan guessed that the coroner was going back to that turbulent, dark night on the Thames when *The Song of the Sword* had been so savagely attacked. At last the coroner gave himself a shake and glanced across at Athelstan.

'The Flesher,' he declared, taking a gulp from the miraculous wineskin, 'Master Thibault had him swiftly arraigned before the justices, and a chorus of King's approvers sang that bastard to his death. He is to hang tomorrow morning at Smithfield.'

'Good lord,' Athelstan whispered, 'so swiftly?'

'Brother, the old King used to dispense justice from horse-back, one hand holding the reins, the other the cross-hilt of his sword. I assure you the condemned were still kicking against the noose as old Edward left. Master Thibault and, of course, my Lord of Gaunt are insistent that judgment be carried out forthwith. They have ordered your parishioner, the Hangman of Rochester, to officiate on the Smithfield gallows.' Cranston paused. 'And they asked you to act as the scaffold priest. I think that would be fitting.' The coroner laughed sharply. 'Moreover, there is no other priest who wants to be even associated with the Flesher. Parson Reynaud was noto-rious, and no cleric wishes to be painted or tainted with the same brush.'

Athelstan held up a hand staring across the room. 'Yes, yes,' he whispered, 'on one condition.'

'Brother?'

'When the Flesher is brought out to be hanged, he is to be closely shaved and shorn before he is placed in the gallows cart.'

PART SEVEN

PART SEVEN

Cage-bird (**Old English**): a prisoner

The execution ground at Smithfield heaved with a throng rarely seen before. The crowd, surging backwards and forwards, had become highly excited, eager to witness what was about to happen. Even the horse traders and cattle sellers had decided there would be no business that day so they had taken down their signs. All of London seemed to have emptied to witness the Flesher hang. The great three-branched scaffold, commonly known as the Elms, the principal gallows, had been well prepared: the long, dark hanging tree rearing up stark against the sky. Braziers flared, their flames leaping greedily. All eyes were on the long, thin ladder propped against the execution post, the 'Judas steps' leading up to the noose, which hung down like some deadly garland at the end of its long rope. The Hangman of Rochester, garbed in black from head to toe, was ready to act as high priest at this grue-some, macabre ceremony. The executioner stood on the edge of the high platform, watching like some tavern host for the arrival of his one and only guest that day.

A sharp, grey morning. The rain had ceased its constant patter, though everything remained wet and slippery. Nevertheless, the grim, grey weather had certainly not curbed either the enthusiasm of respectable citizens or that of the horde of dark-dwellers from the Kingdom of Chaos and the Mansions of Midnight which the Flesher had once ruled. All of London had swarmed out for what was called an 'unholy day'. Miscreants of every kind were eager to watch the hanging of one of their own dark lords: the garishly painted whores in their flame-red wigs and white-plastered faces were hungry for business. These ladies of the night were shepherded by their pimps, garbed in garish rags, sharp, pointed knives pushed through their rope belts, each carrying a small bucket ready to collect the coins of anyone desperate enough to hire a common whore. The conjurors also sought business, clacking their boxes of runes so they could tell the future of anyone stupid enough to believe them. Meanwhile the heralds of the night declared themselves ready to recount blood-chilling stories about the man set to be hanged. Swarms of rifflers ignored these as they pushed their way through, desperate to watch a rival they hated dance in the air as he choked to death. Of course, a hanging whets every appetite, and the itinerant cooks, water-carriers, ale-sellers and wine-carriers bustled about to do business. Guilds and fraternities were also present, chanting psalms and hymns of mourning. The air was riven by chanting, jeering, praying and catcalling. Smoke drifted up from the moveable stoves to mingle with the stench of human sweat and other odours; roasting meat well past its prime, crackling rancid fat, as well as the sweet incense gusting up from thuribles and herb pots. This mass of Londoners could, in the blink of an eye, become an unruly mob, which is why they were cowed by the massed presence of archers and men-at-arms who ringed the scaffold site.

Athelstan, standing behind the Hangman of Rochester, stared out over this surging mass, watching the prisoner and his escort wend their way through the crowd. 'The devil's own carriage,' as the execution cart was called, was surrounded by a screen of men-at-arms, its horses led by the red-garbed custodians of the condemned.

The cart trundled slowly forward and stopped before the steps. The Hangman of Rochester moved back to stand by the ladder. The Flesher, his arms bound, was dragged out. He struggled as he was pushed up the steps, but the archers would take no opposition. The Flesher, shorn and shaved, his ugly face bulging with fury, soon stood in his hanging shroud on the lofty platform. The archers pushed him close to the edge so the condemned man could be seen by the mob, which surged and swirled about like water boiling in a cauldron. All the other riffler leaders, led by the Master of the Minions, had secured the best places beneath the gallows; their henchmen, grouped behind them, screamed a litany of curses, whilst the crowd bellowed its own insults. The Fraternity of the Hanged and the Brotherhood of the Noose tried to chant fresh songs of mourning. Some Friars of the Sack recited the '*De Profundis* – Out of the depths have I cried to you, oh Lord,' but their words were swept away by the raucous noise. The roar of the mob was now constant. The rifflers surged backwards and forwards. A coven of witches, wizards and warlocks fought to get closer, eager to creep beneath the platform, daggers and blades at the ready, for the flesh and clothing of a condemned man were said to contain magical properties, the Flesher's corpse being regarded as a great prize.

The hangman now moved a second thin ladder to rest against one of the gallow branches. He lifted his mask and shouted at the sheriff's men, 'We must do this now or there could be a riot.'

Suddenly a great roar erupted, mingled with curses, jeers and catcalls. Sir John Cranston, who had been overseeing matters at the foot of the scaffold, climbed the steps on to the execution platform. The coroner also sensed the danger. He clapped his hands, shouting at the heralds, who raised their trumpets with a flourish and blew a shrilling fanfare time and time again, until a deep and brooding silence descended like a cloud over Smithfield. A sinister, danger-fraught stillness, as if the milling mob had withdrawn for a moment but was watching, waiting, ready to spring. The trumpet fanfares trailed off. One of the sheriff's men, in a bellowing voice, proclaimed, 'How Simon Makepeace, also known as the Flesher, had been judged guilty of heinous felonies and was worthy of death with no hope of pardon so sentence should be carried out immediately.'

The hangman moved with alacrity. Grasped by the archers, the Flesher was pushed up one ladder whilst the hangman scaled the one next to it. He reached the top rung and, balancing himself carefully, fitted the noose around the Flesher's neck, positioning the knot carefully behind the left ear. He then checked the rope. Once satisfied, the hangman hurriedly descended, the archers likewise, leaving the condemned man, his hands tightly bound, perched on the top rung. A drum began to beat. The hangman seized the ladder the Flesher was perched on and abruptly twisted it. The Flesher fell like a stone and the crack of his breaking neck could be clearly heard. A great sigh echoed from the crowd, a prolonged gasp of breath as this mass of people marked the end of the Flesher's notorious, sinful life. For a few moments total silence, eventually broken by desultory jeering and catcalling. Such insults soon faded as the crowd broke up, now interested in what else might be going on. Athelstan asked the hangman to cut the corpse down.

'I think it's to be gibbeted on the approach to London Bridge, Father.' The hangman lifted his sweat-soaked mask. 'Anyway, those were the orders given to me.'

'Let the friar bless the corpse.' Cranston walked over. 'And I want to scrutinise it. I just want to make sure this sinner has truly gone to God; though,' the coroner added ruefully, 'I heard his neck crack. It was a great mercy for him.' He tossed a coin at the hangman who deftly caught it. 'You showed him more compassion than he did his victims.'

Cranston turned away as a disturbance broke out close to the steps leading up to the execution platform. A coven of warlocks and witches, garbed in their dusty black robes, knives at the ready, were once again trying to creep beneath the scaffold, determined to reach the Flesher's corpse which was being laid out for inspection and blessing. The coroner frightened these away. Athelstan went over and knelt by the cadaver. The Flesher's head was strangely twisted, his ugly face, mottled red and blue, seemed even more grotesque. Athelstan blessed the dead man's body, then asked the hangman to lift the grey linen shroud cloth. Athelstan tried to ignore the sheer ugliness of the corpse as he inspected the dead Flesher's hands, arms, chest, back and face. At last he pronounced himself satisfied. However, he continued to kneel by the corpse, lost in his own thoughts, until a black, glossy-winged raven floated down, only to be beaten off by the hangman. Athelstan crossed himself, rose and told the coroner he was finished. He walked to the edge of the scaffold, watching the crowd disperse as well as half listening to Cranston's instructions. How the Flesher's corpse was to be gibbeted not on the approaches of London Bridge, but in the stableyard of the Devil's Oak tavern.

'A warning,' Cranston grated, 'and a clear proclamation of what has happened.'

'And the Rose Casket? The Twelve Apostles?' Athelstan asked.

'Don't you worry about them, little friar, they are in the kingdom's strongest arca, the Tower of London, guarded by men of the royal household. The Candlelight-Master and the Luciferi have already made their presence felt. Discussions have opened, but those do not concern either you or me, my friend.'

'Sir John, I agree. However, we are not yet finished our business. I need your help. So listen and do so carefully.'

Two days after the Flesher's execution, Athelstan convened what he called 'his own Inquisicio' or Inquisition, after the Jesus Mass in St Erconwald's. Cranston and Benedicta had been invited; Martha the housekeeper, Cripplegate, Curate Cotes and Spurnel were also summoned. Flaxwith and his bailiffs guarded all entrances to the church, in particular the sanctuary where Athelstan had set up this 'Inquisicio'.

He slouched on a stool with the heavy, intricately carved sanctuary chair set before him. Cranston and Benedicta sat on one wall bench, the parishioners of St Benet's on the other. Athelstan intoned the 'Veni Creator Spiritus – Come Holy Spirit;' he blessed all assembled and invited Martha to sit on the spacious sanctuary chair. The housekeeper, garbed in a simple Lincoln-green gown, her lustrous hair covered by a white gauze veil, walked across. She sat down carefully, looking pale and nervous. Her face still bore the effects of the Flesher's attack.

'Brother Athelstan,' she sat rigid in the chair, 'why have you summoned me? Why am I placed here?'

'I have not, Mistress, you have brought about this confront-ation. You are a murderess. You have slaughtered four men and, although I admit they may have been worthy of death, you are still a killer. You are an assassin.' Athelstan raised a hand to still her protests and those of others. 'Mistress Martha, you are bruised from head to toe, the work of the Flesher. However,' Athelstan leaned forward, 'two days ago I scrutinised the Flesher's corpse. He attacked you, yes?' She nodded. 'You resisted, yes?' Again the nod. 'Then tell me, Martha, you are still fairly young and vigorous, you have sharp teeth and even sharper nails. You claimed to have fought furiously, yet I could find no cut or mark on him. Why not?'

Martha just stared back. 'A man attacked you,' Athelstan insisted, 'a veritable brute, a wild animal. You resisted, so you said. But again, there's no sign of that on him. I asked for him to be shorn and, after he was hanged, I inspected the Flesher's corpse from head to toe. I found nothing.'

'He was violent—'

'And you could have been equally violent back, but you weren't. You calculated, quite rightly, that if you laid your allegations swiftly, the law would act, the Flesher would be exposed and left vulnerable. After all, his lawyer Master Copping and his henchman Raquin were dead, murdered by you, of course; whilst he'd been caught red-handed in a crime, the victim of which could not be frightened or cowed. The Flesher had no real defence whatsoever. You planned it carefully, Mistress, as you planned so many things.'

'This is preposterous,' Curate Cotes spluttered.

'You will remain silent,' Cranston snapped. 'Brother?'

'Martha Ashby,' Athelstan continued, smiling gently, 'married as a young girl to a sickly locksmith. He died, and you had no choice but to enter the House of Delights some nineteen years ago. Whatever your gifts or talents, you worked there most reluctantly. You were looking for a way out when you met a young soldier, a Tower archer named Walter Grenel. Both of you fell in love, but there was a problem. Walter was from a respectable family, yet he was consorting with what others would call a common whore. Accordingly, his meetings with you were kept secret. Walter would leave the Tower, or his mother's cottage in Southwark, and go into Queenhithe. I suspect both of you met in the darkness of St Benet's nave, a most suitable place to hide, to talk, to kiss and caress. During one of these meetings, he probably saw the same wall painting I did. The paint is now faded, but it's still a vivid celebration of the story of Lazarus, Jesus' friend, who lived in the small village of Bethany outside Jerusalem with his two sisters—'

'Mary and Martha,' Cotes interjected. 'That's your name, Mistress, but Walter used that painting to hide your true name and calling: Martha from the House of Bethany. He was talking about you. It was his way of hiding the fact that his sweetheart was a—'

'Enough!' Athelstan snapped. 'Mistress Martha may be many things, but she was not, is not, a whore. Young Walter was deeply smitten, wasn't he Martha? And you,' Athelstan pointed a finger, 'had an unwilling hand in what later happened. I say unwilling, because anything else would be truly heinous. You learnt from Walter how a company of Tower archers, himself included, had been summoned to collect something very valuable.'

'Oh Lord and his angels.' Cripplegate got slowly to his feet and walked towards Martha. Sexton Spurnel made to follow, but Cranston shouted at both men to sit down, which they did so hurriedly.

'We were given orders that we were to man the royal barge *The Song of the Sword* on the morning before that night attack. The only other piece of information,' Cripplegate waved a hand, 'is that we were to collect something from a Hanseatic ship.'

'*The Glory of Bremen*?'

'True, true,' Cranston interrupted. 'Only I knew what we were actually receiving, that was made known to me under the Secret Seal. But the Flesher, and I am sure he was responsible for the attack, would have received information from other quarters, some Judas eager for his thirty pieces of silver. The Flesher must have heard how the French had been forced to hand over the Rose Casket and the Twelve Apostles and he would plot their robbery. A scrap of information here, another scrap there and, of course, you don't have to be a brilliant master of logic to see what was happening. A royal barge, manned by myself and a select cohort collecting something valuable from a Hanseatic ship at the dead of night on the Thames?'

'You, you . . .' Spurnel waved a fist at Martha.

'You ruined our lives!' Cotes snarled.

Martha just sat, head down.

'I truly believe,' Athelstan continued, 'you did not act in malice. You simply made a most dreadful mistake. Walter did the same. A young, romantic archer. He wished to show off. He wanted to demonstrate how important he truly was. He probably told you that he could not meet you. How he was unable to keep an assignation with his sweetheart from the House of Bethany because he'd been summoned to serve on board a royal barge, despatched to receive something precious from a Hanseatic ship. You, Martha, a young woman, unaware of the encroaching darkness, must have informed someone in the Flesher's household. Simon Makepeace would simply match that information with what he'd received elsewhere, hence the attack.'

'I would agree,' Cranston spoke up. 'The English Crown's demand for the Rose Casket and the Twelve Apostles was public knowledge. You've seen them, Athelstan, truly beautiful. Every one of them is worth a king's ransom.'

'You now know that, Martha,' Athelstan returned to his indictment. 'You later realised the hideous mistake you'd made. The great battle along the river became common knowledge. I am sure it was discussed in the House of Delights, as it was in the ale booths and taverns both sides of the Thames, but what could you do? You secretly mourned your love. You hid your most grievous hurt. You accepted the hideous damage which you had unwittingly inflicted, but what else? Admit that you were involved in a treasonable act? Who would believe your innocence? You would have been accused of sending your lover to his death, as well as a litany of other heinous crimes. You probably sensed that young Walter would never be returning, that his corpse either lay in the muddy roots of the Thames or was swept out to sea. Within the year you left the House of Delights. You tried to compose yourself as the respectable housekeeper to the priest of your parish. A humdrum existence, yet during it your resentment and hatred for the Flesher only deepened. You mourned. You lusted for revenge, but you could do nothing until Eudo Ingersol, the Sicarius, broke into your life.'

Athelstan paused. Martha was sitting rigidly, yet deeply agitated, fighting to control her tears. 'Ingersol was the

Flesher's emissary to St Benet's. A dark shadow of a man who slipped in and out until he met you. Once again you fell in love. You hated the Flesher. You wanted to be free of his world and so did Ingersol. This only deepened the bond between you. As you know, Ingersol turned traitor, asking Sir John here for a pardon and licence, the opportunity to be free of London and Queenhithe, permission to go where he wished, protected by the Crown. He wanted this for himself and one other – that was you. Yes?' Athelstan paused, staring at Martha who was lost in her own world. 'You both contrived a plot to injure the Flesher and inflict great damage on him. You would rob the arca and take the Flesher's ill-gotten gains to support your new life. Of course, the real obstacle was the arca and its unique locks, one key being held by the Flesher and the other by Parson Reynaud. Eventually you made a decision. You knew the House of Delights, the Flesher's love of bathing in a tub of hot water, his skin cleaned with precious tablets of Castilian soap. You would use that and perhaps the soft, pure beeswax candles which illuminated the bath chamber. After all, both you and Ingersol knew exactly what happened there. You would seize your opportunity and use the candles or the soap to create a duplicate key. And then, by some means, fair or foul, also seize that held by Parson Reynaud. The old priest would not be so difficult.'

'If Copping was here,' Martha glanced up, 'that lawyer would argue that you have words but no proof.'

Despite Martha's paleness, her obvious anxiety and fear, Athelstan caught the mockery in the woman's voice.

'Oh, we shall come to that by and by, Mistress. But to repeat, we were talking about Ingersol. You fell in love for the second time in your life. And, for the second time, your beloved was destroyed by the Flesher. Simon Makepeace was a cunning bastard, well served by Copping and Raquin. At some time, Ingersol made a dreadful mistake and the Flesher discovered that his loyal henchman was hand in glove with Sir John here.'

'And he certainly was,' Cranston interjected.

'Of course,' Athelstan continued, 'Ingersol paid the price, killed barbarously. Another great love of your life snuffed out swift as a candle flame. Somehow you knew Ingersol would never return, so you plotted a most hideous revenge. You would use all the skills you'd been taught. Ingersol, an experienced street fighter, would have feared for your safety. He gave you one of his weapons: an Italianate dagger of subtle design, bone-handled with a cleverly disguised lever to press so that a blade, long, pointed and serrated, would leap out like a dancing flame. He would instruct you on how to draw close to your victim. On reflection you needed little education after your stay in the House of Delights, which honed all the skills necessary for the bedchamber. You watched and you waited. You had the dagger as well as a copy of the Flesher's key to the arca. I suspect he never discovered what had happened. He probably thought that by murdering Ingersol he had nipped any future problem in the bud . . .'

'Lord save us.' Cripplegate would have sprung to his feet, but Cranston growled and he hurriedly sat down.

'On the night of the murders,' Cripplegate exclaimed, 'we left the parish. No one else was expected, either at the church or the priest's house. The only other person beside Martha were the parson and Daventry.'

'She had certainly planned a harvest of vengeance,' Athelstan agreed. 'She chose the night Isabella Makepeace was churched because that woman's corpse was part of her vengeance.' Athelstan pointed at the three parishioners. 'You gentlemen left the church precincts. Thanks to Sir John, we know where you were that night and who you were with, but not you, Mistress. Forget the story of retiring early to bed; you were plotting furiously. You are a mummer, Martha, and you can change your appearance and your manner. A bright gown, a painted face, ready to act all coy and welcoming for the parson and Daventry. I am sure that you promised them sexual favours, taking each man carefully aside. However, not in the house where Curate Cotes or someone else may visit. What better place than a lonely, dark church? Parson Reynaud would act as if he was to shrive penitents, Daventry would be told to wait in the shadows. I doubt if either of them knew what was really happening. You are a consummate lover, Martha, a skilled practitioner in bedroom skills, a wearer of Venus's triple crown. You separated Daventry from the parson. You promised to confer your favours on both of them and they were to wait for you in the church. We know that Parson Reynaud was hot and lecherous for you, whilst a man like Daventry would never refuse such a gift.'

'Unbelievable—' Sexton Spurnel interjected.

'Oh, most logical,' Athelstan cut across the sexton. 'On that night Mistress Martha moved most swiftly. She'd made other preparations but first she had to deal with the living before she dealt with the dead. She crept into the church and softly knelt in front of Parson Reynaud. He expected to fully enjoy her. Martha all smiling and charm, drew very close. In her right hand the Sicarius's dagger. She lifts her head up and, as she does, presses the lever and drives the blade in one swift, killing blow into the parson's heart. Any of you who has served in battle knows such a direct blow kills instantly. No protest, no screaming. Who knows, perhaps Martha covered the parson's mouth as she watched the life glow in the priest's eyes turn to the dull, glassy stare of the dead.

'Martha is well prepared. She wipes the blade on a cloth and hurries, quiet as a shadow, down the nave, where she has told Daventry to sit on the sexton's chair just inside the main door. The nave is long and dark; night is creeping in. Daventry had not seen or heard what had happened at the far end of the church. He would not even imagine it. All he sees is this lovely woman, who has been furtively flirting with him, hurry through the murk to gladden his evening. He is ready, he has unstrapped his warbelt and it lies on the floor beside him. He squats, legs apart, and allows Martha to kneel before him. Martha, you undo the points on his hose. Daventry leans towards you and you strike as fast and fatal as any viper. The Sicarius had taught you well. Another thrust to the heart. You clean the knife, you refasten the points on Daventry's hose, but you are hurrying and you do not do it correctly, I noticed that.'

Athelstan rose to his feet, walking backwards and forwards across the sanctuary. He pointed at Martha. 'Now you turn on the dead. You have Parson Reynaud's keys. You lock that church, make it secure except for the corpse door. You wrench the coffin open and, armed with both keys to the arca, you enter the sacristy and remove the sacks of coins from the chest. Night has fallen. You then do something very subtle and devious. I forget the actual Latin tag, but when translated it reads, "to hide in full view".'

'What!' Curate Cotes exclaimed.

Athelstan just shook his head as he retook his seat. 'Now, it's logical to assume,' he continued, 'that if you have stolen a corpse and intend to hold it for ransom, you would take it to your own very secret place, a stratagem emphasised by reading that note pinned to the empty coffin. Of course, the ransom never happened. You just wanted to hide Isabella Makepeace's corpse and you did so in full view.'

'Where?' Cripplegate demanded.

'Why in God's Acre at St Benet's . . . I noticed,' Athelstan cleared his throat, 'all those pits with mounds of earth beside them. You used one of those many barrows or handcarts which stand around the cemetery to take both the remains and the coins to pits nearest the corpse door: that's where Sir John found them. You buried them there and then returned to the church, locking the door behind you, as you had sealed every other entrance to that benighted church.'

'It's not possible!' Cripplegate declared.

'Oh yes it is,' the sexton interjected.

'You are right,' Athelstan agreed. 'Martha knows that cemetery like the back of her hand. She may have even prepared the pits earlier in the day, only a few yards from the corpse door. To all appearances, just another two mounds amongst many. Who would even think the robber, the violator, would hide his plunder so close?'

'Brother . . .' Cripplegate made to get up, but Cranston loudly coughed and he sat back down.

'Master Cripplegate?'

'Brother, is it true Sir John has found both corpse and coins?'

'Not me personally,' Cranston answered cheerfully. 'Samson, Flaxwith's dog, he has a nose for corpses. Brother Athelstan had a suspicion and Samson proved him correct. Admittedly,' Cranston shrugged, 'it took some time. The corpse was covered in roses which had rotted; their pungent smell masked that of decay, but Samson has the keenest nose . . .'

'And the money?'

'A matter of logic,' Cranston replied. 'If the corpse was buried beneath one of those mounds, why not the money? We searched and we found.'

'Very cunning,' Cotes called out. 'Remember, Mistress, you were the one who claimed it would be highly unlikely that the thief, the assassin, would hide the corpse and coins in or around St Benet's.'

'Hidden in full view,' Athelstan agreed. 'Martha, you didn't really care. You just wanted to hurt the Flesher, inflict as much injury as possible. You were determined he would never recover either his treasure or his mother's corpse.' Athelstan paused as Martha smiled to herself.

'He was hurt,' she whispered, 'grievously so. But what proof do you have that I was responsible?'

'In a while,' Athelstan retorted. 'But on that night you have slain Reynaud and Daventry and stolen both the coins and the corpse. You now move back into the church to set your seal of mystery on those gruesome events. All the doors are locked and bolted. You have replaced one of the arca keys back on the chain around Reynaud's neck. You hold the ring of keys taken from the pocket of his robe. All is finished. You leave the church by the corpse door. You lock it, then insert a pebble you have picked up from the path that will obstruct any attempt to open it in the morning. Only then do you retire to bed.' Athelstan paused, staring down at the ground. 'Clever,' he murmured. 'Oh so very clever. Martha, you are a woman of so many talents.'

'Only in love,' Martha told him. 'Only in love.'

'And so the next morning,' Athelstan continued, 'Martha rises and robes herself. In her pocket she holds the keys and a small metal rod. She prepares herself and hurries out. She has to be first at the devil's door; she carries the key to that.' Athelstan shrugged. 'You know what happened next . . .'

'We broke into the church through the devil's door,' the curate declared. 'We did that at Martha's behest; it was the most logical thing to do. The other doors were of solid oak.'

'The devil's door was panelled, slats of wood easy to remove,' Athelstan agreed. 'And so you break in. You know what you saw. Martha, however, moved swiftly. She hurries to the corpse door and, hidden in that shadowy transept, she draws across the bolts and pushes in the small rod to remove the pebble. She then hastens across to the chantry chapel where Parson Reynaud sits stabbed to the heart, and slips the ring of keys into the pocket of his robe.'

'Yes, yes,' the sexton broke in, 'when we entered the church, all was confusion and scurrying about. Martha, you were flitting here and there like a bat caught in the light.'

'So easy,' Athelstan agreed, 'that long, dark, shadow-filled nave. You three men were startled and shocked out of your wits. Martha, of course, knew exactly what she had to do. Not much: draw across well-oiled bolts, push a pebble out of a lock and slip keys into the pocket of a dead man's robe.' Athelstan pointed at Martha, sitting pale-faced but still composed. 'You'd inflicted grave injury, but were eager to deliver the killing blow when circumstances were in your favour. The Flesher was responsible for the murder of the two great loves of your life and you were determined to settle for both. Oh, by the way,' Athelstan leaned forward, 'I must tell you; we have just given the first of your beloveds, Walter Grenel, a proper Christian burial.'

Martha abruptly lifted her head and, for a moment, swayed in the chair, until she caught its arms, pressing down against them.

'I don't know what—'

'Sir John,' Athelstan turned to the coroner, 'tell Martha what we found in Margo Grenel's cottage. Oh, by the way,' Athelstan gestured at the three men who seemed equally shocked, 'this will stay confidential. Sir John?'

In a few pithy sentences, Cranston described the last few hours of Walter Grenel's life, and how his corpse had been embalmed and hidden away. Athelstan ignored the exclamations of the three men, as did Cranston: the coroner compelled them to swear on the crucifix Flaxwith produced that they would keep this information secret as if it was a matter for the confessional. Athelstan concentrated on Martha, and any doubts about his indictment against her crumbled away. The housekeeper sat back in the sanctuary chair truly shocked, eyes staring wildly, mouth gaping. She had lost all her poise, that calm demeanour which constantly masked her every glance and word. She tried to speak but the words caught in her throat. She blinked furiously, shaking her head, as if trying to concentrate on what Cranston had told her.

'I didn't know, I never knew.' She waved a hand. 'Brother, you'd best continue.' Her voice was strained and hoarse.

'And so I shall, Martha. You were determined on the Flesher's death, but not at your hands. He was to die publicly in hideous disgrace. You'd learnt from Ingersol how many were coming to resent the riffler lord. How the cup of wickedness he'd filled was brimming over. The Flesher had committed foul crimes, but any victim who survived dared not protest. You were different. You bided your time.' Athelstan paused to sip from a beaker of water Cranston had brought over. The coroner had finished taking the vows of silence and came to stand beside Athelstan.

'Your vengeance,' Athelstan declared, 'began the night Flaxwith sent you a message that, on the morrow, he was to bring the corpses of five malefactors and two war dogs for exposure on the steps of St Benet's. Master Bailiff, that is correct?'

'It is,' Flaxwith replied, from where he stood guarding the entrance to the rood screen. 'News about what had happened at St Erconwald's had swept the city and Queenhithe ward. After all, parishioners like Watkin have kin there.'

'True, true,' Cripplegate called out. 'Everyone knew. Many rejoiced but all hid their glee.'

'Circumstances,' Athelstan continued, 'do conspire to impede but also to help. You, Mistress, recognised that the Flesher had been greatly discomfited. He would be wary of appearing publicly in St Benet's after such a setback. You sent a message with a street swallow. The urchin was to inform the Flesher that something had been discovered in St Benet's and that he should come immediately to discover what it was. The Flesher was ensnared. He was desperate for any news about both the missing corpse and his stolen monies. He had little to fear. St Benet's was boarded up, in a sense derelict, which is why he would be accompanied only by Copping and Raquin the killer. The Flesher believed he'd be safe enough. The pack at the Devil's Oak was not too far away, easy to whistle up, and what could the Flesher fear from you three sirs or pretty Martha?' Athelstan smiled at the housekeeper, who was still clearly shocked at what she had learnt. The friar suspected that she was brimming with questions, but dared not ask them, as it would prove Athelstan was correct.

'We were absent,' Cripplegate declared. 'We intended to visit the parish late that afternoon.'

'Whatever,' Athelstan went on, 'on that fateful morning, the Flesher swaggers in. You, Martha, bedecked in all your glory, and I shall come to that later, welcomed him warmly; it was just like the old days. You flirt using all your undoubted skill, charm and experience. The Flesher is roused. A man with a brutal, impetuous appetite, he walks deeper into the trap. At your insistence – after all, you cannot do anything while they are present – Copping and Raquin are despatched to St Benet's; they could squeeze themselves through the devil's door. The Flesher then follows you up to your bedchamber. You are now in full flower, ever so seductive. You serve him a goblet of wine, but then claim you have something to collect from the church. You also want Copping and Raquin to stay there, as they are marked down for slaughter. You ask the Flesher will he wait? And, of course, he is only too eager. You slip out of the house, in your hand the dagger Ingersol gave you. Once in the church, Raquin and Copping think you are on some errand for their master.'

'And by chance I found them separate? I deal with them one after the other?' Martha paused, realising what she had conceded.

'Separate?' Athelstan queried. 'Who told you that they were separated when they were killed? Did I? Did Sir John or Flaxwith?'

'I learnt later.'

'Nonsense, Martha. You've been here in St Erconwald's since we brought you from St Benet's that morning.' Athelstan turned to the three parishioners. 'Have any of you discussed the deaths of Raquin and Copping with Martha?'

They shook their heads, grunting their denials. 'So back to that church, Martha. You are confident and flirtatious. You tell Copping that the Flesher wants the sacristy searched just in case something can be found.' Athelstan pulled a face. 'A message, or something similar to that, which at the time would make sense. No matter. Those two men wouldn't have the slightest suspicion about what you intended. Copping goes off to the sacristy, you lead Raquin into that chantry chapel. You flirt and tease. Raquin cannot believe his good fortune: this lovely woman acting so welcoming. You draw close. Raquin is seduced and distracted. You drive that dagger straight into his heart, swift as a lunging cat. Copping is in the sacristy. He has not seen or heard anything untoward. Again, you draw close, any excuse. Then you strike. Copping collapses, dying almost immediately. To confuse matters further, you draw Copping's knife and place it near his hand. Once satisfied, you hurry back to Raquin, huddled in that corner. You unsheathe both sword and dagger, and position them as if Raquin had at least armed himself against his killer. Of course, it was all pretence, a way of diverting suspicion, indicating that both men had the opportunity to confront their assassin before they died.'

Athelstan shrugged. 'Who would ever have dreamt that their opponent was the sweet, docile Martha?' Athelstan stared at the housekeeper. 'So it was, so it was,' he murmured. 'You'd slaughtered the Flesher's henchmen and returned to the priest's house, where you accepted the Flesher's violent embraces. Painful, humiliating, but the reward was great. Your bedchamber makes an excellent prison: its window is narrow and the door of solid oak. You escape and wait. Flaxwith is coming and you know these three gentlemen here will also be arriving. Meanwhile, at the Devil's Oak, none of the wolf pack would ever dream about what was happening to their master. Moreover, they would be fearful of approaching St Benet's whilst those corpses were being exposed.'

Martha stretched out her hands as if closely studying them, then she lifted her head. 'And the proof for all this, Brother Athelstan?'

'Proof? Oh, I concede you will have to be put to the

question in the press yard at Newgate.' Athelstan steeled himself as the woman flinched in fear. 'Sir John believes there is enough to draw up and present a bill of indictment before King's Bench at Westminster. I am sure the Justices of Oyer and Terminer, not to mention the specially convoked jury, will rule there's more than a case to answer. As for proof? Well, on the night Daventry and the parson were murdered, you were the only one in St Benet's. Our three worthies over there were ensconced in another tavern. We now know that. Ingersol is dead. None of the Flesher's coven had a hand in these mysteries.' Athelstan pointed directly at her. 'You were the only one there. You had the keys, the means, as well as extensive knowledge about St Benet's and its cemetery. Moreover, only someone like you could get close to Parson Reynaud and a fighting man such as Daventry, whose points you were undoing as you edged nearer to stab him. Martha, you also had the motive. By your own admission, you hated the Flesher and all his works—'

'And the next day,' Cripplegate shouted, 'you led us all by the nose.'

'Yes, I think she did,' Athelstan agreed. 'On the morning after, Martha was waiting for you at the devil's door ready to give advice on what to do. The same proof covers the murders of Raquin and Copping. Who else was there? St Benet's was totally deserted, indeed shunned by others. Martha,' Athelstan was determined to bluff his way forward if that was the only path to the truth, 'Sir John, with the help of Flaxwith, has found the street swallow who took your message to the Flesher.'

'I didn't, I . . .' Her voice faltered.

'Yes you did,' Athelstan retorted. 'Let us move on. Copping and Raquin? Who would they allow to draw so close? Who was there to make that approach?'

'Surely they drew their weapons?' she whispered, 'I mean, Raquin was a dagger man.'

'I have asked you this before,' Athelstan replied. 'How do you know those two men were found separate? You have given no satisfactory answer.'

'And you made another mistake.' Cranston took up the questioning as Athelstan drank from the beaker.

'Sir John?'

'When we were comforting you in the priest's house after the Flesher's attack, Flaxwith informed us that Copping and Raquin lay murdered in St Benet's. Brother Athelstan and I were shocked, surprised. You said nothing at all about such startling news. On reflection, little wonder: you already knew. You were responsible for their deaths.'

'I have already referred to further proof,' Athelstan continued. 'I found no signs, no marks, no bruise on the Flesher's corpse, not even a scratch. No sign, no indication that you tried to defend yourself from his brutal assault. Moreover, when I first met you after the Flesher's attack, your face was unpainted. However, when I went into your chamber, I noticed face-cloths smeared with fresh creams and powder. You used those cloths to remove the paint you carefully applied when you were preparing to seduce the Flesher. I also noticed the jug of rich claret and the two goblets lying smashed on the bedchamber floor. Why should there be a jug and two wine cups in your bedchamber? Of course, that was all part of your plot to provoke the Flesher's lust for you. Then,' the friar added softly, 'there's your reaction to our discovery of Walter Grenel's corpse. You were lovers, weren't you? He gave you his wrist guard, the insignia of a Tower archer as a keepsake. Martha, we found it in your chamber. We have it now and it's only a matter of time before our searchers discover the dagger Ingersol gave to you, the one used to kill those four men in St Benet's. Afterwards you hid it away before we arrived. Since that day you have not returned to St Benet's. Consequently that dagger must be hidden, concealed somewhere in the priest's house. Rest assured, we shall find it.'

'You will be arrested,' Cranston intoned, 'taken to the condemned hold at Newgate, the justices will question you closely. Or,' he paused, 'the money stolen from the arca has been recovered. The four men you killed were either felons, associates of notorious felons, or involved in plotting serious felonies against the King's peace. Mistress Martha, in return for your full and truthful confession, there will be no trial, no questioning. You will be despatched to a convent and immured there for life. A comfortable enough existence. You will be well looked after and cared for, but you will never leave that convent alive. Mistress,' Cranston walked across and patted Martha on the shoulder, 'the choice is yours.'

Athelstan remained silent. Cranston and he had agreed to allow Martha a path to the truth by her own confession. She would be given the choice to escape brutal imprisonment and the full rigour of the law at the Elms in Smithfield. The silence deepened. Curate Cotes made to speak but Cranston snapped his fingers and shook his head.

'Can I visit his grave?' Martha lifted her head. 'Can I visit Walter's grave? I would love to. I need to say farewell to at least one of my loves.'

'Of course.'

'And Brother Athelstan,' she raised her head, her face all tear-streaked, 'what Sir John promised?'

'It will be that way.'

'I confess.' Martha crossed herself. 'I confess to a deep,' her voice turned brittle hard, 'lasting detestation and hatred for that devil incarnate Simon Makepeace.' She drew a deep breath. 'I loved Walter Grenel, he loved me. He even gave me his precious wrist guard as a token. He told me, on the morning before he disappeared, how he had been chosen for a very important but secret task, the removal of something precious from a Hanseatic ship, *The Glory of Bremen*. He and others, under Sir John Cranston, were to transport it by barge to the Tower. I was young, immature and stupid. I babbled like a brook and the news must have been passed on to the Flesher. Only long afterwards did I fully realise the effect of what I'd done. But it was too late for anything but grief.' She raised a hand. 'You know the rest. I felt I was in a nightmare but I hid my sorrow, my love, as I did my growing hatred for the Flesher. I kept myself as free as I could from his filthy world. Then Eudo Ingersol entered my life. To put it bluntly, I fell deeply in love with him.'

'You fooled us,' Cotes sang out.

'That was and still is very easy,' Martha retorted. 'We would meet down in that ghostly crypt. Parson Reynaud was correct, no one ever went there.'

'And you plotted your escape?'

'And our revenge, Brother. Eudo would secretly become a
King's approver, betraying the Flesher at every twist and turn.
I encouraged him to approach you, Sir John. I had learnt how
the Flesher and Raquin hated you but also greatly feared you.'

'Good,' Cranston grunted. 'They had good cause to.'

'You know what happened, Sir John. Eudo handed over
valuable information. Both of us prayed, desperate to get the
Crown's protection and licence to go abroad. Of course we
needed money and we dreamed of robbing the arca at St
Benet's. I know I could inveigle Parson Reynaud, use my skills
to seize his key, at least for a while. The Flesher's was a
different matter . . .'

'Eudo made a cast of it at the House of Delights?'

'No, Brother, he made two. One with soap of the purest
kind, the second with beeswax. Eudo acted all dark and secretive but, in truth, he was a merry soul. He thought it was
highly amusing that whilst the Flesher disported himself in
candlelight, being bathed with the purest soap, we would use
both to cast a key and so rob his arca. Eudo was successful,
he travelled to Colchester to get this fashioned.'

'But the Flesher discovered what his henchman had done?'

'No, Brother, he did not. Eudo was very careful. Of course
the Flesher and Raquin realised they were being betrayed. They
believed you, Sir John, was closely involved. For a while they
watched their retainers, the Sycamores, but eventually, from the
little I learnt, they turned their attention to you.'

'Oh Lord save us,' Cranston murmured.

'He may well do, Sir John, but not Eudo. They watched
you meet him and that was it. One day Eudo was supposed
to visit me, then he didn't. Nothing at first but, as the days
passed, I heard rumours. On more than one occasion I eaves-
dropped on Parson Reynaud, the Flesher and Raquin. I realised
what had happened. My hatred became more acute, my desire
for vengeance more sharp. I just waited for the opportunity.
Eudo had told me how the Flesher was ripe for a fall. He'd
also given me his second dagger and showed me how to use
it.' She smiled thinly. 'I had all the skills and experience necessary to draw close to a man.' Her grin widened, as if she were
talking to herself. 'Eudo was correct. It was so very, very easy.

One deep thrust, then step back and watch them die.' She
shrugged. 'For the rest, Brother Athelstan, what you've said
is true. I can add very little to it. You'll find the dagger in a
pouch in the mattress of my bedchamber.' Martha rose
unsteadily to her feet. 'You have what you need. I cannot
answer any more questions. I must see Walter's grave, please?'

Athelstan nodded at Cranston, who told Flaxwith to take
his bailiffs and follow Benedicta. The widow woman would
show them where Walter was buried. The coroner also
dismissed Cripplegate and his two colleagues, warning them
to keep away from St Benet's. At last the church emptied, the
silence deepening. Cranston walked over to the lady chapel
to light a taper. Athelstan knelt beneath the pyx. He was deep
in prayer when the main door was abruptly flung open.
Athelstan scrambled to his feet and turned. Godbless came
hurrying up the nave, almost dragging a young goat by the
leash around its neck.

'Brother Athelstan, Brother Athelstan, Sir John, God bless
you! A miracle! Thaddeus has come back from the dead.'

AUTHOR'S NOTE

*T*he Mansions of Murder is a work of fiction, but I suggest it accurately reflects the political situation in the late autumn of 1381. The gangs of the underworld, the rifflers, did exercise their own authority and could be highly dangerous. One example will suffice. In 1326 Queen Isabella and her lover Roger Mortimer landed at Walton-on-Naze in Essex with the avowed aim of toppling Edward II. Roger Mortimer, through his friends in the city, could summon up the rifflers, and he did so within a matter of days. The London mob surfaced so quickly and so savagely they even surprised Edward's own Treasurer, the Bishop of Exeter, as he rode past St Paul's. Exeter and two of his squires were pulled from their horses, decapitated, their corpses stripped and left to public exposure. The London mob continued to be such a threat for centuries. Indeed, we must remember, that the Tower was built not so much to defend London but to overawe it!

The preservation of corpses, especially the embalming of soldiers killed on the eastern marches, did reach a high level of sophistication, as the knight found at St Bees in Cumbria will attest. The mummification of the dead was not just the monopoly of ancient Egypt. By the fourteenth century, the art of embalming had developed so corpses could be carefully preserved and transported for burial wherever the deceased's relatives decided. Finally, Richard Fitzalan, Earl of Arundel, and his namesake the young King, deeply hated each other. Indeed, during the funeral obsequies of King Richard's beloved Queen Anne of Bohemia, Fitzalan arrived late for the ceremony. The King took this as a deliberate insult, a slur on his wife's memory. He marched down the church and attacked Fitzalan in full view of both court and people. Naturally Fitzalan's opposition to the King deepened and, in 1397, he paid for this with his life. Politics during the reign of Edward II truly was a matter of survival.